CHEATIEBO, THE FOLKLORIST SERIES

3

VOICES CRYING IN THE WILDERNESS

GLENDA SIMPSON

innovo
PUBLISHING

Published by Innovo Publishing, LLC
www.innovopublishing.com
1-888-546-2111

Providing Full-Service Publishing Services for Christian Authors, Artists &
Ministries: Books, eBooks, Audiobooks, Music, Screenplays, Film & Curricula

CHEATIEBO
The Folklorist Series

Vol 3

Voices Crying in the Wilderness

Unless otherwise noted, all scripture was taken from the American Standard
Version of the Bible. Public domain.

ISBN: 978-1-61314-807-5

Cover Design & Interior Layout: Innovo Publishing, LLC

Printed in the United States of America
U.S. Printing History
First Edition: 2022

Has God called you to create a Christian book, eBook, audiobook, music album,
screenplay, film, or curricula? If so, visit the ChristianPublishingPortal.com to
learn how to accomplish your calling with excellence. Learn to do everything
yourself, or hire trusted Christian Experts from our Marketplace to help.

Chapter 1

THE SMITHSON CHILDREN

...Continued from End of Volume 2

All three of the older children assumed he was with someone else. Lizzy quickly sent Ralph toward the road and James to the west where their fort was located. Lizzy headed south toward the slough. "Take a spear with you and watch out for snakes." The three of them were calling out to Peter, and the boys were whistling. Before a half mile had been covered, Lizzy heard Peter crying. When she reached him, he was trying to pull a fawn away from its mortally wounded mother. "Peter, what are you doing?"

"Liz, I saw the mother and baby walking and I followed. The mother is hurt, and she layed down on the ground. I toll the baby to come with me 'cause the momma cain't take care of her. I toll her she could come and live with us." Lizzy saw an arrow sticking in the doe's belly, and she panicked. Peter continued his chatter, "I saw the baby eating some grass so that means she is old enough to keep alive, ya think? How about we keep her for a pet, please, please!"

The sight of the arrow set Lizzy's heart to racing. She Immediately bent down and put her hand over Peter's mouth, "Quiet, Injuns might be back." She surveyed her surroundings but heard nothing more that the song of a meadowlark and buzzing insects. The blood on the deer's body had turned black and was dry.

Lizzy was about to tell Peter that they could not keep the fawn, but then she reconsidered. Lizzy decided the fawn would distract him from reality. It would be fun for all of them. She reasoned that the fawn would die if left to fend for itself, so there was no harm in trying to save it. Since the doe was still alive, Lizzy decided that the animal was edible and could provide them with a lot of meat. Okay, Peter you can keep your promise, here I'll carry her for you, and Lizzy hoisted the fawn under one arm. Lizzy yelled, "Ralph, James, I found Pete!" Both boys ran to meet Lizzy. Ralph took Peter and spun him around and hugged him. Lizzy sent James ahead with Peter so that she could talk to Ralph about butchering the injured doe.

"Ralph, the mother deer is almost dead. It has an Indian arrow in its belly. I didn't hear or see any sign of the Indians but seeing that arrow sure put the fear in me. We have to start being more careful. Do you think we can butcher the doe? Maybe we could slice off some roasts and cut some of it into strips for smoking?"

Ralph scratched his head and thought for a few seconds. Then he said, "We need to figure a way to sharpen the knife, but sure, let's give it a try. We sure need the food."

Ralph sent Lizzy back to camp and he walked back to where the doe lay. Ralph had been along on deer hunts and helped with dressing out the meat. Poppa had insisted that he learn how to field dress game. He was ready to give it his best effort.

Working with the dull, tip-less knife was a huge handicap. Ralph remembered watching both parents use a whet stone and looked around for a big rock that might sharpen the edge. He tried a couple of different rock types without much success. Lizzy was thinking about the dull blade too and it occurred to her that the whet stone might be in the ashes of the burned cabin and be in a useable state.

She knew such items were kept in a bottom drawer in the kitchen. Lizzy waded into the ruins of the cabin with trepidation. She used the shovel to scrape aside the thick layer of caked ashes. She found what was left of the wooden cupboard. It was blackened, but when she pulled on a drawer, some of the contents were not burned.

She removed a stack of scorched cotton napkins, tablecloths, and cup towels. Underneath the charred material Lizzy found even more than she had hoped. Her eyes grew big and she yelled "Ralph" but then remembered that he had gone back to butcher the doe.

Lizzy chided herself for not looking through the ashes of the cabin sooner? At the bottom of the drawer hidden under the linen were several knives, a meat cleaver, a small meat saw, and yes, the whet stone. The layer of cotton material had insulated the tools from the extreme heat of the fire. In another drawer Lizzy found a cast iron skillet with a lid and a long-handled ladle. Some of the cloths on the bottom were useable too. What a find! She was so excited that she ran to tell Ralph the good news.

Ralph used his leather belt to hang the deer by its hind feet and hacked and sawed at the throat until the jugular was opened. He was thinking, how would Poppa do this? Getting the best of the meat cut into small portions for roasting on a spit and cut into strips for drying was going to be —. That is when he heard Lizzy yelling and ran to meet her.

As Lizzy ran toward Ralph she was thinking, Momma always said, where there's a will there's a way. Lizzy hugged Ralph and said, "We can do this! I found the whet stone and some other stuff in the ruins of the cabin. Come see what I found." Walking back to the burned-out cabin Lizzy said to Ralph, "I'm thinkin' we need to cut up the deer away from our camp because the smell will attract animals that we don't want comin' too close." Ralph nodded his agreement. Lizzy and Ralph were able to carry the charred drawer with the scavenged items to the firelight. The sun had set and it was going to be a moonless night.

A jubilant Ralph looked through the find and yelled, "This is great Liz!" James and Peter walked over to see what the commotion was all about. James was carrying the fawn under one arm and Peter was holding on to an improvised grapevine tether. When James heard the good news he said, "I think we are going to make it, hey, when will the venison be ready to eat?"

Peter got a puzzled look and puckered up to cry. "No, no, we are not going to eat my baby, I will never let—."

Lizzy bent down and placed her hand over Pete's mouth and said, "We would never eat your fawn, but what if we eat some meat from the mother, she is hurt and going to die anyway, right? Are you okay with eating the doe? We really need more meat."

Peter sniffed and wiped his nose on his sleeve and nodded his agreement, with some hesitation. "I reckon the baby won't know what we're eating. I always liked ven-sin and I'm very hungry."

Lizzy and Ralph sat down by the fire and worked on sharpening a couple of the knives and the cleaver. With the sharp or at least sharper knives ready, they quickly made a span of rope by braiding three strands of knotted cloth from a towel. Ralph got the idea to make a torch by tying a towel smeared with mashed pecan oil to a long stick. It would light the way to where the deer was hanging. Ralph took along a clay pot of coals to start a fire. He grabbed two of the sharpened spears as an afterthought.

Ralph looked into James' eyes and spoke in a serious tone, "While me and Liz are gone keep Pete safe, keep the fire built up and crack some pecans for your supper. We'll get the meat ready to cook and hurry back fast as we can. Stay right here, real close to the fire." For a moment James looked a little scared but then snapped to attention, nodded and said, "Yes sir!" as he clicked his heels together and saluted the way he did when they played soldiers. Ralph saluted back and said, "At-ease Corporal Smithson."

Lizzy suggested, "Tear several strips of cloth from one of these towels and tie them together to make a leash and offer a drink of water to — hey, Pete what is her name?"

Pete turned his head to the side and said, "I been thinking about that, how about Moses, you know like the one in the Bible? Moses was saved by a woman, and I saved this Moses. I think Moses can be for a girl or boy."

Lizzy said, "Moses it is! Welcome to our family Moses. You sure have pretty eyes."

Lizzy built a fire while Ralph hoisted the doe still higher off the ground. The doe was well bled and ready to be dressed out and skinned. Ralph dug a deep hole to catch the entrails so that they could be quickly covered over. Penetrating the belly hide took all of the thrust Ralph could muster, even with the sharpened cleaver. Ralph asked, "Do we have any of the yucca powder left, Liz? This is going to get messy."

"No more than a handful, so we need to be digging up yucca roots ever chance we get. Second time around making yucca powder should go faster." The deer had begun to bloat and sprayed liquid when the hide was punctured. The stench was overpowering. "Whew, I'm gonna be sick" Ralph said as he turned away and retched. The fumes from the gut sack burned their eyes and induced gagging. They moved back and held their noses while the place aired out a little.

Ralph remembered a trick his Poppa used to mask bad smells. He made a paste of smashed cedar berries and rubbed it under his nose. There were lots of berries in the tree where the doe hung, and the paste really did help. Lizzy decided to do the same. Ralph said, "Stand back while I bury that pile of guts." As he worked Ralph confided, "When I went to cut her jugular, she looked right at me with a terrible fright in her eyes, and she tried to stand. I 'member Poppa saying doin' hard stuff makes men out of boys."

About the time they had finished removing the hide from the carcass, Ralph thought he heard something in the bushes. Ralph stopped and whispered, "Liz, there is something over behind those bushes. They listened for a moment and heard a low growling noise followed by rustling brush. The firelight was reflected in several sets of eyes peering from the darkness. The sight of orange eyes scared them, but they stayed in control of their faculties, and each picked up a knife and spear. As the creatures crept nearer, they recognized them as a pack of 5 or 6 coyotes. Ralph whispered, "The fire is keeping them back but not for long. Let's try to scare them away. First, I'm going to move the deer carcass higher into the tree out of their reach, and then we will run toward them yelling and throwing rocks."

The tactic worked and the pack tucked tails and ran over a ridge. Ralph decided that he and Lizzy should climb the biggest tree and let the coyotes dig up the buried entrails. Ralph threw the hide over his shoulder and started climbing a tree. "Come on up Liz."

Lizzy said, "Ralph, what if James and Peter decide to come see what we are doing, they could walk right up on the pack and might be attacked."

Ralph said, "You're right, we have to back away and hope the coyotes can't jump high enough to reach the meat. Remember, Poppa said to never turn our back or run from animals, we got to face them as we walk backwards and yell at them if they follow." True to form, they slowly retreated from the frightening scene. It was rough returning to the camp without a torch, and they both tripped and stumbled, bloodying their knees and palms. The sound of the coyotes fighting over the gut pile was both reassuring and nauseating.

Upon arrival back at camp Lizzy was relieved to see Peter and James playing with Moses. Lizzy started to pile on firewood and lots of it. It occurred to her that the lion might catch the scent of the deer and come into camp. She figured the coyotes would be gone by morning, and she and Ralph could finish their preparation of the deer carcass. James had both Pete and Moses on his lap. He was singing one of his original songs. James loved to make up songs, and he was surprisingly good at it.

Lizzy said, "James, why don't you and Pete make a bed for Moses inside with us. Pad it with juniper branches and dried grass." The boys jumped up and soon had a bed ready.

Lizzy and Ralph discussed building a drying rack for the meat as they lay in the little shed, trying to settle their minds enough to grow drowsy. They had their spears at their side just in case. Ralph mused, "I had my mouth all set to eat some of the venison tonight." He looked over at Lizzy, and she was watching James and Peter. They were both sound asleep.

Ralph continued, "I helped Poppa with smoking meat a few times. We can increase the smoke coming off the fire with some fresh cut mesquite branches. Poppa said smoke preserves the meat and flavors it too."

At first light Lizzy and Ralph rose without waking the two younger boys. Ralph experimented with a pile of sticks for the best model for the drying racks while Lizzy served up a meager meal. Lizzy told Ralph to stay at camp, and she would sneak down to see if the deer was still in the tree. She arrived just in time to catch a vulture tearing off a chunk of meat. She yelled and threw rocks until it took flight. She made a mental note to discard the meat around the missing chunk. She shouted, "you Buzzards have to be the nastiest creatures on earth." The coyotes were gone, and the pit that held the guts was emptied. Lizzy lowered the carcass onto the skin fur side down and pulled it back to camp. The process of cutting the meat into sections took a full day and left Ralph and Lizzy exhausted. They both conceded it would have been impossible without the meat saw and cleaver.

Lizzy felt a strange sensation when she considered the timing of finding the implements in the burned house and would believe until her dying day it was more than happenstance. She suggested quoting the 23rd Psalm once James and Pete were awake. With each advancing day the Bible passage, especially the ending, "For thou art with me" seemed to provide greater comfort and apply to their situation. Lizzy and Ralph were both determined to eat some of the meat before the day was over.

By sundown there were 20 thinly sliced kabobs of meat suspended over a bed of coals. The larger pieces of meat were suspended about three feet above the main fire on Ralph's rack. Keeping the fire going with the right amount of heat was the current priority. That meant they needed lots of wood both dry and green. Ralph and James stepped up to the task and worked with a maturity beyond their age. The Smithson boys were no weaklings. They didn't quit until they had enough wood piled up to feed the fire for a couple of days. Lizzy bragged on them and helped them wash the filth from their faces and hands. Gathering fire wood was another chore made easier by the tools Lizzy found in the burned house.

Darkness settled over the prairie, and the Smithson children were all four staring at the kabobs. The smoke from dripping fat smelled heavenly. By then all four were weak with hunger.

When Lizzy declared the meat done enough, she asked Pete to say a prayer. With an air of importance, the little rascal said, "Hebenly God, We ain't got no miracles from you yet but finding the deer was purty clost. I hope it tastes as good as it smells. We hope Moses don't figure out what we're eating. I'm too hungry to talk any more so A Man!"

Lizzy and Ralph were forced to look away to hide their amused expressions. Then Ralph said, "Good prayer Pete. Couldn't have said it better myself. James said, "This is cooked just right Lizzy, but it needs salt." The kabobs were devoured quickly directly off the sticks. Lizzy faulted herself for not making more.

Over the next three days, the children took turns tending the fire and guarding the racks of venison. After finding the arrows in the doe and the aggressive coyote encounter, she insisted they stay together and carry spears. Other than hearing the yelping of the coyotes, the nights had been without incident. After a breakfast of nuts and roasted prickly pear pads, all four children stayed together as they gathered firewood, and food for Moses. Lizzy was on edge.

What Moses really needed was her mother's milk. The fawn had developed a case of scours or as Pete put it, "Die-reya." Lizzy recalled a trick her mother had used for the condition and dug up some clay from near the spring and mixed it with water. It took Ralph, James and Lizzy all three to get the liquefied clay down Moses' throat, but it seemed to help. From somewhere in the recesses of her brain, Lizzy remembered her mother feeding rescued baby animals raw eggs. Lizzy told the boys to look for a hens' nest. There should be about four to five hens still alive and living close by. The boys spent hours searching. Lizzy cautioned them, "When you find a nest be careful not to disturb it and leave a couple of eggs there so thar she will continue using the nest." They finally found a nest in some dense brush, and James got all scratched up from the stickers and thorns. When Lizzy showed concern over his injuries, he retorted, "It's times like this when we got to be brave, just give me some of that aloe-vera gel to rub on. That's good stuff! At least I found these eggs."

Later that day they searched and found a second nest. In total they found ten eggs not counting the ones they left in the nests. Lizzy was right, Moses lapped up the raw eggs in an instant and kept licking the pan. Lizzy boiled four of the eggs, one each and kept the rest for Moses. Lizzy broke one more egg into the pan, and it disappeared with two or three swipes of the fawn's tongue. Lizzy thought, we can be watching for bird's nests too. And there might be some turtle eggs at the slough."

Lizzy had been thinking about trying to harvest some honey. She got busy making torches to smoke the nearby hive. Finally ready, Lizzy was shaking when she started smoking the bees. She wrapped up in the blanket and carried coals from the fire. Lizzy noted the direction of the wind and built the fire close to the tree that housed the bee colony. Then she lighted two torches and held them in the lower part of the hollow trunk. As the smoke filled the cavity the bees fell to the bottom and were lifeless. Lizzy sliced off a large chunk of the dripping comb and placed it into the dish pan. Then she spread the embers and covered them with sand. The bees started waking just as she ran from the area.

Fortunately, she was only stung three times and walked away with almost two gallons of dripping honey cone. The cone was good to eat too and made great candles. Lizzy tore strings from the scorched dish towels and braided them to use for candle-wicks. Lizzy had helped her mother make bees wax candles since she was Pete's age. She imagined her father being pleased with her honey harvest.

That night they all four feasted on honey dipped pecans. Lizzy thought it would be okay to give Moses a small taste of honey, and if she was okay afterwards, they could gradually add more to her diet of prickly pear and beaten eggs. Moses made loud smacking noises as she licked the honey from Peter's hand. Because it tickled so much, he started giggling.

Fortunately, the diet of clay, eggs and honey agreed with Moses, and she became frisky and was apt to run off. When Moses was caught nibbling on Peter's roasted prickly pear strips the plentiful food was gradually increased. Ralph and James took the time to build Moses a little pen next to the shed to curtail her wondering.

The amount of meat harvested from the doe came to about twenty pounds, pecans were plentiful, and prickly pears grew everywhere you looked. They were surviving but not quite thriving. Fall was coming. It was getting dark earlier, and the nights were chilly. Lizzy began making moccasins for the four of them from the doe's hide. Ralph and James had trapped two rabbits so far, and they were getting better at setting the dead fall traps.

Lizzy's weaving project was still hit and miss. Trial and error were her teacher. The loom she constructed was small and very crude, but she was thrilled over her first square of fabric. She planned to piece the squares together and use two thicknesses stuffed with cattail down. They needed bedding and clothing quickly, so Lizzy taught Ralph and James to weave. Within a couple of days, they had an assembly line going.

Ralph was making good progress on the rock fireplace. The hard part would be getting the chimney to draw properly. The fireplace was far from finished, but it was shaping up well enough to keep Ralph enthusiastic.

About two weeks after butchering the doe Ralph thought he heard horses approaching. He climbed a tree and saw dust in the air above the trail. He got so rattled he fell the last few feet while coming down from the tree. On the ground, he rummaged through the rocks in his pocket looking for the chicken bone whistle. He started running to where Lizzy was preparing lunch at the fire pit. Lizzy was so preoccupied with her meal she did not hear the whistle until Ralph took hold of her shoulder. She said ouch, and then saw the terror on his face.

Chapter 2

A LITTLE LESS THAN THRIVING

The Smithson children fell to the ground and crawled into the brush. Lizzy motioned for them to be silent. They stopped to listen and moved still farther away. Lizzy rose to a crouching position and motioned for the boys to follow. They were headed for the far side of the hill behind the burnt cabin. After a hundred feet, Lizzy left the boys hidden and peeked over the ridge. The riders were not Indians. There were four mounted white men and one pack horse. Relief flooded over her, but, for the sake of caution, she decided to stay hidden until she got a closer look. The four strangers wore wide-brimmed hats and were heavily armed. Lizzy wondered if they might be outlaws. She whispered, "Yawl stay here and don't make a sound." Lizzy stayed behind bushes as she worked her way to where the men were dismounting. That is when she saw their big silver badges, the very kind that sheriffs and Texas Rangers wear.

Just as Lizzy was ready to reveal herself to the men one of the horses reacted to her presence. The rider pulled his revolver and looked in her direction. Lizzy quickly said, "Please sir, don't shoot, we are just four children that need your help—, I'm Lizzy Smithson." She stepped into the open and started walking toward the men. They were all staring at her with open mouths and shocked expressions on their faces. For a certainty, Lizzy was a pitiful sight. When she saw the men's reaction to her appearance, she became even more self-conscious and tried to brush some of the dirt from her clothing. Her garment was reduced to shredded tatters that barely covered her nakedness. Her mass of tangled hair helped to cover her upper torso.

Two of the men dismounted and walked toward Lizzy. One man held out his hand and said, "Howdy do Mamm." Lizzy straightened her shoulders and shook his hand. She pushed her waist length mane of hair behind her ears, and said, "We are the Smithson children, who might you gentlemen be?"

The one that had shaken Lizzy's hand said, "Cap'n Trainor, Samuel Trainer, Texas Ranger, at your service." He turned and spoke to the men behind him, "Rudy, fetch me that blanket I have tied behind my saddle. Looks like this young lady could make use of it." While Trainer helped wrap the blanket around Lizzy he continued speaking. "Peers you had a might of trouble; where's your folks?" Lizzy started to speak, but the words did not come out right away.

She shuffled her feet and choked back tears. Finally with a quivering voice, "Comanche come while us kids was out pickin' fruit. Killed Momma and Poppa and then stole everthing and burned our house."

Captain Trainor spoke with shock in his tone, "How long has it been?" Overcome with excitement and curiosity Peter burst into the open and stared at the men, as though they were an apparition. He was quickly followed by Ralph and James.

Ralph said, "Hello, Sir. I can answer your question. I been marking off the days, and I'm up to 57, yep 57 days."

Captain Trainor exclaimed, "57 days, did I hear you right, almost two months? You children have managed to survive out here all this time on your own? That is amazin'; you must be some tough little buckaroos."

Ralph stood at attention and saluted, "Yes sir, we are Texans!"

Obviously impressed, Captain Trainor smiled and returned his salute before saying, "There is no doubt about that!" Trainor began introducing the three other Rangers. "This is ole Melvin, and this'n is John, and the ugly one over thar is Rudy." Lizzy noticed that Rudy was just a kid in his late teens. While she looked him over, he blushed and shifted in his saddle. She noticed that his ears turned red. The two older men tipped their hats and nodded. Then Capt. Trainor said, "Good thing you put that sign at the road, or we might have gone on by without stopping."

Lizzy introduced herself, "I'm Mary Elizabeth Smithson, folks call me Lizzy and this is Ralph, and he's James, and this'en, lit'l Peter.

Peter interrupted and corrected Lizzy, "I'm big now. This is our pet; her name is Moses." Everyone had a good chuckle over Peter's tug of war with Moses. The frightened fawn was trying to stay hidden behind a bush.

Lizzy said, after a long sigh, "We're sure glad you Rangers come along. We been havin' a hard time of it. We buried Momma and Poppa down by the wash and since then, well we're jus try'n to stay alive. We've been turble scared't tha Injuns might come back. You reckon you could give us a ride into some town where we could get some help?" Captain Trainor agreed with a hearty, "Ya got it, little miss, but first it looks like you might enjoy some grub."

The Rangers made camp and right away cooked up a meal fit for a king's table. The hungry children were polite in responding to questions but were obviously focused on the cooking food. They kept sniffing and moving a little closer to the fire. James asked if they had salt for the food and smiled when the one named Melvin said, "Got plenty of salt." Once the food was done cooking Captain Trainor dished up plates of food for the children first. Then, barely in time, when the Rangers were lifting their first bite of food to their mouths, Peter enthusiastically volunteered to lead a prayer. The men all lowered their plates of food, removed their hats, and bowed reverently while Pete addressed the Creator 'Peter style.'

"Dear Hebenly God, boss of miracles, thanks for sending these Texas Rangers. Be sure Momma and Poppa know we are safe now. It was a long time till we got this miracle, but ya did good keepin' the Injuns away and helpin' us find food. This Ranger food smells too good to say a long prayer, so thanks for our blessings. A-Man."

When Melvin saw how fast the food was disappearing from the kid's plates, he quickly started a second batch of biscuits and gravy. Melvin and Captain Trainor watched the children eat while they waited for the second batch of food. Perhaps the breeze had kicked up some dust because all four of the big, burly Rangers developed a sudden case of watery eyes.

With full stomachs and contented expressions, everyone relaxed and enjoyed the warmth of the fire. The rangers handed blankets to the boys since there was a chill in the night air. Peter responded to Captain Trainor's playfulness and in no time was sitting on his lap. Peter and Moses decided to provide some after-dinner entertainment and kept the whole bunch in stitches with Peter's personal accounts of survival. The biggest laugh getter was when Pete told about James putting the fish in his trousers. They seemed to like the story about the gold at the end of the rainbow. Pete was enjoying being the center of attention. A strange feeling of relief settled over Lizzy. The appearance of the Rangers had taken a giant weight from her shoulders.

The Texas Rangers slept on the ground around the fire with one at a time standing watch. For the first time since the Indian attack Lizzy felt safe. Lizzy took the boys and Moses to sleep in the shed as usual. Lizzy was about to blow out the candle when Captain Trainor rapped on the shed. Lizzy said, "Come in."

Captain Trainor stuck his head in and looked around at the hammock and the unfinished fireplace. "I just wanted to say good night, you youngin's did a good job fixin' this shed up, kinda homey like. Looks like you wuz gittin' ready for cold weather and doin' a good job of it. Get rested up 'cause we have a long day tomorrow. Goodnight buckaroos!"

The Smithson brood had trouble getting to sleep. The uncertainty of their future was looming large. They welcomed rescue, but the status quo, was about to change. Lizzy felt she was ending the ordeal without a satisfying conclusion. Abruptly riding away would be disquieting. Perhaps it was that she was abandoning Ida and Jonas' homesteading dream. And what about maintaining their graves? Lizzy reasoned that such thoughts was borrowing trouble and decided to think positive thoughts. Before drifting off she thanked the Lord for sending the Texas Rangers.

Before the children awoke the Rangers discussed what to do with the fawn. Who would take it when they got to town? Even a bigger question was who would take the orphaned children with times being so hard. The aroma of breakfast cooking woke the children. The blanket clad youngsters filed out of the shed and took a seat on a blanket per John's instructions. "Breakfast coming right up, hope you like biscuits, ham and red eye gravy."

Ralph grinned and reminded everyone that James was hoping there was still some salt for the gravy. John said, "Yep, plenty of salt, and if you want to give me a hand with stirring the gravy, I might share my jar of strawberry jam."

"Wow, real jam, strawberries! James had to hurry to beat Pete to the chore who wanted to share in the jam.

While James stirred John gave Pete a good tickling on the ribs while he assured him, "It's a big jar of jam, enough for us all." James and Peter tied Moses to a shrub near a green spot where water spilled from the cistern. The fawn was getting better at eating grass on her own and had mostly recovered from the scours, information the boys decided not to share with the Rangers.

After the meal Lizzy seemed confused, and tears welled up in her eyes. She asked if she could bring a few things. The captain agreed and volunteered to help her gather up what she had in mind. Lizzy said, "Oh there's not much, I was thinkin' about bringing our dried venison and some of the tools that belonged to our parents. Lizzy used one of her clay-lined baskets and packed up the plant-fiber fabric she had been weaving and two pairs of doe skin sandals she had made. James and Ralph insisted on taking the clay shoes that were still curing. She packed up the yucca soap and the fish comb. After almost starving to death, Lizzy felt compelled to bring the uneaten food. The Smithson's would be obsessive about food, possibly for life, common for victims of starvation.

Lizzy approached Captain Trainor, "Sir, can you give us time to say a prayer at the grave of our parents? It's hard leaving them out here all alone." The rangers stayed with the horses as the children walked to the grave and had a farewell prayer.

Peter's farewell prayer was short and apprehensive. "God, my tummy is hurt'n and I'm a little skiered. If you decide to do a miracle and let Momma and Poppa cum back to life, help 'em find us wherever we are. A-Man"

It was time to ride away, and Lizzy took one last look around. Captain Trainor was lashing Lizzy's baskets and bundles to the pack animal. He set Peter in front of him. Ralph climbed on behind Melvin and Lizzy rode behind John. James and Moses were seated behind Rudy's saddle.

The children were solemn on the ride into town. Pete dozed off, and Moses disgraced herself on Rudy's horse, requiring a swath of grass and splash from a canteen. Upon reaching Gainesville Captain Trainor took the Smithson brood directly to the stucco shanty that served as the Cooke County Sheriff's office. On the ride into town, John engaged Lizzy in conversation on the latest news about the Comanche's return to the war path. Lizzy asked if there was news of Cynthia Parker. John speculated that she was likely dead from cruelty and over work or a married squaw. Her age had been at the cut-off for adoption into the clan. He mentioned a circulating rumor that she had been adopted and was suffering the 'fate worse than death' in the eyes of white folk. It was mid-afternoon when they dismounted at the hitching post in front of the city jail. Trainor said, "Rudy, why don't you and Melvin go and reserve us some rooms at the hotel."

Melvin said, "Ya got it, Capt'n." The captain tied his horse to the rail next to the others, within reach of a large watering trough. The thirsty horses began drinking. He and John lifted the children down to stand, except for Peter who had a choke hold on Captain Trainer's neck. They entered the open door of the sheriff's office. Captain Trainor was reminding Peter to be brave like a big boy. Still, Pete started to pucker up.

"Ah. Come on, don't be scared. I'll stay with you 'til you git settled in." Trainor found the sheriff kicked back with his boots on the desk, and his sweat-stained hat covering his face. It appeared to be the Sheriff's siesta time. Trainor slammed his fist down on the desk and watched as Sheriff Bozeman fell over backwards in his chair.

As Gil Bozeman was floundering about on the floor and reaching for his holstered revolver, he saw Trainor. "I should'a knowed, why you hunk of buzzard bait. What brangs ya to these parts?" Trainor walked behind the desk and extended his free hand to help Bozeman up off the floor. "Good to see you again, Sam. Who's yur fine lookin' sidekicks?"

Bozeman shook hands with the amused Rangers, "John, Sam, good to see you two, pull up some of them chars ov'r thar."

After pulling the chairs up to the desk, Sam started by saying, "Comanches back on the warpath, Gil. Done right smart killin' and burnin'. We found four homesteads burned out. These young'ens' the only survivors"

The three men chewed the fat for a few minutes and exchanged the latest about some mutual acquaintances, a couple of them featured on wanted posters with bounties on their heads. After half an hour, the Sheriff rose, and said, "Stay put, I need to ask around."

Gil Bozeman first thought of preacher Rhodes, but then he got the idea to ask Jesse, his wife. After eight years of marriage, Jesse Bozeman had lost three pregnancies to miscarriage. Maybe helping these children would get Jesse's mind off the most recent loss, only two months before. He walked to his house and found Jesse kneading a wooden platter of bread dough. "Gil, what are you doin' home at this hour?"

"Jess, wipe your hands, and sit down, we got to talk. Sam Trainor just showed up at my office. He has terrible news. The Comanches is raid'n agin. Found four farms burned out, most everbody dead. You ever meet the Smithson family from out west of town aways?"

Jesse answered, "Yes, once at church, a few months back, oh no, not them, such a nice family. The best behaved children—." Then Jesse said, "Here, give me a minute." Gil waited while she covered the dough with a damp cloth and sat back down.

Gil explained, "The kids was out pickin plums when the Injuns hit so they survived. Mr. and Mrs. Smithson was killed. The four children are settin' in my office. From the looks of 'em, they been through a devilish hard time. Ya want to help me figure what to do with em?"

Jesse said, "Oh my, those poor children. I don't think we have anybody in town that can take on four more mouths to feed. Maybe the preacher and his wife? Oh, but she's been so sick and all. No, that will not do. Gil, how about if we let them stay with us 'til we find some of their relatives?"

"Jess, I was thinkin' the same thing. They are a pitiful bunch. Been livin' like scared rabbits for eight weeks. It is a wonder they made it." Then Jesse stood and said, "Give me a minute, and then I want you to take me to them." Jesse walked into her bedroom and removed her apron. She wet a towel and washed the flour and perspiration from her face. She quickly ran a bore bristle brush through her long brown hair and wound it into a knot on top of her head. Jesse didn't have a vain bone in her body. Much of her comeliness was that she was totally unaware that others found her attractive. Her lightly creased face exuded thoughtfulness and a peaceful spirit.

Jesse and Gil held hands as they walked the two blocks back to the jail. "Jess, are you sure that you're up to takin' this on? It will be a lot of work."

"Oh Gil, I'm fine, never felt better. You worry too much."

When Jesse and Gil walked into the office, Peter was still sitting on Sam's lap. Lizzy and James shared a chair, and Ralph was walking about the office, checking out the two empty jail cells and the rack of rifles.

Jesse walked over to Lizzy and held out her hand. "Hello dear, I am Jesse, Sheriff Bozeman's wife."

"Hello Mamm, I am Lizzy Smithson, and these are my brothers. It's very nice to see you. I think we met at church a while back."

"Yes, we did meet. It is nice to see you again. I hear that you lost your parents. I am so sorry. Terrible loss, just terrible. We'll talk later, I am a good listener. Maybe the Sheriff and I can help you find your way in the world. We will do what we can. For now, Sherriff Bozeman and I want to invite you to stay with us. First, we will set yawl down to a hearty meal and then a hot bath. In the meantime, Sheriff Boseman will send his men around town and find you some clean clothes."

As soon as the words were out of her mouth, the children all looked at each other and smiled. Then Lizzy said, "Peter, James, Ralph, will it be okay if we go to this nice lady's house?" Ralph decided to speak for himself and his siblings. "Thank you, Mrs. Bozeman, that all sounds too good to be true. We been praying for help, just what you are offering to do, so I believe you are an answer to our prayers."

Jesse took James and Ralph by the hand and walked out of the building. James almost asked if she had plenty of salt but decided against it. Suddenly Peter began yelling, "Wait, we got to bring Moses with us! I ain't leaving without Moses."

Captain Trainor said, "Calm down Pete, Moses can come too." The ranger untied the fawn from the hitching post and tucked it under his arm. The children were silent on the walk, but Jesse talked non-stop, in an attempt to reassure the youngsters. She said, "I have four loaves of bread rising. I reckon you kids like fresh baked bread? And I have a big pot of beans with a ham bone simmering on the stove. Our tomato vines are loaded right now, and we have a jersey cow. She is fresh, and we have more milk, cream, and butter than we can eat. Oh, I almost forgot, I made two apple pies earlier today. I will be interested in hearing about your ordeal, but we will save that for later when you are ready. I'm amazed at how healthy and strong you all look."

Jesse continued the one-way conversation, "Oh, by the way, we have a cat named Roscoe. He lives under our house and keeps the mice away. He loves for children to pet him. As soon as we get to the house, we will put some water on to heat, and at least one of you can get a bath while I pop the bread in the oven and fry up a big skillet of potatoes with onion to go with the other food." The children walked without responding, obviously overwhelmed. The looming unknown was heavy on their little hearts. Lizzy was thinking, things could be much worse, Ralph was excited about living with a lawman, and James was glad to be in a town where they were safe from Indians. Peter was curious about the house and of course the cat. At the entrance to the cottage, he smelled the beans cooking and whispered to Sam that he was hungry. Sam whispered back, "I'll see if I can get you something to hold you over." The children were big eyed and smiling when the cat came from under the porch to check out the visitors. When she saw the fawn, her back humped up and she hissed. Moses was frightened and tried to squirm out of Sam's arm. Ralph spoke up and suggested, "Mamm, I would like for Lizzy to be the first to get a bath. She hates being dirty more than anybody I ever knew."

Jesse said, "Good idea Ralph, and I will let her use one of my dresses." Lizzy smiled at Ralph and mouthed, "Thank you."

The Smithson youngsters became a part of the Jesse and Gil Boseman family for the next two years. A few months after the Smithson children were rescued, The Texas Rangers were able to arrange a pow-wow that culminated in a peace treaty with the Comanche Tribes including the notorious Nokoni. After the latest round of violence, the good people of Gainesville and surrounding area would be tentative about its durability. During the truce process Comanche Chief Peta Nokoni was told the remarkable survival story of the four Smithson children.

The chief was skeptical but decided to investigate the incident. His approach to learning what really happened was ingenious. He would meet with the heroic children face to face. Prior experience with white people had proven they often spoke with forked tongues.

Without advance notice Peta Nokoni, his interpreter, and two lesser war chiefs rode into Gainesville under a white flag. Their sudden appearance cleared main street of townspeople and brought out the sheriff's deputies with shotguns at the ready. Before they made it all the way to the jail house, they were stopped and frisked for weapons. Their bows and knives were promptly confiscated. There was no odor of alcohol, and they were quite docile. Gil Boseman spoke briefly with the woman interpreter, "Come to see the children of Smithson. We hear them tell. Say sorry for dead parents, cabin burn."

Gil ordered his two deputies to escort the four Comanche to the hotel lobby to wait until a decision was made over a meeting. Gil didn't sense any hostility from the serious and dignified chieftain. There was nothing threatening about the Indians, but he instructed his men to keep close watch. This visit was a huge surprise to Gil.

Gil rushed to his home to speak with Jesse. The Bozemans lacked proper medical terminology, but they were blessed with reasoning and wisdom. Gil and Jesse spoke among themselves at length. They decided to leave the final choice on meeting with the Indians to the children themselves. They wanted to set the stage for the meeting without revealing that the Comanche were already in town.

Gil began by asking, "If you could talk to the head Comanche in these parts, would you want to? Do you know what you would say to him?" Immediately all four children perked up and began speaking at once. Gil said, "Wait a minute, so by your reaction it seems that you would like to speak with the Chief, am I right?"

All but Peter nodded and Ralph said, "Long as they don't hurt us or nothing." Gil and Jesse looked at each other with surprise.

Gil said, "There are four Indians here in Gainesville right now, and they came to speak with you, but you don't have to go near them unless you want to. They heard about your tragedy and how brave you are. They are Comanche, but these are not the ones that killed your parents." The three older children opened up, and their pent-up emotions spilled over with accusations, questions about motive, and curiosity. "I am so impressed with your bravery, but take a few minutes to reconsider. I don't want to make matters worse for you."

Lizzy said, "Jesse, I think it will be good to see them. We have them built up into super devils, and it might help to see that they are only people, dirty, ugly, mean, and not so smart people. I know what I want to say to them."

Ralph spoke up next. "I have plenty to say to them."

James said, "Me too! And they won't like it."

Pete had fallen silent and looked away. "Maybe I am not ready to be a big boy yet. Jesse, do you think I can go back to being little just for today while the Indians are here?"

Jesse rushed to Peter and lifted him into her arms. She hugged and kissed the boy as tears began streaming down her cheeks. "Peter, you get to decide. Talk or not, it will be fine. We will protect you so there is nothing to be afraid of from these Indians or any Indians, not ever again." Jesse continued reassuring the Smithson children. "I have a notion you will want to dress in your church clothes. Show them how civilized children look and how you behave. Show them how brave your parents taught you to be. Show them how sad it is that their lives were cut short for no good reason. Okay, then start working on what you want to say. This is your one and only chance. Make it count."

Ralph asked Jesse, "Do you think Momma and Poppa will be able to see us talking to the Indians from up in heaven? I sure hope so."

Jesse and Gil left the room and spoke. Jesse said, "Gil I'm surprised the kids are so eager to meet the Indians. It might help them to heal faster. I think they've been pushing their anger back rather than dealing with it. It might be good for them to face the Indians."

Gil said, "I agree. I'll watch and step in if it starts to get out of hand."

Back with the kids Gil said, "It is important that you understand that Indians are all different, some good and some bad. These Indians came a long way to meet you. Maybe they came to apologize and see if you really are as brave as they've heard. If you get scared, I will make them leave and never come back."

Ralph looked at James and then Lizzy and said: "Yes sir, I would like to tell them how it felt to find our parents dead. It might be a little scary, but I want to try and find out what went wrong! Why all the killin' and, and all that turble stuff?"

James nodded and said, "Same for me, I'm ready to face the mangy buzzards, and I ain't takin' no excuses." (James was already borrowing folksy nomenclatures from Gil Bozeman.)

Lizzy piped up and said, "Sure, I would like to look them in the eye and ask how they can live in the same tribe with terrible murderers. I want these Injuns here today to punish the killers! After what we been through, ain't much that can scare me. Take me to them."

Gil and Jesse helped the children dress in their Sunday go-to-meeting clothes. As a family unit they all held hands and walked down Main Street to the hotel. Word of the Indians had spread throughout Gainesville like lightning, and folks stepped out to the board walk to show support for the Smithson family.

Peta Nokoni and his companions were seated cross legged on the lobby floor. Bozeman's deputies had searched them a second time and sniffed for liquor. A small assembly of important townspeople had been granted permission to attend the meeting. They were seated at the back of the lobby. The preacher, the mayor, and the doctor were seated in the second row of chairs. There were chairs waiting for Lizzy and the boys, but Lizzy crept slowly to within a few feet of the Comanche and seated herself on the floor facing them. Ralph and James followed Lizzy and lined up next to her. The striking appearance of the Indians' garb and feather headdresses was intimidating. Peter hid his face in Gil's shoulder too terrified to watch what his siblings were doing.

Chief Peta Nokoni sat on the left and forward of the other Indians by about two feet. His appearance was wildly exotic. The angle of his chin and his posture established superiority. He was confident, his gaze was intent and missed nothing, and his general demeanor was one of exceptional intelligence.

The Indian Woman seated to his left and back wore a cape that covered her head. The reason for her concealment was not immediately apparent. She looked to be young and in robust health. She was tanned and weather beaten. Her hyper-vigilance indicated that she was uncomfortable with her surroundings. As the meeting progressed, it became apparent that she felt kindly toward the children. During the course of the discussion, the veiled woman revealed an agenda of her own and that was to explain to the children that atrocities had occurred on both sides. Once when she shifted positions, her enlarged midriff showed her to be in the late stages of pregnancy. When she interpreted for the chief, her English was slow and halting. Waiting on her to find the correct words took patience for the listeners.

Gil introduced the children. Lizzy waited for the expected apology that never materialized. Finally, Lizzy decided that she was expected to speak first. She stood and looked directly at the Chief. Her voice was loud enough to be heard throughout the large lobby as she launched into a most detailed account of finding her murdered parents. She described their mutilated bodies in graphic terms. "Poor Momma was propped up on the door step and was smoking from the heat." Lizzy stopped to wipe away tears and made a deep sigh. "The shock I felt when I walked up on my Momma and Poppa, well there ain't no words. It made me sick at my stomach. Momma was naked and scalped and covered with bruises and cuts all over. As soon as I pulled their bodies away from the heat of the burning cabin, bugs swarmed over them. My Poppa was barely still alive but died right away. Momma's body had been left to show what had been done to her womanhood, the cruelty she had suffered before she died,—it was rape, and worse! Do Indians really do that to other humans? Animals are not that cruel!" The assembled group of white people groaned with shock. "Poppa was scalped too and had been stabbed and beaten. The heat from the burning cabin was so hot my hair got scorched. And the smell, I will never get that smell out of my nose. I didn't want my little brothers to see them like that, so I made them stay back."

Lizzy walked back and forth using her arms in sweeping gestures, "That first night we put boards in a tree to sleep on. Coyotes came up close and scared us real bad. At daylight I drug Momma and Poppa to a gully and caved the soft sides off to cover them: hardest thing I ever done. I had to beat off the critters, used rocks and sticks. They refused to leave at first. The worst was vultures and armadillos. By then the smell was even worse!"

"We were starving to death most of the time, scratched up and filthy, and scared to death for two long months." But we came through it alive! Here we are stronger for the experience. Mr. Nokona, it was cruel, savage, what those Comanche men done, I mean did to our family, and I need to hear why you did not control your braves. Do you have the power to prevent this from happening again? Why did those men hate us so much? It is only fair that your tribe pay for our burned house. I will be wait'n for your answer. There, that is what I wanted to say." She sat back on the floor.

Just as Lizzy sat back down Peter wiggled from Gil's arms and ran from the building. Then he stuck his head back in the door and said, "I'll be right back. Gotta go to the outhouse." When Pete finished at the outhouse, he saw Moses and decided to take her back with him, on a leas, of course.

Gil asked, "Sorry folks, guess Pete couldn't wait. Sure hope you don't mind the break." The crowd was nervous and silent for the most part. Pete was gone about ten minutes.

Being emboldened by Lizzy's statement the five-year-old walked to stand directly in front of the Chief. Pete was so small and cute in his short pants and jacket and knee socks. Certainly, small in physical stature, the boy spoke with such awesome bravery and delivered his poignant plea of indignation with great force. His words cut to the heart every man, woman, and child in attendance. The listeners were breathless from the impact. Pete kept eye contact as he spoke. The blue of his eyes was intensified by the window light coming in from behind the Indians. He pointed his right index finger directly at Chief Nokoni. The Chief cocked his head to the side and eyed the small boy with a raised eye-brow and an incredulous expression. Peter took in a big breath and in his small high-pitched voice spoke, "Sir, do you see this little fawn, well her mother died with an Indian arrow in her belly, and this baby had to see her mother like that. Babies should not have their mother murdered! And you need to know how sad I am without my Momma and Poppa. We needed them to raise us. There weren't no need to kill nice people like them. You should say you're sorry!" Peter waited and then stamped his foot with anger and shouted "Well, say it!" Peter started to cry, and he wasn't the only one in the room weeping. Gil rose from his chair and walked over to Peter and carried him back to the chair. "Good job, Pete, they got your message."

Ralph stood and glared with intensity as he raised his closed fist, "Sure we was scared, but we got a lot braver and you Injuns better watch out when I'm around. We thought we was going to starve to death. We had to eat food that was terrible. Sometimes we didn't have any food at all. I believe in forgiving others, but it's gonna take me a long time, so you Injuns better sleep lightly!"

James was blinking back tears when he spoke, "Shame on all of you Injuns. Ida and Jonas was good people! They didn't deserve to die like they did. Wild Animals ain't that mean. We kids thought you wuz gonna come back and kill us or capture us. One night a mountain lion come and killed our pig. The noise we heard will stay in my memory forever!" He glared at the Chief and said, "That was the second scariest time of my life. And a storm hailed so hard it almost knocked down our shed. What those Injuns done weren't human? God will punish those men for what they done!"

The interpreter was possibly part white. She understood English well, but her vocabulary was limited. It wasn't until later that the woman was identified as the captive, Cynthia Ann Parker. Because she wore head covering and kept her face shaded, her Caucasian ethnicity went undiscovered. None of the white people in Gainesville knew that Chief Peta Nokoni had taken Cynthia Ann Parker to be his wife.

Chief Nokoni and Cynthia Ann were left big eyed and definitely surprised. The Smithson Children's ferocity had been verified in a most dramatic way. There was no doubt that they were indeed extraordinary children. Peta Nokoni did not speak, but as a show of respect placed his forearms across his chest and bowed. Then he raked his hands together as though brushing dust from them, indicating that the meeting was over. He had come to see the brave children, and now he knew the reports were true, absolutely accurate.

Cynthia Ann leaned toward her husband, and they conversed in a whisper for several minutes. Then she announced, "Brave Children, sorry. We talk." Cynthia rose and walked over to Lizzy and helped her to stand. The boys stood in like manner. Cynthia Ann encircled Lizzy with her arms and then approached the two older boys and embraced them in a motherly manner. She whispered, "Sorry, very sorry, war bad. Much Nokoni people die, bad whites killers, war bad." Then the Indians abruptly rose and filed out of the lobby, took possession of their weapons, and rode in the direction of the setting sun.

A few days later a crude letter arrived from Cynthia Ann. There was a poke of silver coins and a letter. The juvenile printing was messy and hard to read. "Brave children, Chief Nokoni sorry. Some Warriors bad. And white men much bad, see, on both sides"

Lizzy responded to the woman's letter thanking her for her kindness and for the bag of coins. Lizzy had no way of knowing if the letter would reach its destination. She also revealed her intention to inhabit the family ranch and invited the woman to visit. Lizzy closed her brief letter with, "Please, no more killing! Nokoni will be welcome to draw water when passing by. We need peace not war. My brothers and I are trying to forgive the murderers that killed our parents, but it will take a long time. Lizzy"

When Mary Elizabeth turned seventeen, she married Rudy Jones, the youngest member of Texas Ranger rescuers. She and Jesse spent weeks sewing a whimsical, princess style, floor length gown of white satin and lace. The small wedding ceremony was held in the Bozeman's backyard next to a lovely flower garden. Sheriff Bozeman gave the bride away. For a girl so young, Lizzy's exquisiteness was deceptive; her 'porcelain doll' appearance belied an emotional toughness whetted by unimaginable hardship and tragedy.

Samuel Trainor was in attendance and served as the best man to Texas Ranger Rudolph Jones, his former apprentice. Shortly before the wedding Rudy had satisfied the informal training and was duly sworn in as a full-fledged officer of the law serving with the elite Texas Rangers.

Within days of the wedding the newlyweds began work on restoring the family ranch and after a couple of weeks were camping out full time on the property. The young couple invited Ralph, James, and Peter to live with them. The community of Gainesville showered the orphans with love and volunteered the manual labor to organize a house and barn raising. Several local businesses donated building materials. The entire able-bodied community spent a couple of weekends getting the cabin and barn in the dry. As time permitted other improvements to the property included a fenced burial plot, a deep-water well with irrigation ditches to the garden. The following year Lizzy gave birth to a baby girl who just happened to be the mother of Asa McCawl, my grandfather.

Chapter 3

LORNA, A FAIR LADY

Spread before me lay land deeds, death certificates, high school diplomas, a large family Bible, and Lorna Fulton Maxwell Long's water-stained and tattered journal. The following section of the novel "Cheatiebo" contains Lorna's compelling life's narrative.

The Maxwell family arrived from the British Isles in the mid 1780ies. They settled fertile ground that bordered the coastal grasslands of Chesapeake Bay. Their farm was situated near a hamlet on the outskirts of Williamsburg. The farm's soil was suited for growing tobacco and cotton. Samson Maxwell arrived in the new world an astute farmer. Success through trial and error rewarded his hard work. Like the other farmers of that era and locale, Samson acquired a sizable African slave workforce.

The Maxwell's quickly abandoned the established state religion of the British Empire in favor of Calvinistic Protestantism. They left behind a disease-ridden society, over-crowded cities, and farmland depleted of crucial minerals. Samson and Dorothy Maxwell were well educated, socially refined, and civic minded. Samson, a natural leader, was destined to serve his community.

Samuel and Dorothy Maxwell's two daughters and four sons grew up in a well-disciplined household. The five older Maxwell siblings were required to contribute manual labor and apply themselves to the schooling offered. They grew to be well-adjusted and industrious adults. Most families have at least one black sheep among them, and the Maxwell family had John Silas. The community of Williamsburg was minded to overlook the Maxwell's rogue son, preferring to stay on a friendly basis with such an influential family.

Dorothy conceived John Silas during menopause. A child so late in life was a strain on her health and disrupted her social life in the community. Dorothy, being a kind hearted woman, soon accepted the notion of rearing another son. Dorothy had always kept a tidy home, but during her difficult pregnancy she shifted her workload to her domestic staff. Dorothy had the trappings of a privileged existence: a two-story mansion, a well-manicured lawn, a productive vegetable garden, and an adequate number of domestic slaves to maintain the mansion and grounds.

Dorothy had her hands full caring for the colicky John Silas. As he grew into a toddler, he was unusually cute and angelic looking. She unwittingly established a pattern of catering to little John Silas. The man that began as a fretful infant matured into a narcissistic, lazy, and obnoxious embarrassment to his parents.

As a teenage boy, John Silas was apprenticed to his mother's brother, Winton, the local blacksmith, but the arrangement didn't work out. Though John Silas possessed the intelligence and dexterity to learn the trade, he was hopelessly lazy. The working environment of the forge was objectionable to the self-centered lad. This created a serious dilemma for Winton. Dorothy was his closest sibling. After a couple of months, Winton threw up his hands in frustration and replaced John Silas with a younger boy from the village.

Dorothy asked John Silas' oldest brother, Gordon to put him to work on the family plantation. Gordon accommodated his mother and assigned John Silas to work as a supervisor over the workers in the tobacco drying sheds. After a few days working in the sizzling sheds John Silas began shirking his responsibility. Gordon found the workers assigned to John Silas unsupervised and slacking in their duties. Nearby he discovered an inebriated John Silas, sound asleep under a shade tree.

Gordon's reprimand failed to elicit the necessary contrition. John Silas was transferred to the less accountable task of field monitor. The assignment required John Silas to supervise the field hands on horseback. Right away John Silas became complacent and took liberties that affected the harvest. The final straw came when a vigilant Gordon realized that John Silas was missing from his field. He tracked his wayward brother and discovered him cavorting in a local swimming hole with a lady of dubious reputation. At that point Gordon lost all hope that his youngest brother would ever be reliable. After the latest infraction Gordon called a family meeting and was successful in banning John Silas from ever working on the plantation.

Dorothy offered excuses for her lackadaisical son, but agreed to follow the family mandate. When Gordon told John Silas of the decision, he made a great show of contrition and offered the well-rehearsed and disingenuous promises to do better. Heavy heartedly Dorothy and Sam informed John Silas that he could temporarily occupy a vacant cottage in the slaves' quarters and was welcome to take his meals with the family while he pursued other career paths. John Silas had apparently burned his last bridge to family privileges. As usual John Silas rationalized his situation and attributed Gordon's contempt to sibling jealousy.

John Silas was incredulous over being fired. Did his family actually expect him to go out and find work like a common ruffian? He soon realized that was exactly what they had in mind.

John Silas told Dorothy, "Me and my girlfriend, Lorna will be moving far away. You will never see me again." Within a week, John Silas proposed to Lorna. Dorothy hoped to avoid a scandal and volunteered to organize a wedding ceremony. Dorothy got permission to use the nearby Baptist chapel. She wanted to keep the unpleasantness hidden from the community. The informal and private ceremony went off without embarrassment.

John Silas found living among the slaves humiliating and even hazardous. He had always treated the servants with contempt and was reaping what he had sown. Some mysterious warnings had John Silas afraid of his own shadow. A dead rabbit was found at his door. A few days later a voodoo doll full of pins was discovered underneath his pillow. The fetish indicated that he was under a curse of some kind. Burrs under his saddle sent him flying into a hedge row. John Silas' first and only attempt to partake of the family meal was so awkward it ended with Dorothy running from the table in tears. His charmed existence was history.

With a wife and a baby on the way, John Silas had complicated his situation. He went to Dorothy and fell weeping at her feet. When she said there was nothing else she could do, he renewed his threat to leave the area forever. He thought that would be enough for his mother to intervene on his behalf, and the ploy worked. Dorothy hatched a scheme and finally convinced Sam to go along.

John Silas' bride, Lorna, was attractive and intelligent. Lorna had fallen victim to John Silas' powers of persuasion, a vulnerable flower for his picking. Lorna, a child of poverty fell in love with the image John Silas presented. A suave, fast-talking John Silas used Lorna's emotional neediness to capture her affections.

Well before John Silas entered the picture, the village schoolmarm, Lilly Ratcliff recognized Lorna's above average intelligence. She would often spend personal time with Lorna and encouraged her to take full advantage of the schooling available. Early nineteenth century Williamsburg was more progressive than many communities when it came to educating girl children. Lorna did not disappoint Miss Ratcliff. In fact, Lorna became Miss Ratcliff's star pupil and helped tutor the other students. Lorna's teaching talent and patience with children had developed from years of caring for her own younger siblings.

As Lorna became more comfortable with Miss Ratcliff, she gradually revealed the truth about her dysfunctional parents. Miss Ratcliff confided her own sad start in life. The teenage Lilly's intelligence was repulsed by the illiterate yokels that showed an interest in courting her. Sadly, she was not blessed with the physical beauty that attracted the sort of men that make good husbands. Rather settle for just any man, she chose the lonely life of a spinster schoolmarm.

Lorna fell behind in her school work because of her sporadic attendance. Miss Ratcliff took pity and tutored Lorna privately long enough to realize just how bright she was. Right away they bonded as kindred spirits. Lilly vowed to help Lorna mature into a proper and educated young lady. The girl was much too intelligent to go through life uneducated.

One day Miss Ratcliff surprised Lorna with enough fabric to sew a stylish frock and matching bonnet. The lonely spinster had plans for Lorna that she didn't reveal until the dress was almost finished. As their friendship deepened Miss Ratcliff insisted that Lorna call her Lilly, with the understanding that Lorna should still call her Miss Ratcliff at school. The two of them shared many happy hours sewing the dress.

Even a casual observer would recognize that the schoolmarm was attempting to live vicariously through her young protégé. They satisfied a certain emptiness for companionship in each other. The careless and inept Fulton family, perpetually dealing with crises, hardly noticed the changes in Lorna. As long as she was careful to finish up her chores, she received no notice from her preoccupied parents. It was their lack of attention that freed Lorna to devote the necessary time to her schooling.

When the frock was almost finished, Lilly mentioned the coming 'Changing of the Leaves Ball' that she would be chaperoning. After much cajoling, Lorna agreed to attend the annual community dance. Lilly started preparing Lorna for the dance well in advance. She taught Lorna the importance of posture and moving gracefully. Lorna spent hours walking about Lilly's house with a book balanced on her head. "Lorna, this is important, when you are conversing pay attention to what people say. You must be able to discuss the topic by responding with a comment or question. Keep your eye contact subtle and always be friendly and kind hearted."

Lilly announced, "Lorna, shall we dance? We will start with the waltz and go on to the minuet. Lilly's poor feet suffered being trampled upon until Lorna got the steps ingrained in her mind. In no time Lorna was swaying and whirling about Lilly's living room. Lorna had the mechanics down but needed practice on gracefulness. Lilly put a book on Lorna's head while she danced and that worked its magic. Preparation for the ball became more frantic as the time grew near. There was still so much to teach Lorna in such a short time. They quickly covered when to courtesy and the proper handshake. The two women staged introductions and giving and receiving compliments in a gracious manner.

Lorna learned to eat as though she wasn't hungry. Lilly kept reminding her, "Tiny bites and space them out. Slowly sip no more than a spoon full at a time. Oh, and remember to lightly blot your mouth with your napkin. I recommend eating before you go. Lilly had Lorna practice folding her hands in her lap, holding her knees together at all times and crossing her feet at the ankle when sitting. Be sure and let it be known that you are having fun, but keep your laughter soft and reserved."

As the day grew near Lilly was apprehensive over Lorna's readiness for the dance. She didn't want to leave any details to chance. Lorna would never forgive her if she inadvertently embarrassed herself. She thought of one final instruction, "Lorna, always stand back and allow the gentleman to open doors and wait for him to assist you when exiting a carriage."

The day of the ball arrived, and Lilly began styling Lorna's hair around noon. Lorna had the kind of thick and healthy hair every 16-year-old girl hoped for. Lilly wanted to frame Lorna's lovely oval face by parting the hair that covered the top and sides and tying it at the crown. She used a hot curling rod to form cascading ringlets that fell over the remainder of Lorna's glistening waist length hair. At the crown where the hair was tied, Lilly fastened a beautiful diamond and gold broach that had belonged to her mother. The final touch was to pull a few tiny strands of hair to hang in curls around her ears. Lilly commented that Lorna's complexion was so clear and bright there was no need for makeup. Just some highlighting. Lorna had perfectly shaped brows and lush lashes. Lilly applied a thin coat of lanolin to Lorna's face and neck. She mixed some red pigment with a drop or two of olive oil and applied it to Lorna's lips and cheeks.

Lilly loaned Lorna her mother's string of pearls and a diamond dinner ring. The style of her dress was straight from Paris, France. The sky-blue gown had an empire waist and a long flowing skirt. The gown had a deeply cut square neckline with a modesty panel. The short puff sleeves barely cupped her shoulders. The light weight fabric was topped with a floral pinafore made of pastel blue chiffon edged with a delicate lace. Peeking from beneath the floor length gown were white satin slippers tied at the ankle with white ribbon. The final touches were an oriental fan and a compact beaded hand bag with wrist bands.

The finished image of Lorna caused Lilly to catch her breath. Lilly was standing behind Lorna as she sat before the vanity mirror. Words such as captivating, enchanting, and endearing spilled from Lilly's mouth. Her eyes were flashing with affection. While Lilly dressed for the ball, she reminded Lorna to eat a quick meal so that there would be time to brush her teeth and re-apply her lip rouge. Lilly wore a navy-blue two-piece garment made of polished brocade. She wore gold ear loops and a golden chain that reached to her mid chest. Lorna remarked, "Oh Lilly, your suit is quite fine and very distinguished. You will be attracting plenty of notice yourself! You are lovely!"

Lilly and Lorna were equally excited and nervous on the way to the ball room. Lilly accurately predicted that the other young ladies would be green with jealousy when they saw their latest competition.

Lilly was required to report an hour early. She assigned Lorna the task of affixing name tags as the guests arrived at the door. Being busy helped Lorna control her nervousness. Her heart had been jumping rope inside her chest all afternoon. When they first arrived, Lorna felt a moment of panic and almost ran from the building. But then she looked at Lilly and realized how much her cowardice would disappoint her mentor and beloved friend. After all, Lilly had spent hundreds of hours at considerable expense preparing Lorna for the evening.

Lilly noticed that Lorna was genuinely enjoying the dancing. That made all of her effort worth the effort. Lorna's hair was even staying put.

As soon as the music began, Lorna was surprised at the succession of young men inviting her to dance. Now she understood why the dances were so popular. She didn't want the evening to end. With so much attention from the gentlemen, Lorna's expectations for the future took a dramatic turn, full of romance and adventure. She was thinking, *now that I am a proper lady just perhaps—*. Her private reflection was interrupted by a rather handsome gentleman who introduced himself as John Silas Maxwell. She took his hand as he led her to the dance floor. His obvious admiration was almost brazen. He held her closer and kept her captive between songs. She was mesmerized by the intensity of his gaze. He appeared to be older than the other young men and was certainly more gallant in his mannerisms. Lorna's lack of experience with courtship was well disguised thanks to Miss Ratcliff. Her stylish attire, erect posture, and poise had worked their magic. It was an evening Lorna would remember for the rest of her life. Being the bell-of-the ball was heady stuff for Lorna, already predisposed to romantic fantasy.

Lorna had never heard of the Maxwell family or anything about the notorious exploits of John Silas. When he asked if he could walk her home, she readily agreed. A courtship began that progressed to an engagement in short order. John Silas was accomplished at flattery and seduction. He had an ulterior motive for the romance. A girl like Lorna would figure into his scheme to be rescued by his mother. He was confident all would return to normal.

Even in everyday dress Lorna was appealing and curvaceous. She had a cute turned-up nose, smiley eyes of a dark blue color, and perfect teeth. Lorna's emotionally immature parents had shifted too much of their rightful responsibility to Lorna. She was determined to escape their clutches as soon as her siblings were old enough to care for themselves. At just the right time, John Silas entered her life.

Lorna's story book marriage was short lived. She had traded one bad situation for another. She was forced to give up on her dreams and quickly resigned herself to a loveless and abusive marriage.

Dorothy Maxwell found Lorna awkwardly shy. She would have preferred that John Silas pick a wife from one of the other wealthy plantation families. But Dorothy was soon wooed by Lorna's sweet and unassuming nature. What Lorna lacked in pedigree was compensated for in her kindly spirit.

As an adult John Silas had embarrassed his family with escapades involving womanizing, laziness, and public drunkenness. Williamsburg made allowances for the errant son since none among them were prepared to cast the first stone. After pleading with John Silas not to leave the area, Dorothy offered him the deed to a rundown farm. The abandoned home site was located a few miles inland from the Maxwell plantation. Dorothy made the offer to John Silas and Lorna with mixed reaction. John Silas immediately recalled the site and realized the work it would require to make the place livable.

While John Silas was hatching a scheme to strike a better bargain with his parents, Lorna leapt from her chair and placed her arms around Dorothy's neck and kissed her cheek. "Thank you, sweet Dorothy, how will we ever be able to thank you enough! A little farm, just what I have always dreamt of. I promise to do all I can to make it a proper home and make you proud of us. John Silas, you have the most wonderful parents! Can we go now and see the farm, I don't think I can wait, please take us there."

As soon as Lorna saw the little cabin and ten acres of farmland, she was beside herself with gratefulness for the opportunity the property provided. John Silas decided to go along with Lorna's excitement and tried to appear excited too. Dorothy found Lorna's excitement over the little homestead appealing and was prompted to do even more than she had planned. Lorna clasped her hands and squealed, "Wishes really do come true!"

Dorothy suggested Lorna look through the shed where spare household furnishings were stored and available to slaves and hired-help on first come basis. Most of the furniture was nicer than what Lorna had grown up with. The items she selected quickly filled a large wagon. Dorothy instructed the driver to take Lorna to the farm and off load the cargo. At the last minute, Dorothy decided to ride along. When Dorothy saw Lorna's face light up as the sad little shack came into view, an urge came over her to help get the little cabin in shape. Dorothy rationalized getting involved because of the coming grandchild. Dorothy relished the prospect of having a mission, something to occupy her time and a source of excitement. It would be fun to work with Lorna in the remodel. Dorothy had the resources to make the farmhouse into a weather tight and safe place very quickly.

The following day Dorothy arrived with a crew of Negro carpenters and a wagon loaded with roofing material, lumber, a roll of wool carpeting. The first day the well was cleaned out, weeds cut down, and a garden plot plowed. The crew of men had come prepared to camp at the site and the following morning the roof was totally resurfaced with new shake shingles. Glass windows replaced the shutters, and the doors were replaced. The interior walls were lined with pine lumber and then varnished. The front porch was rebuilt and the fireplace and chimney re-cemented. After only three days the place was ready for Lorna to move in and spend the night.

Lastly the lean-to style barn was repaired. The fourth day Dorothy sent a servant to deliver a milk cow with new calf, a dozen laying hens and rooster, and a mother sow with a litter of piglets. Dorothy's guilt was assuaged as far as John Silas' punishment, and she was having a delightful time getting to know her new daughter-in-law.

Privately Dorothy was coming to grips with her parenting of John Silas. She pondered the difference between children that are catered to and grow up the center of attention like John Silas, as opposed to neglected children like Lorna that are forced to fend for themselves and are deprived of adoration. From times eternal, parents like Dorothy have struggled with the same emotional pain and guilt when their offspring go astray. Unable to undo John Silas's early years, Dorothy settled on helping her son one last time.

It was late January, and Lorna launched herself into making the place a real home she could be proud of. Preparing for spring planting came first on her to-do list. She spread manure from the Maxwell corrals on the garden patch. Lorna was now in her second trimester with child, but the pregnancy did not deter her from hard work. Dorothy offered to help with anything at all, but Lorna wanted to do as much on her on as possible. She repaired the crumbling milking stall, fixed a leaky henhouse roof, and reinforced the fence around the pigsty.

John Silas complemented Lorna's improvements, but never found an opportune time to actually pitch in on the manual labor. Lorna invited her younger brother, 15-year-old Rodney to sleep over and give her a hand with the renovation. She was determined to provide a better setting for the coming child than the sad home she had grown up in. Lorna contacted her laundry patrons and informed them that she was available but from a new location. Several of the customers began using her services. She knew how to be frugal and used the meager coins she earned to purchase building materials.

Lorna invited her 11-year-old Sister Betsy to come to stay when delivery was eminent. Lorna asked Dorothy to send her a book on childbirth, and she and Betsy studied the pages and gathered the suggested supplies. In early May, a girl child was born to Lorna and John Silas. The labor had progressed quickly, and Lorna and Betsy successfully delivered the child. The baby was full term and healthy. Lorna chose the name Dora Jane, after a character in one of her favorite books. Lorna was full of the new awakening that comes with a first child. The blessed event represented a magical transition. The love she felt for the tiny person entrusted to her care left her breathless.

Lorna tried to share the wonder of parenthood with John Silas, but he didn't react to the baby as she would have hoped. She grudgingly admitted that John Silas was too immature to make a good father. Dorothy was a regular visitor and showered Lorna with a layette and garments of the finest quality available. There was lots of lacy blankets, and ruffled comforters, silver spoons, and bonnets. Lorna had never seen such lovely baby things. They literally took her breath away.

Very early in the marriage Lorna adjusted her expectations for John Silas, who made it plain that he would do as he well-pleased. A few weeks after the birth of Dora Jane, John Silas was celebrating at a village tavern until after midnight. The company he kept, the community's most rowdy and drunken rabble, factored into John Silas's troubled life. John Silas' propensity toward dishonesty and law breaking was about to sweep the innocent Lorna and Dora Jane along into a life of lawlessness.

One late night in early June, John Silas stumbled through the door, and without regard for the late hour, jabbed his sleeping wife in the ribs, and asked, "How'd you like being rich? Wake up Lorna, you have to hear this!"

A drowsy Lorna whispered "Quiet, you're gonna wake up Dora. Come on to bed."

Because Lorna failed to show the desired interest, John Silas removed his boots and threw them across the room. Reeking of alcohol, he angrily shouted, "Never mind, no one believes in me, not even my own wife. I'll show you, and the rest too." Fully clothed, John Silas fell into bed next to Lorna. A startled wail came from the crib. Snoring within a few seconds, the drunk was oblivious to the crying baby. Lorna stumbled from her bed to the crib and then on to a rocking chair. Lorna changed Dora's diaper on her lap and then lovingly offered her breast.

For the next month, John Silas was gone from home most of the time. Lorna threw herself into her work, refusing to dwell on the disappointing reality of her relationship with John Silas.

On a mid-summer morning, near sunup, John Silas ran into the house, and loaded his rifle. He whispered to Lorna, "We alone? Start packing, we got to move away from here." Parked in front of the house was a large buckboard hitched to a team of 4 mules. John Silas was acting in the most bazaar manner. His facial expression frightened Lorna. As he scurried about gathering household items that he piled onto the bed, he growled for Lorna to help him pack and to hurry. He drew buckets of water and filled a barrel bolted to the side of the wagon. Lorna placed her hands on her hips and said, "Before I start packing, I need to know why. What has happened? How can we just pick up and leave our home?"

John Silas rang his hands and said, "You know that Constable Winslow, well he tried to arrest me, and I tried to get away. Winslow tripped and fell against a rock wall and hit his head hard. I checked when he didn't get up. He was out cold, and I held my ear to his face, and he wasn't breathing so I panicked and hid. I didn't mean to kill him, but I would for sure be blamed for murder. We have to leave before folks find his body. Here, I will help you." He started piling clothes and quilts onto the bed and tied them into bundles. He removed a drawer from a wardrobe and started filling it with pots, skillets, and tin ware. He packed a trunk with clothing and bedding. The commotion woke the baby, and Lorna had to stop and care for her.

As Lorna fed the baby, she asked, "Why did the constable want to arrest you?"

John Silas paused to answer, "It was over the whiskey I been making and selling folks. Remember, I tried to tell you 'bout it that night. Old Winslow claimed I been poisoning folks. Not nothing wrong with my brew, I been drinking it myself. Here, look at the money me and the boys made." Eyes flashing with greed, he pulled a poke of gold and silver coins from his pocket. Then Lorna said, "John Silas, you need to go back to town and explain what happened. Surely, they will understand that you did not intend to kill the constable. John Silas whirled around and pointed at Lorna, "When did folks in this community ever give me the benefit of the doubt?" Lorna realized that he was right. Then Lorna said, "How about Dora and I stay here, and when you get settled, you can send for us."

To this John Silas' anger exploded. "You and Dora are coming with me! You are all I have left." Then he said, "If you refuse to go, I'm taking Dora with me. It's your decision." Lorna knew that it was an empty threat, but was afraid to resist.

"John, calm yourself, we have to think straight. You're right, we will go with you." Then she asked, "Did you hide the body?"

He answered, "Well, no, —you think I should? I just wanted to get away before someone saw me, so I stole this wagon and team from the livery stable."

The gravity of the situation started to dawn on Lorna. "I think you need to go back, and if it hasn't been discovered, hide the body when no one is around. It will give us a head start."

John Silas paced back and forth a couple of times. He repeatedly ran his hands through his sandy colored, shoulder length hair. "You're right; I'll go back and hide the body. I can unhitch one of the mules and ride through the woods."

Lorna's mind was racing. *While John Silas is gone should I run away and hide? This is bad, no good choices! Oh my. My parents might take us in, but that is not what I want. My life is ruined forever if I go with John Silas. The law will be after me too. I will be giving up this farm.*

What if I ask Miss Lilly for help? Yes, that is what I should do. Lilly will hide me until John was gone. Then she could tell the Head Constable what happened and ask for protection. Maybe Dorothy would let me stay on the farm. Lorna took a big drink of water, filled a bottle with water, and stuffed a bag with diapers and baby clothes. She took her hidden coins from the hole in the wall, and just as she was ready to make a run for Lilly's house, she got scared John Silas might catch up to her.

Could she walk that far carrying a baby and the bag on such a warm day? John Silas is a dangerous man, capable of anything. He is sure to come after me and even kill me? Dora would be left without a mother. For the moment Dora needed to nurse and have a diaper change. She supposed John Silas would be gone for 3 to 4 hours. That gave her time to make up her mind on what to do. Lorna decided to her change clothing and put on better shoes for walking.

After only an hour and a half, John Silas returned catching Lorna leaving the porch about to run into the woods. She reentered the house and pretended to be packing.

John Silas jumped from the horse and said, "I hid the body, but to be safe we need to hurry in case someone was watching."

Lorna avoided eye contact and asked where. He replied, "You know that old well at the Beecher place? I just dumped him in and covered it back. Ain't nobody lived there for a long time now, at least five years."

By midafternoon, they were ready to leave. As they rode away, Lorna was overcome with fear and sadness. She broke down and wept aloud. Dread of what lay ahead caused her to wish she had stayed single. In addition to the household goods, John Silas made room for the copper kettle, coils and other paraphernalia for operating the liquor still. A last-minute decision was made to take the cow and calf. They could be sold if need be. John Silas tied the cow to the back of the wagon but left the calf free. Travel with the cow and calf was slow, but it didn't appear that they were being pursued.

After two days of almost non-stop travel, an exhausted John Silas and Lorna pulled off the westward leading trail near a creek and hid the wagon in a dense grove of willow and cottonwood trees. After taking time to sleep for several hours, John Silas walked to a high point to see if they were being followed. Satisfied that there were no pursuers, John Silas went to work constructing a frame over the bed of the wagon. Then he left Lorna and Dora and rode one of the mules in search of enough waterproofed canvas to cover the wagon frame. He was gone overnight, and when night fell Lorna huddled in the bed of the wagon, frightened by the night sounds. She was thankful that it wasn't raining.

When John Silas finally returned, he had a big roll of canvas and a dozen jars of preserved food. She asked, "Where did you get the canvas and food?"

"It found me and wanted to come along." he answered. It disturbed Lorna that dishonesty was second nature to John Silas. He seemed to derive satisfaction from preying on others. At this point Lorna's primary concern was for Dora, and the stolen canvas would keep them sheltered from the elements. As she worked over a cooking fire, she imagined what Miss Lilly would think of her if she knew about the thievishness.

Lorna asked John Silas, "Where are we going?"

He answered, "It don't matter none as long as it is far away from here. I think we ought to join up with a wagon train and start using a different last name. How 'bout we be the Jones family from the Boston area. Howdy do Mrs. Jones." John Silas removed his hat and bowed, with a silly sideways grin on his face. Lorna managed a fake smile and quickly turned back to the food preparation.

Lorna decided to stay busy and keep John Silas happy best she could. It didn't take much to get him riled. Right off she arranged the living space in the bed of the wagon. She cleaned out a drawer from the chest and padded it for Dora's bed. She fixed a bed for her and John Silas at the head of the wagon bed. All items needed for stops along the trail were stowed just inside the tailgate. Lorna hung a clothesline high in the frame of the canopy for drying diapers. Getting organized distracted Lorna from the terrible reality. It helped her deal with a sense of impending doom. Lorna nervously hummed a little tune as she worked.

John Silas remarked, "While I take a little nap how about you fixing up some supper? One of those jars of food looked like beef stew. That sounds good. Oh, and coffee with that, Mrs. Jones." His laughter was too loud and frightened Dora. Lorna gathered the baby into her arms to soothe her.

"John, hun, you feel like dragging up some firewood before you lay down?"

"Ah, Lorna, I just got my boots off, look right over there, I see some wood that you can use close by. Wake me when the food is ready."

After only four days, a small wagon train overtook the "Jones family." The trail boss was a tall, barrel-chested man called Jack Long. While engaged in conversation with John Silas, Lorna observed Jack Long's piercing gaze as he sized up John Silas. Long mentioned that he had been hoping to add another wagon or so to his group. He felt that the larger the train, the less likely that they would be attacked by Indians or outlaws. Long's scrutiny made John Silas uncomfortable, and he fidgeted and looked at his feet. He had an uneasy feeling about this Trail Boss. He thought, *His kind is hard to get anything over on.* Next Boss

Long looked at Mrs. Jones and the little one and tipped his hat. Then Long proclaimed, "I'm the boss of this wagon train, you got a problem with that, speak now. This train is made up of fine, God-fearin' folks. We don't abide no drinking or gambling." John Silas was a little too quick to agree, "Yeh, yeh, we won't be giving you no trouble."

Trail protocol dictated that the Jones wagon be assigned to the end of the line. At first the dust wasn't bad because of a series of summer showers, but as the road dried, John Silas went to Jack Long and asked to move up in the line. Jack, with an air of absolute authority said, "Sorry, but I can't have that. We all hate the dust, but it would be unfair to the wagons that signed up before you. Try tying a wet kerchief over your faces. If the dust gets too bad, drop back a bit." John Silas bristled at the pronouncement, but waited until Jack was out of earshot to express his anger. As usual, Lorna became his whipping post and meekly absorbed his outburst of vitriol.

When the train stopped to camp that first evening, it was Lorna's chance to meet the travelers. She craved companionship and hoped to get acquainted with the women of the train. She took a minute in front of her tiny cracked looking glass to neatly braid her long hair and coil it around the crown of her head and then washed her face. Lorna thought, "This could be a new beginning, a clean start. The trip west would provide an opportunity to escape John Silas' reputation." In the past John Silas' knack for offending people had resulted in social isolation for Lorna. That first evening, the wagon just ahead in the formation invited Lorna and John Silas to share their meal.

Sally and Lindsey Trenton introduced themselves, along with 15-year-old Bert. They served dutch-oven biscuits and a vegetable and ham soup. As the two families sat around the campfire, John Silas did most of the talking and embarrassed Lorna with his boasting. Lorna kept her eyes lowered to hide her embarrassment. John Silas misrepresented himself as a businessman and indicated that he would be opening an emporium in Kentucky. The Trenton family was politely reserved. Lorna could tell that they were not likely to cultivate much of a friendship with John Silas.

Each evening, just before bed time John Silas would take a walk into the darkness and soothe his addiction with a draw from a bottle of his home brew. Mornings found John Silas feeling nauseous with a throbbing headache. It never occurred to him that chemicals in the liquor were gradually poisoning him. Officer Winslow was right about the brew he had been peddling in the community. Being hung over accentuated John Silas' belligerent nature, resulting in a growing wedge of resentment in the marriage.

Westward progress was slow but steady under the guidance of Boss Long. Jack had made the trip west twice before at the head of a wagon train, but this time he planned to settle in Kentucky. His surroundings back in Massachusetts reminded him of the painful loss of his wife and child. He was hoping new scenery would help to dull his pain.

In spite of John Silas' obnoxious nature, Lorna was making friends with the travelers. So far, she liked them all. There was the middle-aged, childless couple, Lyla and Kingston Bullard. The Bullards were searching for a new start after fire had wiped them out. Lyla was a confident and industrious person with a kind and thoughtful personality. She was a natural-born leader. She had worked as a battlefield nurse during the Revolutionary War, and that made her an important asset to the group. Lyla was the closest thing to a doctor the Long Expedition would find. Kingston was a hard worker always ready to do his part. He was at least ten years older than Lyla, but the age difference didn't affect the close bond between them.

The Trentons, Lindsey, Sally, and Bert were planning to settle near some relatives already situated in Kentucky. Their dream was to settle on property near their family and establish a dairy farm. Sally loved to have people around her. She had a lively personality and was quick to see the humor in mishaps. She was the optimist's optimist. The lines on her middle-aged face graced her with a permanent smile.

The Olsen family, five in all, was shy, but once they became acquainted was warm and endearing. They were Methodist immigrants from Sweden. Abraham and Lucinda were affectionate but strict parents. God had blessed them with two boys and a girl. Both Abe and Lucy sported the characteristic curly blonde hair and blue eyes of Scandinavia. They had a thick Swedish accent that was hard to decipher. Lucy had lost her girlish figure but had a comely face. Other than time spent cooking and doing laundry, Lucy's hands were perpetually busy at knitting. The entire family wore the authentic ethnic designs of their mother country. She had stowed away in their Conestoga wagon a wooden box stuffed full of woolen yarn. Among her handcrafted creations were multicolored sweaters, caps, mittens, socks, shawls and two-sided comforters. The women of the group loved to watch Lucy turn out articles with her dexterous, rapid hand movements, and some were learning the craft themselves thanks to Lucy's instruction. Abe was over six feet tall, lanky, and his poor posture caused him to walk with an awkward gate. The smile lines that mapped his sun-damaged face reflected his good nature. The eldest child 14-year-old Ian was a genetic copy of his father: the middle child, Helga, a sickly 10-year-old shared her mother's enthusiasm for knitting and was already turning out perfectly crafted items. The youngest, little Rolf, aged 6, pretty much stayed in trouble with his stern Father, and though mentally bright, he suffered from a hearing deficiency. His cuteness and mischievous facial expressions generated a degree of tolerance the two older children had not benefited from. Ian was at the gawky stage of adolescence and was plagued with a squeaky voice and pimply face.

Before joining the wagon train, Lucy and Abe decided to supplement the children's traditional education by teaching them about the New World on a firsthand basis. Both Lucy and Abe wanted the children to sense a spirit of adventure all along the trek westward. Abe compared the family's journey west to Father Abraham's travels from Mesopotamia toward the Fertile Crescent. The children took the hardships of the journey as part of a great adventure. They were cultivating an appreciation for the grandeur of the landscape. The two older children played a game of imagining all sorts of adventures that lay just beyond every crook in the trail. Before long the adventures of the trail became all too real.

Tommy Thacker and his 18-year-old son Walter were in search of a new beginning. Tommy was a jack-of-all-trades and had extensive experience in trading and trapping on the frontier. He was an expert at recognizing edible and medicinal wild plants. Everyone called Tommy 'Old Tommy,' though he was only in his mid-forties. He was a likable cuss and loved to joke and play his harmonica. Old Tommy had a bum leg, the result of time spent fighting with the Virginia Regulars. Needless to say, he didn't have much use for the "blankety-blank" Red Coats. Fifteen years before, Tommy's wife had been abducted as she worked in her vegetable garden, most likely by a Creek raiding party. A pain-maddened Tommy left three-year-old Walter with neighbors and unsuccessfully searched for his wife among the tribes in the northeast.

The more folks got to know Tommy, the more they respected and trusted him. He would turn out to be an important member of the wagon train. Young Walter Thacker was a tribute to Tommy's parenting. The lad had grown up working hard and was a quick learner. It was unfortunate that he lacked a formal education because he would have excelled in the classroom. Walt had a slightly twisted sense of humor and was known for his love of practical jokes. The women of the group sometimes discussed his good looks and the fact that he would make some young woman a prize catch. Walt had a muscular frame and was well coordinated. His brown eyes and dark brown hair and beard made him appear to be older than his eighteen years. Tommy could not have been prouder of Walt, but treated him with gruffness. Jack Long enlisted Walt to drive his wagon when he rode ahead to scout out the trail. Walt took Jack's trust and confidence seriously and would have gone to any length to justify Jack's faith in him.

Finally, there were the newlyweds, Jane and Jonathan Macintosh. Following a traditional Irish wedding, they had sailed for the new world in search of cheap farmland. Economic times in Ireland held little promise for the young couple. The delight the newlyweds took in each other was a reminder of the days of young love. The presence of the love-birds served to remind the other married couples of their own honeymoon days. Jon was self-conscious and stammered when forced to speak before the group. His fair complexion and blond sun-streaked hair gave him a boyishly handsome appearance. Jon was prone to blushing at the slightest mention of wedded bliss. Jane had a beautiful soprano singing voice and loved to sing as she worked. Among her repertoire were the ancient songs of the Motherland like "Barbara Allen" and "The Wagoner Lad." Compliments on her voice encouraged more singing. Jane's curly head of fiery red hair reached to her waist and complimented her exuberant charm.

> *"Oh-oo hard is the fortune of all womankind,*
> *She's always controlled, she's always confined,*
> *Controlled by her parents until she's a bride,*
> *A slave to her husband the rest of her life."*

> *Oh, my parents don't like him because he is poor.*
> *They say he's not worthy of entering my door.*
> *He works for a living, his money is his own.*
> *If they don't like him they can leave him alone.*

> *Your horses are hungry, go feed them some hay.*
> *Then sit down here by me as long as you may.*
> *My horses ain't hungry, they won't eat your hay.*
> *So fare thee well, darling, I'll be on my way.*

Chapter 4

GETTING ACQUAINTED

After a few weeks on the trail, Lorna and Jane became fast friends. Jane's openness and kindly nature appealed to Lorna. Jane recognized a certain kinship with Lorna and frequently confided her most private thoughts. Jane was open about her desire for a large family. Jane adored Dora. and Lorna could always depend on her to give a helping hand with the baby.

Boss Long was traveling alone. A person who kept his own council, Jack would only say that he needed a change of scenery. He was consistent about enforcing his rules. Lorna could not help but be curious about his past. After a couple of weeks on the trail, shortly after John Silas and Lorna had gone to bed, Boss Long approached their wagon and called out, "John Silas, I need to speak with you, come on out here."

A long-john clad John Silas climbed down from the wagon and asked, "What the hell do you want at this time of night?"

Jack reminded John Silas that it was his turn to stand watch for the first half of the night. "Did you forget or what?" Then Jack said, "What is that I smell on your breath?" John Silas made up a story about a medicinal elixir for his cough and glared back at Jack with exaggerated indignation.

Letting the matter drop, Jack said, "We need you to walk the outer perimeter, and don't forget your gun. We could run into Indians anywhere along here. They like to steal stock and sometimes take women captive." John Silas moaned and fussed under his breath as he pulled on his clothing and boots. Next John Silas fished out his side arm. It wasn't loaded so that delayed his arrival at the muster site. Lorna pretended to be asleep so that he would not lash out at her.

The next day John Silas asked Lorna to drive the team so that he could catch up on his sleep. Sleep was something he seemed to need a lot of. She handed him a sleeping Dora, and he put her in the bed next to him. Within a few minutes Dora was crying. John Silas cursed and handed the baby back to Lorna. Lorna almost asked him to switch places, but sensed that he was still angry over having to stand guard and held her tongue. She laid Dora across her lap and began feeding her, forcing her to handle the reins one-handed. The mules quickly realized that Lorna was not able to control them and veered from the trail and stopped to graze.

Out of frustration she stood and flicked the whip on their rumps and shouted, "Get-up, move it, ha!" This woke John Silas, and he raised his head to see what had happened. He saw that Lorna had allowed the team to leave the trail, and he flew into a rage. Without considering the consequences, he decided to put some fear into the mules and fired his pistol into the air.

The gunshot caused the mules to rear and then bolt. As the wagon bounced over uneven rocky ground, Lorna along with Dora held in a fabric sling were catapulted from the wagon seat. Mother and child landed in a heap, with Dora on the bottom. At first Dora was silent and appeared to be unconscious. Lorna watched as she turned blue. The baby revived but could not breathe. It was several seconds before she took a breath and then began a cry that was more like a scream. Lorna sat up and gathered Dora into her arms. She removed Dora's blanket and checked for injuries. The baby had a cut on her cheek that oozed blood, and Lorna noticed as she was moving both arms but only one leg. Dora was not moving her right leg! Lorna saw a large bruise already turning black on Dora's right hip. When Lorna touched her hip, she screamed even louder. "John Silas, Dora is hurt bad, please get help!"

There was no doubt that Dora was seriously injured. It was hard to tell how badly. Then Lorna felt a stab of pain. She was hurting in her back and ankle. When she tried to stand with Dora in her arms, she realized that her right leg would not bear her weight. She collapsed back to the ground. A wave of nausea caused her to retch the contents of her stomach.

Boss Jack spurred his gelding to the scene of the accident and was followed by several others. Jane ran to Lorna and offered her apron to use as a wrap for Dora. Lorna, drenched in perspiration, collapsed on the ground. Jane knelt beside Lorna and reassured her with soft words. Lucy brought a cup of water and a wet hand towel. While the women tended to Lorna and Dora, John Silas was angrily stomping through the grass, gathering the spilled items and tossing them back into his wagon. He stopped and shook his fist at Lorna and yelled, "Stupid woman, what was you thinkin'—?" Then Boss Long interrupted the tirade and asked, "Who fired the gun?" John Silas lied and claimed that it had gone off accidentally. The others were astounded that John Silas showed no concerned for Lorna and Dora. He ignored the fact that they were still lying on the ground and instead focused on the belongings that were scattered about. After repacking the wagon, he calmed the mules, untangled the tack and hitched them back to the wagon. John Silas brought the wagon to where Lorna lay and said, "Git in the wagon, and hurry up."

Once again Lorna tried to stand but cried out with pain and almost fainted. Lorna begged, "Please, John Silas, you need to help me. My ankle is hurt, and look at Dora, I think she broke her hip. She needs a doctor."

John Silas walked over to see Dora's injury. He pulled back the apron covering her. "She looks okay to me, just scart from the fall. Besides, where do you think I can git a doctor?" John Silas took Dora, still screaming and placed her on the bed in the wagon. He took Lorna by the arm and pulled her to a standing position, steadied her as she hopped on one foot to the wagon. The movement was so painful she had tears streaming down her face but managed to avoid crying out. John Silas boosted Lorna into the wagon, and she managed to crawl to the mattress to lie beside Dora. John Silas looked toward the cluster of concerned traveling companions and shouted, "Show's over!"

Lorna was certain that her ankle was broken, she actually felt the bone break when her own weight snapped it. The foot and ankle were swelling before her eyes. Lorna removed both shoes and attempted to place a pillow under the injured foot. Faintness and nausea swept over Lorna when she moved the ankle. The fractured bones were off-set and grated against each other. Lorna knew to elevate her leg to lessen the swelling but was otherwise helpless. The foot was off-set to the side. Lorna turned her attention to Dora. She tried to comfort Dora by cradling her in her arms.

Nothing seemed to calm Dora. Lorna placed the infant on the bed. The jolting of the wagon brought both of them terrible pain. Dora continued her tortured crying for hours, and it was well past dark before she would take some water from a dropper. When the train finally stopped to camp for the night, Lyla administered doses of laudanum to Lorna and Dora. She asked Boss Jack to help her splint Lorna's ankle. While John Silas sat by the fire, Jack and Lyla examined the injuries of both mother and baby. Dora soon relaxed and fell into a laudanum-induced sleep. Lucy, Lyla, and Jack treated the cuts and bruises.

Setting Lorna's ankle required stretching until the fractured bones went back into the right configuration. Jack helped Lyla wrap the ankle and suspend it from a sling tied to a rafter that applied traction but without cutting off circulation. A second dose of laudanum helped Lorna fall asleep.

Over the days that followed, the painful ride over the rough trail tried Lorna's spirit. Constant worry over Dora's condition, her own physical disability, and the way John Silas was behaving gave Lorna such emotional distress she was beginning to question if she would come out of the crisis with her sanity.

Lorna spent the next few weeks in a haze of pain and mental anguish. The roadway seemed to be growing rockier, and there were many creeks to ford and hills to climb and descend. It was days before Lorna and Dora's pain began to subside. John Silas became more annoyed and brooding. He was descending ever farther into the clutches of paranoia. His demon possessed face was constantly distorted. The whites of his eyes had turned yellow. Lorna's efforts to soothe John Silas with kindness and reasonableness were rebuffed. It was apparent that he had lost his grasp on reality. Boss Long and several of the ladies in the train did what they could to provide for the needs of Lorna and Dora but avoided John Silas as much as possible. His obvious drunken state was ignored for the time.

John Silas was speaking to himself aloud and interacting with hallucinations. Because Boss Long was keeping a close eye on Lorna and Dora, John Silas accused Lorna of being flirtatious. Flirting with a man was the last thing on Lorna's mind. John Silas was insane and not responsible for his actions.

In other circumstances Lorna would have made a mental note that Jack Long was a handsome figure of a man. He was ruggedly attractive with his straight-lined nose, strong jaw line and prominent chin. His muscular neck and broad shoulders coupled with a trim lower torso reflected strength and agility. By far the most attractive attribute of Jack Long went beyond his outward appearance. He wore the mantel of authority and decisiveness so comfortably.

From the start, the travelers naturally looked to Jack for directions and organization. The admiring glances of the women did not escape Jack's detection, but of course he pretended not to notice. The passage of time had done little to dull Jack's sense of loss. So far, he wasn't actively pursuing the opposite sex although he was sorely aware of his normal biological needs.

The women were taking turns caring for Lorna and Dora's needs. John Silas had become so ill that he had very little appetite and stopped hunting. He figured if Lorna got hungry enough, she would barter with the others for something to cook. He saw through her poor-me act and the constant nagging was becoming intolerable. Besides, missing a few meals might take off the weight she gained during pregnancy. Lorna was exceedingly grateful for the kindness of her lady friends. They helped with her daily hygiene and laundry. The well disguised bundles of food they brought got past John Silas at first, but he soon learned to intercept them. Once when John Silas saw the food, he accused Lorna of not sharing with him. "You think I don't need to eat?" He snatched the food from her hands and took it with him into the woods.

Only weeks after the wreck, Dora started suffering the effects of Lorna's limited diet. John Silas was too self-absorbed to be concerned for the welfare of Lorna and Dora. When he brought food to Lorna, it was bread and whatever roasted meat the hunters were willing to share. Lorna feared that without better food, Dora would have to start eating solid food and cow's milk.

Jack was on edge over John Silas' sullenness. He knew that trouble was brewing. Unbeknownst to John Silas, Jack and the other men decided to expel John Silas as soon as the wagon train reached a settlement.

The Long Expedition had reached the section of trail notorious for hostile Indian attacks. Jack warned, "Starting right now I want everyone to be watchful. It's important to stay together, keep a weapon handy, and be ready to repel surprise attacks. I am doubling the night sentries." John Silas was left off the guard duty roster citing Lorna's helplessness as the reason, but in truth he was deemed totally unreliable.

The following Monday morning an Indian attack occurred at daybreak. A war party in full battle regalia, managed to surround the encampment under the cover of darkness. The savages fired arrows into the center of the circled wagons. An alarm was sounded, and the settlers scurried to cover. They returned fire with the women reloading the weapons as soon as they were discharged. The crack shots knocked several of the Indians from their mounts. The wounded were rescued by their cohorts and carted to cover. The excellent marksmanship of the trekkers resulted in so many casualties that the attackers retreated to regroup and reconsider their plan of attack.

The attack continued for a half hour, but after losing about half of their number, the Indians turned their attention to the livestock. They singled out the mules, kept in an easily accessible rope corral. The raiders left behind the cow, calf, and saddle horses. Since they didn't kill those animals, Jack knew they were planning to return. Wisely Jack had insisted that the horses be individually hobbled. When Jack ran toward the corral, firing at the raiders, they herded the mules ahead of them into the rolling hills to the south. The retreating war party celebrated with jubilant whooping and brandishing of weapons, but considering that they had chosen Jack Long's party as victims, the victory party was premature.

As soon as the attack ended, Lyla found Sally Trenton lying beside her cooking fire semi-conscious with an arrow lodged in her neck. She frantically called for help. Poor Sally was the only injury, but the ground and wagons held the chilling sight of near misses, imbedded arrows. Sally had been tending a cooking fire when the attack came. As soon as the savages rode away, Boss Long quickly assessed her injury. The arrow had gone into the side of Sally's neck. Jack realized that the wound was life-threatening. He carried Sally to her wagon and left her in the care of Lyla and the other women.

Jack beat upon a pan to summon the men together. "Our first order of business is to chase down the mules and bring them back. If the Indians get too far ahead, the tracks will be gone." Jack with hat in hand walked to stand beside Lindsey and placed an arm over his shoulder. "We got to get the mules back or we're in trouble. I want you to stay here and take care of Miss Sally."

Jack decided to leave Walter, Bert, and John Silas behind with Lindsey. While the pursuit was being organized the women stood by as Lindsey and Bert hovered over Sally. Jack encouraged the men to pack wisely; "We want to go weapon heavy, in other words, they were to bring rope, extra pistols and swords, hunting knives, and bayonets, and anything else that could strike a lethal blow." Jack told the men, "Choose an alternate mount to carry gear and serve as a back-up in case of lameness."

Jack packed his field glass and a signal mirror and his keepsake armored vest. The vest went on over the head and fastened under the arms. It was constructed of double layered oxen hide lined with multi-layers of woven silk fabric, one of the strongest fibers known to mankind. Only people of wealth were able to attain rare silk fabric. Jack had learned that silk is woven from the fiber that makes up the cocoon of specific Chinese moth larvae. Though not capable of stopping a musket ball, the vest would be good protection from Indian arrows. Jack figured it might come in handy and concealed it in the wooden gear box that rode in a saddle tree on his alternate mount. He had a partial plan in mind for attacking the Indians.

Lyla was tending to Sally, but there wasn't much she could do. Lucy and her three children were gathered at the rear of the Trenton wagon. Jane, Bert, and Walter armed themselves and hid from view on the camp perimeter. John Silas was unaccounted for.

A chill fell over the small group as they watched the men ride away. Once Lyla was able to examine Sally's injury, she realized that it was much worse than first thought. Lindsey and Lyla discussed the best way to remove the arrow. Lindsey told Bert to go outside and stand guard, partly out of fear that the Indians might return and partly to protect the boy from the seriousness of his mother's wound.

Lindsey bathed Sally's brow with a damp cloth, and said, "Hang on, Sal, we're gone git that arrow out, you're gonna be okay." Sally nodded her head to acknowledge Lindsey, but she sensed that she was losing the battle to stay conscious. The bleeding was minimal, but the arrow was impeding the flow of blood to Sally's brain. The arrow had gone almost totally through her neck. The point could be seen protruding under the skin on the opposite side. Lyla called for Lucy to look at the wound. The two women looked at each other and shook their heads. Sally had a peaceful look on her face, and hoarsely whispered, "Call Bert." Sally's voice was so weak and hoarse it required placing an ear over her mouth to hear.

Lucy climbed down from the wagon and took the gun that Bert was holding. "Zour Muder zis asking for zou, z'll stant guart."

Inside the wagon, Bert knelt at the bedside and said, "Momma, I'm here, can you hear me, you just gotta git better," then he turned to Lindsey and said, "I hate those Injuns! Why did they want to do this?" Lindsey placed his arm around Bert's shoulders, and they prayed silently for God to save Sally.

Sally looked at Bert and then at Lindsey and in a hoarse whisper said, "I'm gonna be okay, take good care of each other." Lindsey leaned forward to kiss her just as she lost consciousness. It was decided to saw the shaft off at the entry point and then force it out the opposite side of Sally's neck. It is doubtful that even the most experienced physician could have saved Sally. As soon as the arrow was removed, uncontrollable bleeding caused the already unconscious Sally to lose all color and stop breathing. Lindsey and 15-year-old Bert, kneeling beside the bed were unable to accept that she was gone. After a long silence, Lyla, in a soft voice said, "We did all we could, dear Sally has gone on to a better place." Lindsey and Bert looked at each other and flung their arms about each other. It was beyond their ability to comprehend losing Sally. They refused to accept the obvious, and Bert tried to rouse Sally by shaking her and rubbing her face. Bert continued speaking to Sally, "Momma, can you hear me? Wake up, we're gonna help you get better."

Lyla asked Jane to come into the wagon and comfort Lindsay and Bert. Lyla lovingly folded Sally's hands onto her chest and covered her with the blood-soaked quilt. Bert quickly uncovered her face and said "No, I can tell she is still alive." Then Lyla said, "Lindsay, we're gonna let you and Bert have some time alone with Sally. There is nothing more we can do." The women embraced the devastated man and boy. With heads bowed, the weeping women retreated to their own wagons. Lyla briefly spoke to Jack before the men departed and told him that Sally had died. Jack was crushed at the loss of such a dear friend and had to pause a moment before he could continue packing his gear.

Before two hours had passed, John Silas went on the prowl. He was rummaging through Boss Long's footlocker sitting by the fire pit. Before leaving, Jack had told Walter to keep a close eye on John Silas. When Walter confronted John Silas about snooping in Jack's trunk, John Silas claimed that he was retrieving a tool that he had loaned to the trail boss. Walter, not wanting to provoke a confrontation, pretended to accept the explanation.

The search party was gone for three full days, and during that time John Silas was sullen and complained about the recovery team taking so long. Without provocation, he would fall into fits of irrational anger. John Silas whined, "Why, if I was in charge, we could've been back with the stock by now. That Boss Long is the poorest excuse for a trail boss I ever seen."

Jack pushed the recovery team hard, riding non-stop except to rest and water the horses. The trail was easy to follow at first, and they made good time. Jack, knowing something of how Indians think, decided to determine the general direction of travel and then followed out of sight of the actual trail. He was certain they would be watching for a pursuit, and he was right.

Once the war party had ruled out a pursuit, they slowed their pace and left an easy-to-follow trail. Jack could have attacked them along the trail but was worried some would get away. His inkling that the Indians were planning a second attack on the train was weighing heavy on Jack. He decided it would be better to follow them back to their encampment where he planned to incapacitate the village. By mid-afternoon Jack spotted the smoke rising from a small but well-concealed encampment. Jack crept on foot to an overlook to spy out the defenses of the village. He wanted to preserve the element of surprise, so he planned to attack the encampment from the south. The camp was nestled into a low place that had an area that held water when it rained and was surrounded by cottonwood trees and low bushy willows. There was a pool of runoff about half full. The entire area was surrounded by randomly strewn boulders perhaps from volcanic explosions.

Jack used a long stick to diagram his plan of attack in the sand and explained, "First we cut down on the number of fighters we will face and to do that I have an idea to draw a party away from the camp into a trap. Then we will attack the main camp. Since both Tommy and Abe are our eagle-eyed sharp shooters, they will take out the sentries."

Jack left the others behind and hiked on foot to spy out the camp with the field glass, but it was hard to get a good grasp of the number of people or the organization of the camp. He scouted the narrow path leading to the village from the south and saw that it was perfect for staging an ambush.

Jack said, "Boys, remember the old rope trick? We can raise a hidden rope in front of the charging Indian horses; I saw just the perfect place to pull that off not far away. What 'cha thinks boys; got any better ideas? The feedback was unanimous in the positive, "My idea is to create a decoy for them to chase into the rope trap."

Jack went into more detail for drawing a war party into a trap with a decoy. He looked at Jon and smiled, "Jon I'm thinking of sending you to build the fire and then be the decoy. The smoke from the fire will cause them to dispatch a war party to investigate the smoke. When they encounter you on the road, you will whirl around and ride away at top speed and lead them into our rope trap. That horse of yours will outrun anything the Indians have, and I have an armored vest for you to wear. Are you willin' to lead the Indians into our trap? It's a dangerous proposition."

Jon had been sitting on a knee-high rock all slouched down and relaxed until Jack asked him the question. He sat up straight and became very alert, "Jack old friend, with the request coming from you, my answer is an automatic I reckon! But what was that about an armored vest?

Jack walked to his pack horse and took down his gear box. When he held the vest up, there was silence; the boys all had open mouths and walked to get a closer look. Tommy said, "I heared about these things but never seen one, for shore not on this side of the Atlantic. Jack, where did you get this?"

Jack grinned and said, "I sort of inherited it from an uncle that fought at the Battle of Trenton with General Washington back in '76. In fact, he was in the second boat across the Delaware River. He took it off the body of a Hessian officer after dispatching him to the next life. I did some asking around, and supposedly the garment has woven silk fibers from China between the two layers of oxen hide. It's not likely to stop a ball fired from a long gun but should stop arrows. I kept it for a novelty and keepsake, but I figure it will give Jon some protection from arrows, so if you agree Jon, you are welcome to wear it."

Jon stepped up and said, "Jack, can I try it on to see if it restricts my movements? I'm a mind to wear it." Jack helped Jon on with the vest and fastened the buckles under each arm. Jon bent over, twisted from right to left, and raised his arms over his head and nodded in a positive way. "It allows plenty of movement so yes I will wear it, thanks Jack."

The plan called for Abe and Tommy to take up positions in the rear of the war party and kill any Indians that escape the initial shoot-out. Jack once again diagramed his plan drawing in the dirt. "This is where the rope we brought comes into play. One rope will go on the ground and be covered with dirt. Upon approach the rope will be pulled to the right height to unseat the riders. A second rope will be ready behind the first to unseat riders that stop in time to avoid the first rope. They will be unseated as they turn back. On out ahead and out of sight of the rope trap will be a place to trap the rider-less horses. There is a stretch of the path almost totally enclosed with boulders except for the trail. We can close off the few feet of the trail with brush and fallen wood. Then we can hobble the horses and hide them back from the trail. I want to take them back with us or shoot them if need be."

Jack maintained eye contact as he spoke with an intense tone, "From there we advance on the unsuspecting village. Under the cover of darkness Abe and Tommy will take up their sniper positions and wait for the signal. It is important to fire simultaneously. Boys, we need to make sure that not one of the warriors escapes alive! Not one! This is a camp and not the main village, and we don't want the larger group to send reinforcements. And now there is one more thing to discuss. There will be no vengeance killing, the women and children and old people are not to be harmed! Need I repeat myself? No harm to the children, women, or old people, unless they come against us armed. I just hope our mules are still alive."

Once Jack had finished laying out the plan, he got some raised eyebrows, and Tommy said, "Jack, you got a lot of 'ifs' in the plan. But heck, beats anything I could think up, I say give her a try." The others all indicated that they were on board with Jack's plan. "Jon, you're up. Ride hard and make that a smoky fire. We will get the trap all set and enclose the trap for the Indian horses."

The plan mostly worked as planned. The devil was in the details as usual. The rope was too low and upended several of the horses. For a minute or two the Indians didn't know what had just happened. Pandemonium set in; some of the horses were down and struggling to stand, others were wildly bucking and kicking causing the Indians to dodge the flying hooves. The shocked braves were shouting at each other while they searched for their bows and quivers. There was no place to find cover from the gunfire raining down on them. The attack was over quickly. Jack's strategy had worked despite the minor miscalculation. The horses that avoided the brush corral were shot on the run to prevent them returning to the village rider-less.

At daybreak Jack worked his way to the village, and with the help of the field glass could see that four of the mules had been slaughtered and were being butchered by many squaws. The older children and old men were helping prepare the meat for the drying racks. They worked with a sense of urgency, constantly looking about. At first Jack was curious about the vigilance until he realized the village dogs were giving them away. Jack was forced to attack sooner than he had planned because they had mostly lost the element of surprise.

With the drop of the flag, two shots rang out. Both sentries dropped, dead upon impact with the ground. That was the signal to charge the village firing at will. During the time it took for the few Indians capable of fighting back to arm themselves, most were shot or stabbed. For a few short minutes there was hand to hand fighting, but the Long team with their sabers and bayonets prevailed. The surviving and wounded warriors were finished off by blades to the body. The rest of the people were restrained with rope bindings. Some teenage boys and several women had jumped into the battle and lost their lives as a result.

Before leaving the village, Jack stood in front of the restrained Indians and used sign language as he spoke to indicate that they were being spared. "We leave mule meat, you not go hungry, we take horses, if you follow us, we shoot you! If you try to come against our wagon train, we will kill all of you. We do not make war on women and babies or the old and sick. Your men killed one of our women. We only kill when attacked. We want peace!" The squaws glared at Jack, showing no appreciation for his generosity. He wasn't sure how much they comprehended.

As the Long party rode away from the village, an adolescent boy stepped from behind a bush and shot an arrow into Kingston's leg. The boy who looked to be about twelve years old dropped the bow and ran to hide in the brush. Jack yelled at the kid and then spurred Bones to Kingston's side to look at the injury. The arrow had pinned a muscular strip of Kingston's calf to the saddle skirt but did not appear to sever any major blood vessels or impact the bones of his leg. Jack said, "Kingston, we have to hurry. Are you alright with me removing the arrow and wrapping the wound tightly to slow the bleeding? You gonna be able to ride?"

Kingston said, "I can ride with no problem, and yes, get that arrow out of my leg. Jack don't worry about me, I signed on to be tough! Kingston managed to remain silent while Jack removed the arrow, but his face turned purple, and it was undeniable that he really was a tough son of a gun. Thanks Jack and give me the arrow to keep for a keepsake. The trip back to the wagon train only took about four hours by pushing the horses hard.

John Silas was threatening and irrational while Jack was gone. He grudgingly prepared food and helped bring in firewood. Lorna was weary of the constant barrage of criticisms and complaints but was too afraid of John Silas to speak her mind. All along Jack and Lyla had both insisted that she avoid putting full weight on the fractured bones for at least another month. She thought, "for the sake of Dora I must control my anger, this is no time to argue with John Silas." Lorna was doing as much as she could to help with food preparation by scooting on her knees inside the wagon bed but anytime the ankle wasn't elevated it hurt and throbbed.

The state of fear back at the camp was quickly relieved when the men arrived from their successful sortie. They were coated with dust and exhausted. They had recovered all but four mules, and the only human injury was to Kingston Bullard's leg. The horses were heavily lathered and on their last legs. The men dismounted all except Kingston, and Jack went to help him down from his horse. When Lyla saw that Kingston was hurt, she let out a loud "KINGSTON" and ran to help Jack support him back to their wagon. Jack asked if Kingston had any liquor, and Lyla pulled out a bottle she had hidden away. Kingston said, "Ah, so that is your hiding place." Lyla returned a dirty look at Kingston. Jack held the bottle out to Kingston, who gladly took a big swig.

Jack irrigated the wound with the whiskey and watched as Kingston turned purple again and did some sputtering and shook his head. Jack went to put a couple of knives in the coals of the fire. Jack asked if Lyla could cauterize both sides of the wound while Jack held Kingston down, and she assured him that she could. Jack was relieved because Lyla was much more experienced in such things. Once the knives were glowing orange, Jack prepared to literally cover his body to hold him motionless. While Kingston was preoccupied with reaching for the whiskey bottle, Jack fell across his body and Lyla quickly held the blade to the entry wound. Kingston let out a terrible scream, bit his tongue, and fainted. Lyla turned his head to the side to allow the blood to drain from his mouth and lovingly held his head and blotted the blood from his mouth. Jack handed her the second knife, and she treated the exit wound before Kingston regained consciousness. While Lyla bandaged the leg, Jack told her about the Indian boy shooting Kingston, and Lyla chuckled and said, "he hasn't heard the last of that." Once Kingston was fully awake, Lyla asked, "You want to describe what it was like to be bested by an eight-year-old Indian kid with a toy bow and arrow?"

Kingston looked at Jack and said, "I will get you for that, watch your back Jack Long." Then Kingston looked at Lyla and said, "The kid was at least 12 years old, and that weren't no toy bow and arrows he shot me with."

The three of them had a good laugh, and then almost as an afterthought Jack said, "Lyla, I figure you should loosely bandage the wound, and check on it twice a day, we have to watch for blood poisoning." Jack put his arm around Lyla and said, "Lyla darlin', it pears to me that the bones ain't damaged, and the wound is purty clean." Lyla agreed and told Jack it should heal up just fine. "Thanks, Jack, for taking care of Kingston."

Jack told Jane about Jon's heroism and how he had executed his part of the ambush with precision. Jon was fascinated with the armored vest and modeled it for the whole group before giving it back to Jack to be stored away.

The owners of the retrieved mules took their animals back to the corral, but John Silas didn't see his two mules. He marched to his wagon and walked in circles, gesturing angrily as he spoke to no one in particular. He returned to where Jack was standing and spoke in a threatening tone, "I want to know where my mules are?"

Jack explained that by the time they caught up to the Indians, they had reached their village, and several squaws were already butchering four of the mules. "Isn't that right, fellars?" Jack asked. The other men nodded. Without a word, John Silas assumed a wide legged stance and slowly placed his hand on the grip of the pistol tucked into his belt and asked, "Does that mean you're gonna leave us here stranded all alone?" John Silas and Jack had a staring contest going when Jack responded by carefully moving his right hand to the handle of his own sidearm. John Silas had chosen the wrong man to intimidate.

Jack spoke in full voice so that everyone could understand, "John Silas, if you think it was easy for the five of us to sneak up on a camp of Indians and attack them, you're not thinking straight. You will not be left behind. You will have to use some of the Indian ponies to pull your wagon. We will all help you. The loss of your mules is unfortunate, but we did the best we could under the circumstances so get used to it." After a very uncomfortable standoff, John Silas blinked first and whirled around and went back to his wagon.

Dora was whimpering and inconsolable, even though Lorna was rocking her. Already in an irrational fit of temper, the sound of the crying baby prompted John Silas to shout from the rear of the wagon, "You better keep that kid quiet." The sound of John Silas' harsh voice startled Dora, and she began wailing. Lorna's face turned red with anger, and the look she gave John Silas prepared him for what followed.

In a shrill, desperate voice Lorna screamed, "What is wrong with you? Dora is in pain you idiot; you know I can't stop her from crying." Several others overheard Lorna and waited, trying to decide if they should intervene. Lorna knew that she had stepped over the line with John Silas. Lorna's angry outburst triggered a violent response from John Silas.

He shouted, "You know better than to raise your voice to me." Then John Silas literally exploded with a string of profanity. He jumped into the wagon, shoved Dora aside, and straddled Lorna. Next, he began slapping Lorna in a sideways motion that snapped her head from one side to the other. Over and over, he slapped her. The tantrum escalated into tearing at her hair and clothing. Finally, he began to choke Lorna. "I'll teach you a lesson, you stupid, ugly bitch, you need to know who's the boss around here, you don't appreciate nothing I do. Lorna futilely tried to remove his hands from her neck. John Silas pinned them under his knees and then continued battering Lorna about the head and chest. "How does that feel? Want some more?" Then he stood, still astraddle Lorna, and gave her a kick in the side.

Chapter 5

TWO FUNERALS & A CAVE

From behind, John Silas heard the low, deliberate voice of Jack Long, "John that will be enough. STOP IT, NOW! Step out here, and we'll talk this through." Totally without reason, the wild man that John Silas had become whirled toward Jack as he drew his pistol from his belt and fired pointblank at Jack. The shot narrowly missed; Jack felt the air turbulence from the passing bullet upon his face. Before John Silas could reach for a second weapon and fire, Jack in one rapid movement placed his shot dead center in John Silas' forehead, dropping him on top of Lorna and Dora. The already crying baby screamed in pain. Lorna tried to shove John Silas to the side, but his limp body didn't budge. Jack sprang into the wagon, and with one fluid motion rolled the dead man to the side, grabbed his lifeless body by the belt and tossed him from the rear of the wagon as though he were a sack of potatoes.

Others of the group were gathering at the back of the wagon and had to jump back to avoid the flying body of John Silas. They were stunned into silence. Jack knelt beside Lorna and gently smoothed her hair and turned her face toward him. "Let me see, looks like your lip— is split, and uh, oh— Lorna, how could he do this to you? I'm so sorry, so, so sorry!" Lorna was bleeding from the mouth and had a cut under her left eye. Red imprints on Lorna's neck began turning purple. Clumps of hair had fallen over the bedding where Lorna lay. Lorna whispered, raspy from the choking, "Give me Dora! Is she hurt? Then she looked at Jack and asked, "Are you hurt?" Jack said, no, the shot missed, I'm fine. Lorna groaned when she sat up. Her hand went to her rib cage where the kick had landed.

Lorna began to sob. Jack knelt beside her and held her in his arms. After a few minutes, Jack said, "Lorna, we need to see if you have broken ribs before you move around much." Lyla climbed into the wagon and knelt beside Lorna. Lorna was going into a state of shock and hardly acknowledged Lyla's presence. Lyla unbuttoned Lorna's dress and unlaced her camisole exposing only the injured area. Jack carefully traced each rib with his fingers. He looked at Lyla and said, "I don't feel any breaks, but they may be cracked. See what you think." Lyla also felt of the bruised ribs and said, "I think her lungs are safe. I will prepare some poultices for the bruises. Jack backed off and let Lyla take over with Lorna."

Lyla said, "Lorna, you have some bad bruising. You need to lie real still and settle your nerves, you poor, dear girl." Jack gathered Dora into his arms hoping to quiet her wailing. He carefully unwrapped the baby and looked for new injuries. As he ran his fingers over her tiny body, she continued her mournful wailing, thrashing with her little arms and legs. Dora's injured hip could move but not normally. He told Lorna, "Looks like she's just scared." When Lorna looked up at Jack, she noticed that a tear escaped his glassy eyes and ran down his cheek into his mustache. Lorna placed her hand on Jack's arm, and her look communicated what she was incapable of articulating. Still holding Dora, Jack leaned down to embrace Lorna. Then he wiped his eyes with his shirtsleeve.

Jack stood beside Lorna and rocked Dora, patting her on her well-padded bottom. "Shu, shu, little one, it'll be okay, we're gonna take good care of you and your Momma." Lorna, with a faint quavering voice said, "thank you, Jack."

Jack replied, "Lorna, I'm sorry about John Silas, he must have gone mad, totally crazy. I had no choice." Jack knelt on one knee and gently placed Dora beside Lorna and covered them with a quilt. "I'll be back after I talk to the men."

That night Jack hardly slept. During the War for Independence, Jack had served with the Continental Army as a teenager. He was battle hardened, but this was different. He was shaken to the core by the brutish and demonic rage so incomprehensible to a reasonable man like Jack. What kind of evil had possessed him? Jack thought, "I knew that he would confront me sooner or later. Lorna and Dora will be better off without him; maybe they can lead a normal and pleasant life. Jack offered a silent prayer, "Oh Lord, comfort Lorna. And please Lord, lift the burden of my act of violence from my heart." Jack lay in his wagon with a racing heart throughout the night. During the brief periods when he was able to fall asleep, mental pictures of John Silas beating Lorna, John Silas' expression the moment the bullet struck him in the forehead, and the sound of Dora's screaming kept playing repeatedly. The incident reminded Jack of the torment he suffered following the loss of his wife and infant.

Jane and Lucy decided they would take turns caring for Lorna and Dora. Lyla went to be with Kingston who was feeling considerable pain in his leg. Lucy and Jane felt so inadequate at comforting Lorna. Only time would heal Lorna's wounds. Lorna's tearless face stared into space with only slight recognition of their kindnesses. Jane cleaned and applied salve to the cuts and bruises on Lorna's face and then insisted that she drink a cup of soup. Lucy placed the tip of her little finger in Dora's mouth and rocked her to sleep.

When the men searched the body of John Silas, they discovered a money belt with his hoard of gold and silver coins. It was the money he had earned from the whiskey making enterprise, and in a trouser pocket they found a gold pocket watch with a chain. As one of the men held up the watch, Jack said, "Wait just a minute that looks like my dad's watch." That is when Walter said that he had caught John Silas looking through Jack's belongings while they were gone.

Jack walked over to the back of Lorna's wagon and asked, "Lorna, are you awake? Sorry to bother you, did John Silas have a gold watch like this?" Lorna answered, "No, not that I ever saw." Jack tucked the watch into his pocket and passed the poke of coins to Jane to stow in Lorna's trunk. As darkness fell the men unceremoniously took shovels and buried John Silas' physical remains in an unmarked and shallow grave.

It was a miserable group of campers that evening. The following morning the men dug a grave for Sally.

Jack asked if Lorna felt up to coming out for Sally's funeral, and she said, "Oh yes, I must, dear, dear Sally." Thinking of Sally caused tears to well up in Lorna's eyes. Jack climbed into the wagon to comfort Lorna. He used a corner of her quilt to dry her tears and then pulled her to his chest and held her tight while shushing her weeping. Jack knew that the tears were a sign that Lorna was recovering from the psychological shock that had followed the incident with John Silas.

When it was time, Jack carried blanket-swathed Lorna, holding Dora from her wagon to sit upon a box. Jack stood beside Lorna, ready to steady her if the box tipped. Absent from the internment service were the two posted sentries on guard duty. Jack assessed the situation; the small group of travelers had gone from 18 members to 16. The number of wagons would be five as opposed to the seven they had before the attack, hardly enough to form a defensive circle, and the number of mules shrunk by four.

Jack officiated before the grief-stricken party. It would be difficult to imagine a more morose group when Bert spoke up. "I have something to say." Jack nodded to Bert, and the boy started by saying, "Momma told me funerals should celebrate the good times too. Now my Momma had lots of good times. She kept Poppa and me smiling most of the time. She was a happy person, and that is what I want all of you to remember about her. As you all know Momma's eyesight was not good. Ever once in a while she would get the wrong spice for what she was cooking. One time she ruined a perfectly wonderful apple pie with the tin of chili powder she confused with a similar shaped tin of cinnamon. She tried to feed the pie to a neighbor's dog, and when it took a sniff, it sneezed and backed off and hid under the porch. And I'll never forget the frog pajamas. It was Christmas time, and she loved to give funny joke gifts and handmade sweaters with strange designs and colors. When I was about Rolf's age, she made me some green knitted sleeping long handles that had frog feet and big black eyes sticking up on top of the hood. I liked wearing them so much I took to wearing them in the day time. I was the envy of the other kids." Once Bert and Lindsey started to laugh, the gloom was replaced with humor and happy memories.

Jack said, "Bert, your comments are so fitting, Sally was a happy person, and it rubbed off on all of us. She was a blessing to have around for sure. Thank you for reminding us of that."

With hat held behind him, Jack raised his face heavenward as he spoke. His white, bald head reflected the midday sunshine and contrasted with his deeply tanned lower face and neck. Jack's baritone voice made even huskier with emotion, recited the Twenty Third Psalm. Next, he led the group in singing, "Blest Be the Tie That Binds" and "Amazing Grace."

"Blest Be the Tie That Binds"

By John Fawcett
Blest be the tie that binds
our hearts in Christian love;
the fellowship of kindred minds
is like to that above.

Before our Father's throne
we pour our ardent prayers;
our fears, our hopes, our aims are one,
our comforts and our cares.

We share each other's woes,
our mutual burdens bear;
and often for each other flows
the sympathizing tear.

When we asunder part,
it gives us inward pain;
but we shall still be joined in heart,
and hope to meet again.

By John Newton

Amazing grace, how sweet the sound
That saved a wretch like me.
I once was lost, but now I'm found.
'Twas blind, but now I see.

'Twas grace that taught my heart to fear
And grace my fears relieved.
How precious did that grace appear
The hour I first believed.

When we've been there ten thousand years
Bright shining as the sun,
We've no less days to sing God's praise
Than when we first begun.

Amazing grace, how sweet the sound
That saved a wretch like me.
I once was lost, but now I'm found.
Was blind, but now I see.

Jack asked Abe to say the closing prayer. Abe was so racked with emotion he was unable to speak more than a few words, "Got da Fadder, ve tank ze that, for Sally be'n vith us, and it vil be hart to not zee hert. Lord, ve askt de blessn't on Lindsey and Bertz peeze heal da paint vith sher passzn. Ament."

Lindsey and Bert watched as Sally's casket was carefully lowered into the grave by ropes. Then they each tossed a handful of dirt onto the rough wood surface of the casket that contained the already decomposing body. Lindsey and Bert wiped tears away, leaving their faces streaked with dirt. Jack once again removed his hat and led the group in a short but earnest prayer, "Dear Lord, we need your protection from murderous Injuns as we pass through their hunting grounds, look down upon us with favor as we continue this dangerous journey. We praise you for the blessings you have provided. We're sure gonna miss our Miss Sally. Please give her a special place there in heaven with you. Please Lord, help Lindsey and Bert to someday find peace over their loss; help Kingston's leg to heal up real good, Lord, we ask that you protect and bless our Miss Lorna and her little Dora. In Christ's name we pray. Amen."

The following morning Jack called the men together and said, "First off, we need to double the night sentries. Don't need to tell you to stay alert and keep your weapons loaded and close by. We kilt most of the band that attacked us, but there are others all around. From now on we keep the mules hobbled too and closer to our camp. Since we are short of mules, two wagons must be left behind. That will be Miss Lorna's and Jon and Jane's wagons." Secretly Lorna welcomed leaving the stolen wagon behind. It helped her to part with some of her guilt.

Jack announced, "I'm moving Lorna into my wagon. I'll sleep in my tent under the wagon. I propose that the Macintosh's move in with Lindsey and Bert." Jack continued, "Folks, as you all know, it is late in the year. Besides getting' a late start, we been slowed by some unfortunate things nobody saw comin', and we need to move on by tomorrow. Let's change the belongings around before bedtime so's we can git an early start." The men went to work cannibalizing anything they might need from the discarded wagons. Walking away, Jack spoke over his shoulder, "Take it all, anything we might need like wheels, canvas, water barrels, you boys know." After a couple of hours, Jack said, "Ever body, git some rest," but he kept on working.

Jack took his belongings and stacked them at the front of his wagon so that he would have access without climbing into the bed of the wagon. He placed Lorna's trunk just behind his belongings, opening into the wagon bed. He went through the other belongings in Lorna's wagon and found the components of the whiskey still. He asked Lorna, "What you want to do with the still?" Lorna shrugged and said, "That old still caused us a lot of trouble. I don't want anything to do with it." The still and John Silas' personal items were off loaded, and anyone from the group was welcome to help themselves. Jack advised Lorna to keep the guns and tools. "You just might need to sell them, worth a purty penny out here on the frontier." Lindsey and Bert decided to take the still, since they figured making whiskey might be a real money maker in Kentucky. In fact, Lindsey had some experience with a still and jumped at the chance to take it off Lorna's hands. To make room for the still, Lindsey decided to give Lorna most of Sally's personal belongings. Lorna acknowledged Lindsey's generosity with a smile, but she wasn't ready to look through them yet. Lorna was heart sick over her death.

Jack fussed over making a comfortable bed for Lorna and Dora. As soon as the group ate a quickly prepared meal of venison stew, Jack carried Lorna and Dora to his wagon. Satisfied that they were resting comfortably, he walked the perimeter of the camp, stopping often to listen to the night noises.

Jack had an idea. He took his axe into a nearby thicket of trees and cut two strong, straight saplings. Within an hour he had fashioned Lorna a pair of crude crutches. He padded the tops with a folded piece of blanket and then nailed rawhide over the padding. He used his hunting knife to smooth the rough spots. Just below waist height, he hollowed out a hole to insert a dowel handhold. Jack was eager to see if Lorna would be able to use the crutches as they were or would he need to adjust them.

Jack prepared to sound the "forward ho" signal after checking in on Lorna. He told her, "No need to get up, I'll bring you some coffee and a plate of food." After the meal, Jane helped Lorna with her morning lavatory. Jack planned to show Lorna the crutches when they stopped for the noon meal.

The day started off overcast and foggy, but by mid-morning the sky cleared, and the wind became gusty. The trail was rough but mostly level, and they made good time. Jack decided to appoint young Bert hunter for the day. Jack wanted to distract him from his grief. Jack surmised, "Bert must be thinking that he will never see his mother again, or even her burial place. Bert, with his dad's muzzle-loader, walked well in advance of the column of wagons and a hundred yards behind Jack.

Jack rode astride his gelding, Bag of Bones, a large and powerful dappled roan of mixed blood lines. When a whitetail buck sprang from a thicket, Bert got off a hasty shot and missed. Only a few hundred yards ahead, the boy got a second chance. This time a young doe was standing in some brush and gave him a clear shot. Bert spun around to face Jack and smiled before following the blood trail. Bert could field dress his kill, but with a lot of advice. Jack exclaimed, "Bert, that's gonna be some good eatin'. Yes sir, you've got what it takes to be a hunter." The men congratulated the 15-year-old on bagging his first deer, a rite of passage. Lindsey was sitting in his wagon, disabled with grief, out of touch with reality. The men's cheerfulness was contrived, but Bert accepted the effort for what it was, love and concern.

Dressing out the meat took much longer with all of the advice, but the job got done. Bert needed to rest and spend time with his father. Tommy walked over to Bert and said, "I think we may keep you on as a hunter! Good job!"

Bert gave the men a tear-streaked smile and said, "Wish Ma would be here to eat some of my first deer with us."

Jack decided not to stop for a noon meal, since they had lost so much time with Bert's deer. That evening, Jack chose a clearing next to a small, rain-swollen creek for the overnight camp. Jack posted three sentries. A portion of the venison was sliced into very thin steaks to speed the cooking time. The skewers threaded with meat lay suspended over the coals on a rack made from green saplings. Bert volunteered to turn the meat as it roasted. While the meat cooked, the men hurried about topping off the water barrels, checking on the livestock, making repairs to gear. By this point in the journey, the men were well organized and shared the big tasks. The creek water was murky and required straining and then filtering. Downstream, hidden behind a stand of cattail and pussy willow, the women and children went to bathe, actually immersing in the creek water. Getting a good bath lifted the spirits of the women. Only Lorna and Kingston missed the bath. The chilly stream water beckoned to the men as well, and as soon as the shivering ladies made it back to the fire, the men took their leave. Next to the shallow crossing there was an outcropping of flat limestone, perfect for doing laundry. The women worked past twilight doing laundry. They were no different from other pioneer women. Their rough and calloused hands were cracked and bleeding by the time the laundry was finished. Walter and Ian each held torches so that they could finish the wash and then jumped in to ring out the excess water and helped to spread the clothing over bushes and limbs. Wagon wheels and ropes strung between tree limbs. Most of the clothes would still be damp at daybreak, but they would be spread inside the wagons to finish drying. Jane added Lorna's laundry to her own. Dora had run out of anything close to a diaper. Lorna and Dora sponge bathed in the wagon. After the dishes were washed, the livestock was led to the stream and allowed to drink their fill. Jack moved his foot locker near to the fire. Then he brought out Lorna and Dora and seated them on the trunk.

Since the venison needed more cooking time, Jack decided that it was the perfect time to show Lorna the crutches. He carried them hidden behind his back as he approached her. Lorna was perched on the box and was patting and humming to Dora. The baby was resting her tired little head on her mother's shoulder.

"Miss Lorna, I made something that might be a help to you. Try these here crutches out."

Lorna brought her free hand to her mouth and said, "How did you know? I've been wishing for crutches. Here, let me try." Jack took Dora, kissed her, and then handed her to Auntie Jane. Jack held Lorna by the arm as she stood on one foot. A crutch was carefully placed under each arm, and she took a step. Lorna's face still bore the signs of the terrible battering but was starting to heal. Lorna gave Jack a big smile, and then the others, making eye contact one at a time. She was thinking how she loved these kind-hearted people. Lorna took a few more tentative steps, and then she started walking with some confidence. Luckily, Jack continued to hover just behind her with outstretched hands, knowing that crutches take a lot of getting used to. It was dark, and Jack asked Walter to add wood to the fire. Lorna made a trip around the fire, and as she started around the second time, she failed to see a critter hole hidden by grass and lost her balance. As she started to fall, Jack was able to spring forward and keep her upright. "Lorna, I got ya, you had enough for now? Sit back down, looks like the food is ready."

Lorna patted Jack on the arm and said, "Thank you for the crutches, they will sure help me get around better."

Lyla announced, "Food's ready," and then Abe offered a prayer before serving the meal of venison. The first to be served were the watchmen on duty, and then the others settled down to some serious eating. Between mouthfuls, the hungry travelers heaped still more praise upon Bert.

Tommy asked, "Boy, where did you learn to cook like this?" Bert lowered his head and shrugged and then said, "Mom, she would always ask me to give her a hand."

As Lorna settled down for the night in Jack's wagon, she realized that for the first time in a long time, she felt safe. Jack had placed extra padding under the bedding, and both Lorna and Dora were able to sleep in comfort. It was comforting having Jack guarding the wagon just outside the rear of the curtained wagon bed.

Jack was thinking, "Anyone intending harm to Lorna and Dora will have to first get past me first." It felt good to have someone to watch over again. Ever since his wife had died in childbirth, Jack had felt adrift, without purpose.

The farther west the Long expedition progressed, the more difficult the trail became. The grades grew steeper, and there was a succession of streams to ford. The more western mountains of the

Appalachian chain, with peaks of more than five thousand feet, had an early blanket of snow by the first of October. The westward route Boss Long had chosen meandered near the borders of Virginia, Tennessee, Kentucky, and North Carolina. Off to the north the travelers kept snow-capped Mount Rogers in view as they approached the place where Virginia narrowed to a point at the Kentucky-Tennessee border. Jack, referring to the lay of the land, gave a preview of the well-known Cumberland Gap that lay straight ahead.

On a crisp Sunday morning in mid-October following their regular worship service, Jack called the men together for a meeting. "Winter is catching up with us. Didn't make as good a time as I expected; the signs predict a bad winter." He proposed that the group search for a sheltered valley with good water and plentiful wood. They would need to construct a shelter of some sort. It was not unusual for travelers to lay over for the worst of winter before continuing westward. The men unanimously agreed that it would be too dangerous to travel much longer.

The next morning Jack decided to saddle Bones and scout ahead to search for a place to hole up for the winter. Walter was always willing, even eager to drive Jack's wagon. It was a thrill to have the respect of a man like Jack Long. For someone so young, Walter was an impressive young man.

Only five miles ahead, Jack came upon the Clinch River. The canyon created by centuries of running water was a scenic place of red rock cliffs and a fast-flowing boulder-strewn river. Where the trail crossed the river, the water was only six inches deep and clear of large rocks. From debris collected on the trees and brush, it was obvious that the Clinch flooded and would make crossing impossible after heavy rain or snowmelt. Along the banks of the Clinch were shelves of dense timber and small patches of rich grass fertilized by periodic floods.

A hundred yards north of the crossing Jack's attention was drawn to a vertical cliff with an east-facing opening. Ancient boulders were strewn about, and partly obscured the opening in the cliff. Descent from above would be impossible since one large chunk of granite formed an overhang to shelter the opening. Jack gave Bones a chance to drink from the Clinch and graze on a patch of grass near the water's edge. He stroked his beard and looked at the hole in the cliff.

After assuring himself that what appeared to be a cave opening was well above the flood line, he decided to hike up to see if it was really a cave. The grade to the opening was a steep, rocky climb that wound among the boulders. Jack took note of a grassy flood plain covering about two acres just north of the cave's entrance. To the north of the field, elevated a good 25 feet from the river bottom, a grove of pines mixed with some oak and cedar abutted the vertical canyon wall. The grove would be a good place to park the wagons. The stand of trees would also be a good place to construct a corral and lean-to for sheltering the livestock.

With some work, the approach to the opening could be smoothed. The hole was about ten feet wide and led to an oval shaped room about twelve feet high in the center. The floor was mostly level and sandy. The room had an approximate diameter of fifty feet. Judging from the blackened ceiling, the cave had been used as a shelter before. It would be simple enough to drive poles into the sandy ground across the front of the cave and close off most of the opening. At the back of this cave there was water seeping from the rock wall. Jack recalled how common it is for caves to have a water source. Jack sampled the water and found it to be free of strong minerals, and it had a pleasant taste and was odorless.

The cave would be close quarters and certainly a larger living space would have been preferable, but it would work. Jack decided to ride back to camp and ask the others how they felt about sheltering in a cave.

Jack arrived back at camp after the evening meal was over, but Lyla had kept a plate warm for him. Jack called a meeting to discuss his discovery. He described the cave and asked if anyone had objections to wintering in a cave.

Old Tommy rose from his seat and said, "I always wondered what it would be like to live in a cave. Heaven knows I have been called a blankety-blank caveman, and right about now it don't sound too bad; the fellars must have been prophets. Sure sounds better that trying to spend the winter in these here wagons. We might have to rout any bears or lions 'fore we move in." As soon as the words were out of Tommy's mouth, he saw the look on Rolf and Helga's little faces and quickly said, "Of course I've been told that all of the dangerous animals have moved to warmer parts. I say let's give it a look-see."

Chapter 6

A COLD JOURNEY HOME

With sunrise came a gale, straight out of the northwest. Breakfasts were hastily prepared and carried back to be eaten in the shelter of the wagons. As Tommy served the steaming food, he said, "Better hold your biscuit in your mouth before it blows away like Lyla's did."

When everyone was huddling in the wagons to eat, a red-hot ember blew from the cooking fire and landed on top of Lindsey's wagon. Jack, on guard duty, noticed the smoke. He took a wooden bucket and filled it from his water barrel and doused the flame before it did much damage. Next Jack scattered the burning embers of the cooking fire and covered them with sand. The hole in Lindsey's canvas would need to be patched immediately, based upon the look of the sky.

Jack didn't like the looks of the approaching cloudbank and walked to each wagon and told everyone to prepare to move out. "There's no time to waste. We move out in ten minutes!" Lindsey had pulled his wagon aside and removed the damaged canvas. With cold numbed hands, they sewed a large patch over the irregular hole. Jack's decision to head out was a difficult one, considering the Indian threat, but as leader, he was forced to come down on the side of the group's best interest. Bert stood guard while the patch was completed. Lindsey drove his mules hard and within two hours had caught up to the others.

The wind increased as the day passed. The travelers had to push the mules into the wind against their will, lashing their rumps with rawhide whips. By mid-day horizontal sheets of sleet slowed the wagons. At four in the afternoon, Jack stopped to gather fire wood and prepare for a night of misery. He had the wagons form a tighter than usual circle on the eastern edge of a stand of trees. The trees gave some relief from the sleet and wind. The animals were led into the woods and confined by ropes stretched around the trees. Old Tommy, who had a way with the sometimes-cantankerous jersey cow, pulled an armload of dried grass for her to feed upon while he milked her.

Jack dug a hole and ringed it with an extra high stack of rocks for building the cooking fire. The big iron pot was suspended over the fire, and enough stew to feed the entire group was cooked up. The stew was made from finely chopped venison, browned in bacon fat, and then boiled with potatoes, onions and some turnips. A handful of cornmeal thickened the hearty stew. It was becoming the norm to prepare communal meals. John Silas had been the only divisive personality, and with him gone the group was functioning more like a family. By dark, the worn-out trekkers took shelter in their beds and prayed for protection from the storm. As they slept, a dry snow fell and blew into drifts.

Jack had raised his tent and then took the first watch. By the time he was ready to enter his little tent, he couldn't find it. Jack used a torch to search under the snow and finally found the flattened tent over fifty feet away almost hidden by the snow. When he checked inside for his bedroll, he found it to be dry thanks to the below freezing temperature. Jack decided to ask Tommy and Walter if they could make room for him inside their wagon that just happened to be parked next to where Lorna was sleeping.

The howling wind drowned out most noises, but not a howl of a different sort. The mournful sound of timber wolfs made their presence known. Jack woke Kingston and sent him to stand guard over the stock. Kingston built a large fire and paced back and forth. The tactic worked, and the howling stopped. Loss of any more mules would be devastating. At midnight, Tommy and Lindsey took over as watchmen. Jack collapsed upon his bedroll just inside the tailgate of

Tommy's wagon but didn't get to sleep right away. He was listening for the wolf pack.

At first light, the men hitched the mules to the wagons and prepared to move without cooking breakfast. The temperature was well below freezing, and in spite of the discomfort for both man and beast, footing for the mules was made easier by the hard frozen mud. Visibility improved when the wind settled down to a breeze. Snow started coming down in big wet flakes and was quickly accumulating. Jack rode ahead to make sure that they were on course to reach the cave.

By mid-afternoon, the train reached the crossing at the Clinch. The water was frozen solid and caused the mules some slippery footing as they crossed. On the west side of the river, Jack led the wagons up the river bank into the stand of pines just north of the cave opening. Clearing a path for the wagons was hard work. Mules were unhitched and used to drag aside fallen logs and boulders. A temporary rope corral was strung around a group of trees. The wagons were parked side by side in the cover of the cliff and the trees. Jack told Lorna, "Put Dora inside your clothes, next to your body. There will be a hard freeze tonight. Bundle up everyone!"

Jack advised the women to stay in the wagons and prepare for a very cold night. Once a large fire was burning Jack put Bert, Ian, and Walter on rock detail. He carefully explained, "We will need to have hot rocks in our bedding to stay somewhat comfortable. Don't pick up any rocks close to the river. They have moisture trapped in their pores and will explode like a bomb when they get hot. Pick rocks about this big and pile them around the fire to be heating up. We will switch them out as they cool."

The evening meal was quick and easy. It started with a boiling caldron of water. About four pounds of fresh finely cubed venison was dropped in, and then the liquid thickened with cornmeal. Onion and bacon were added for flavor, and the final ingredient was a huge pan of dough mixed to make drop dumplings, made of flour and cornmeal with salt and baking powder and fresh cream. The meal was ready within an hour and was eaten in the relative protection of the wagons. Jack took a swig of his soup each time he went back to the fire for more hot rocks. He advised everyone to sleep bundled up wearing socks and caps.

Once the crew was bedded down, Jack left Abe walking the perimeter as watchman, and Jack asked Tommy if he would like to walk up to see the cave. Tommy said, "Ya betcha, I am curious as a ring-eyed coon." The snow reflected some light though there was no moon. The two men decided to take a lantern on a pole and that turned out to be a wise decision. The way up to the cave was icy and steep. At the entrance they were shocked by what they found. Before reaching the entrance, a sick feeling came over the two men. There was light and smoke coming from the cave opening. Jack whispered, "Someone is here. Now what do we do?"

Tommy said, "Come on Jack les'see who it is in thar." They entered with Jack calling out, "Hello, anyone here-bouts?" The only sound was that of guns being cocked. Jack and Tommy stopped midstep and raised their hands.

A gruff voice shouted, "Drop the weapons and keep your hands up." The appearance of the two occupants shocked Jack and Tommy. Never had they seen such unkempt, bedraggled men. Their faces bore the marks of hunger and exposure. The strangers told Jack and Tommy to sit down. "What you fellars mean walkin' in on us?"

Jack spoke up, "We are traveling to Kentucky and need a place to get our women and children out of the storm." The larger of the two fellars said, "Well, this here's our cave, so you'ins need to keep going if ya know what's good for ye." Jack decided to try strike'n a bargain with the two men in spite of their hostility.

Jack cleared his throat and said, "How's bout we share some of our food if ya let us crowd in here with you? Our women are good cooks, and we brung along a milk cow." The men slowly rose and walked a few steps away and put their heads together. They came back and the spokesman asked how many in the group. Jack said, "There's sixteen altogether, six be youngins." Jack didn't tell them that three of the youngins, Bert, Ian and Walter, were about grown.

"How many women you got?"

Jack replied, "Four."

"Okay, the grub sounds good, and we need a might of money to buy our stake next spring.

Jack said, "We might could spare a few pesos when we part company, assuming you are hospitable enough. We'll go back and talk it over with the rest of our group." As Tommy and Jack made their way back to the wagons, they both had an uneasy feeling.

Tommy said, "We are likely to get robbed by those ruffians and worse done to the women."

Jack replied, "As I see it, we don't have much of a choice. We chance freezing to death if we don't take shelter in the cave." When Jack and Tommy got back to the wagons, they made the circuit and explained their dilemma. Jack spoke to each wagon separately, "We will meet and discuss what to do at breakfast. Keep your guns by your sides tonight. Those fellars in the cave just might try to rob us."

When morning came Jack stood before the group of shivering souls and laid out their choices. "We are faced with two choices, both bad. We can try to travel on and look for shelter elsewhere, or we can hole up in the cave and risk being robbed by those rapscallions. They want food and money to let us share the cave with them. Ever-one that wants to move on and look for another place, raise your hand." Abraham Olsen was the only one to raise his hand. Abe, Lucy, and their three children were the most private and shy of the group, never causing any trouble and always willing to do their share of the work.

Jack respectfully said, "Abe, out with it, what you thinking?"

Abe, so tall and thin with wisps of blond hair peaking from under his green and yellow knitted wool cap, stepped forward and cleared his throat, "Ya, zee way I seed tit, that, just might be anutter cave like zeez one ups zee creek, then."

Jack said, "That's a good point. Abe, how soon can you be ready to explore the river bed? You can choose someone to go with you. Take gear in case you are caught and forced to be gone overnight. In the mean time we will hunker down here and wait till you get back before deciding." Abe asked Tommy to go with him. They quickly packed for their departure and quietly rode away. The only sound was that of the crunching of the hooves in the crusty snow. The animals snorted and blew white plumes of condensation from their snouts.

Jack placed more rocks to warm around the fire, and put a pot of venison soup to boil. The snow had stopped and the sky was crystal clear. A clear sky meant colder temperatures. One good thing about the snow cover was that it would show tracks if the men from the cave came sneaking around, and of course snow would, to some degree, insulate the canvas wagon covers.

Jack was still on his feet patrolling the camp at mid-day. For the present he was confident that everyone had hot rocks in their cocoon of covers. Jack added snow to the water pot. He added some arrowroot powder to the soup pot for thickening and flavored the soup with some minced onion and salt pork. Once it was boiling and thick, he would start delivering it to the wagons. With Abe and Tommy gone to look for another cave, Jack had to keep going in spite of his fatigue. Jack felt responsible for everyone's safety. His feet felt like chunks of ice and there was no feeling in his fingers or ears. Jack was starting to panic over their situation. He cautioned each family, "Cover up your heads as much as you can. Brace for an even colder night tonight." Jack was especially concerned about Lorna and Dora. He carried some of his own bedding for Lorna to add to the coverlets she was using. "Let me know when your rocks cool down so I can change'em out."

Afterwards Jack asked Jon Macintosh and Walter Thacker to take a turn patrolling. Jack quipped, "Just need to get off my feet for a spell." Before taking a rest by the fire, he walked to each wagon and suggested that most of the money they carried be carefully hidden. "Keep a few coins out in case we need to give them fellars something at the point of a gun if you know what I mean. Hide extra weapons on your body, say, in your boots, for sure out of sight in case they jump us. The women need to be ready to fight too. It would be good to sleep with one eye open tonight." Jack, not wanting to let on how cold and tired he felt, sat down on a warm flat boulder and elevated his numb feet toward the blaze. The heat hurt so he backed them off a little. After sipping a bowl of steaming soup, he became drowsy. As soon as he leaned his head on his knees, sleep overtook him. Lorna, seeing him huddled by the fire, hobbled on one crutch from the wagon with a down coverlet, and draped it over his spent body. Her gratitude for the goodness of this man was beyond description. While Lorna hobbled back to the wagon, she was forced to acknowledge that what she felt for Jackson Long went beyond simple gratitude.

Jack woke with a start; it was almost dark. He wondered how he had slept so long. Then he realized that the noise that awoke him was a wolf pack howling. They were nearby! He figured they were the same pack and had been following the wagon train.

He sat up, and recognized the blanket covering him as one from Lorna's bed. He gathered it up and started to return it when a shot rang out. Then, Walter ran into the camp, and shouted that wolves were stalking the livestock. Jack tossed the blanket to Lorna and ran to help frighten the wolves away from the stock. He told Jon and Walter to build four fires around the corral. Wood was dug from under the snow and dead branches broken from trees. Burning embers from the main fire ignited the new fires. Jack took cover behind a large tree and waited for a shot at the marauders. After several minutes he spied what looked like the alpha male, a large crouching wolf. As it crept closer the bonfires clearly illuminated the animal. Jack took careful aim and dropped the wolf with a slug in the chest. The animal sprang into the air and let out a shrill yelp before falling dead. When the pack quickly retreated into the darkness, Jack surmised he had hit the alpha male. Jack gathered the men together and said, "I think I kilt the pack leader. If we drag his bloody body in a circle around the corral and camp, the scent should keep the rest of them at a distance. We got to remember; them wolves ain't our only worry. You fellars that's been out here the longest, go on back and get warm, I'll patrol till midnight. Tommy and Abe should be back tomorrow."

All was quiet until daybreak. Jack kept his feet from frostbite by frequently warming them by the fire. Every few minutes he would cycle by the fire to add wood and exchange heated rocks. He carried a hot mug of soup for energy and to keep his hands warm. He was battling extreme exhaustion. Jack was beginning to worry about Abe and Tommy. He figured they should be back by now.

Jack kept checking on the women and children. "You got to hang on a little longer, here's some rocks for your bed." Jack's confident, fatherly tone worked its magic and kept spirits hopeful. He took a moment to replenish the large water pot with snow. He insisted they all stay in bed when not patrolling or gathering wood. "Be sure to move around under the covers to keep your blood circulating and drink a cup of water every hour or so. You girls should use the chamber pots for urinating. It's going to be dark soon and bitter cold so prepare to be brave one more night. The Lord will take us through this trial just as He has in the past. Recite the Twenty Third Psalm and pray!"

The hours passed with no sign of Tommy and Abe. Jon, Lindsey, and Kingston had been gathering firewood for hours, and Jack sent them to warm up in their beds. Lyla climbed out of her wagon and ran to hug Jack. She was out to empty her chamber pot and was going to make the rounds and empty the others while she was at it. She was shocked at the sight of him and said, "Jack, you look terrible! Have you rested at all? Get in your bedroll and rest for a while. I am rested and warm, so I will take care of delivering rocks for you."

"Lyla dear Lyla, I'm gonna take you up on the offer. If you are going to be out in the open, you need to be armed and be sure to watch out for wolves and those fellars up in the cave. Wake me when———." Just then a shot rang out and then a second. Jack and Lyla stopped what they were doing and strained to listen. "It sounds like the shots are coming from up at the cave," Jack exclaimed under his breath. "Stay here and guard the camp, I'm gonna sneak up there and see if I can find out what's goin on."

Jack checked his two pistols and returned them to his waistband. Halfway up to the cave, he heard a man crying out in desperation, "help—oh, God help me——." Jack continued up the rocky passage to the cave entrance, crouching behind rocks and rushing across exposed spaces. When he cautiously peered around the side of the cave opening, he saw one of the men sprawled on the cave floor and the other sitting against the cave wall all bent over. Jack approached the men with a pistol in each hand. The taller of the two appeared to be unconscious and bleeding from a throat wound. The man sitting against the wall was shot in the upper abdomen. He was slumped forward with both hands pressed against his belly. A copious amount of blood was seeping from between his fingers. Jack walked up to the unconscious man, kicked away his gun, and probed his side with his boot. He appeared to be dead. He approached the other man and asked, "What happened here?" Jack quickly removed the man's pistol and placed it in his own belt.

Between breaths, the wounded man managed to gasp, "Old Cory— shot me. Last night we was play'n poker and -ee' got drunk, never could hold—liquor. I won fair, but -ee said I cheated." The wounded man's words were becoming fainter, and Jack had to kneel in order to hear him. "Last night we bout come to blows, -ee backed off and then passed out. Whent -ee woke, -ee comp'te steal my winnin's, figured -ey still sleep'n, but -ad' my gun under my blanket. I opened my eyes and aimed my gun at him, that's when he shot me. I yelled 'Cory, what the hell,' and then I fired back. Oh, my God, I can't stand this pain! I need whiskey, can you git—?" Just then the pitiful man slumped over and died. Jack thought how sad for a man's last words to be taking the Lord's name in vain. Jack was recalling the verse in the book of Philippians that promised that "every knee will bow before God." Yep, Jack thought, sure won't be no unbelievers standing before God on the judgment day.

Jack thought, with these two dead everything changes. He checked for a pulse, and they were definitely passed on to the next life. He decided to hurry back to camp and tell everyone to prepare to move into the cave. We may need to go looking for Tommy and Abe.

Even Jack Long, a mountain of a man in the prime of life, had endurance limits. As he trudged through the mid-calf deep snow, progress became slower with each step. The walk back to the wagons seemed so far away, —now which direction? Maybe I'll stop and rest. Jack was disoriented. Then he tripped over a hidden branch and fell into a snow bank. His surroundings seemed distorted and unreal. He recognized the signs of hypothermia, but was too exhausted to continue. A restful sleep claimed him. Suddenly someone was shaking him. It was Bert. "Jack, wake up, here, git up, I'll help you." The boy pulled Jack into a standing position and supported him as they walked back to the fireside.

On the way back Jack managed to tell Bert, "Them boys kilt each other; both of 'em dead."

As the two neared the camp, Lindsey saw their approach and hurried to help. Lorna was horrified when she saw the two men almost carrying Jack. Then Lorna called out to Lindsey, "Bring him to me." The two men hefted Jack onto the wagon bed. "Quick, get me more hot rocks. Jack, Jack! Can you hear me?" Jack was unconscious so it was a struggle for Lorna to pull his limp body to the mattress on the floor of the wagon. She loosened his belt and covered him with a stack of blankets. She reached underneath and removed his boots and gloves. She placed her hands underneath the covers and started massaging Jack's cold feet and hands. She was panicked on what to do first. As she worked to revive Jack, she began to weep and pray. Dora had been asleep during most of the crisis, but now she was awake and squirming inside Lorna's sweater. She took the time to blot the melting ice from Jacks face and beard and cupped his ears in her palms. She knew not to warm him too fast. Just when she was seeing some improvement in skin color, Lyla appeared at the wagon gate. "How is Jack? Need help?"

"Yes, will you take Dora to Jane and come back and help me. I don't know what to do. Lyla, he is unconscious!"

"Calm down Lorna, I'll be right back." Without Dora Lorna could maneuver about on her knees better. Lyla brought a cup of warm broth back for Jack. The two women worked over him, massaging, and moving the warming stones around. Lyla whispered, "I think he is suffering from exhaustion more than from the cold. He has been pushing himself too hard, and it caught up with him."

"Oh, Lyla I can't bear to see him like this, not Jack—."

"I am enjoying listening to this, but I'm awake now so I reckon I better warn you." Jack opened one eye and grinned at the two women. "Got anything to drink? I'm thirsty." Lyla was on one side of Jack and Lorna on the other. Their reaction was instantaneous, and they both bowed to give Jack a kiss on the forehead but cracked their heads together.

Jack said, "Ouch! This makin' on over me needs some organization. Lyla, you go first, and then you Lorna. Don't forget the drink of something. And I think I would recover a lot faster with some hugs." The laughter was so loud that Bert, Kingston, and Lindsey were suddenly at the tailgate looking in.

After more laughs, some hugging, and smacks on the forehead, Lyla stepped into the role of boss that came so naturally to her. She said, "Jack, this was a warning shot over the bow, so take heed and rest in here where Lorna can keep you warm. The wolves are gone, and we are all managing what needs to be done. Go on back to sleep after you hydrate and eat something. That is an order!"

Jack raised a hand to his forehead and saluted Lyla and then gave her a big loving smile.

Lindsay decided to go after Tommy and Abe but before he had gone a mile, he met them coming back. They had heard the shots and decided to return. The cold air had carried the sound along the river bottom. As the men converged on each other, Tommy asked, "What the heck was all of the firing about?"

Lindsey told them of the shootout between the two ruffians in the cave and said, "Come on, boys, let's get the women and children moved in. And by the way, Jack got too cold, and is sleeping in his wagon. We bout lost him."

Abe and Tommy helped Lindsey and Jon wrap the two dead men in their blankets and drag them down to a small sandy shelf where they attached a rope to the bodies and pulled them into the forest where the ground was soft. After removing any valuables, they buried them together in a hastily dug grave. Back at the cave the men went through the dead men's belongings. They found two unopened whiskey bottles, several pokes of lead balls, and two horns of black powder. Other than these items and a few coins and their weapons, the rest of the dead men's belongings were burned outside the cave.

Within three hours the women were brought up to the cave, except for Lorna and Dora. Lorna refused to move as long as Jack slept. Inside the cave, the men restarted the fire. Tommy decided to load up one of the wagons with the most important trunks and boxes. He arranged them so that they were stable and helped the women and children to seats on the top. At the bottom of the steep walkway, he transferred everything to a quickly constructed travois-like sled to be pulled by one of the mules. The women and children walked up the incline to the mysterious looking opening. They didn't know what to expect, but with candles and a large fire illuminating the interior, they were pleasantly surprised. The interior was chilly, in the high fifties, but that was almost balmy after the days of below freezing temperatures. Shutting off the opening with a canvas curtain would keep the heat generated by the fire inside and raise the temperature by five degrees or so. That all depended on the smoke being sufficiently vented to the outside.

Everyone got to work making the cave into a home. Tommy decided to bring the cow up to the cave. "We can fence her off at the entrance. Glad we have the ole gal. Hope she stays fresh a mite longer see'n we have no way to breed her."

After sleeping about six hours, Jack awoke, "Lorna, why didn't you wake me? I need to be helping with moving our gear up to the cave."

"We all need you alive and healthy, you big lug! We almost lost you because you would not take time to rest."

Embarrassed, Jack sat up and started pulling on his socks and boots. He didn't bother with building up the fire but brought hot rocks for Lorna's bed and then struck out to join the others. Before leaving Lorna, Jack handed her a pistol and asked, "I reckon you know how to use this?"

Lorna gave Jack a big smile and said, "Thanks Jack, yes, I can shoot."

Bright sunlight was warming the air and melting the snow. Jack took long strides and felt rested. When he reached the cave, he was quick to admire the progress being made. The men greeted Jack with back slaps and warm handshakes, and the women all hugged his neck.

Tommy with a mischievous smile asked, "What you been up to?"

Lyla ladled a bowl of stew for Jack, and Jane carried him a mug of milk. As soon as Jack finished the hurried meal, he asked where they were planning to put Lorna and Dora. The women directed his gaze to a stack of boxes that formed an L-shaped area at the back of the cave. "Looks good, ladies. I'm gonna bring Lorna and Dora up on my horse. We'll be back as fast as possible." Jack hurried to the corral and saddled Bones. He led the gelding to the back of the wagon and told Lorna not to worry about bringing anything, but to dress warmly. Jack went back a second time and packed up Lorna's belongings and carted them up to the cave.

On the second day the invigorated workers constructed a more permanent corral for the mules and horses. A water barrel was placed in the enclosure. When the weather let up the animals would be hobbled and allowed to graze the riverbank during daylight hours.

The cave was divided into sections. Just behind the entrance was the kitchen area, and back from there was the fire pit with a long table and seating improvised from crates and boxes. The individual sleeping areas were located along the circular backside of the cave where the ceiling was lower. Dividers and drapes gave each area some privacy. A water barrel was placed under the water seeping from the cave wall.

Outside the cave, the men built a privy. The brush structure was covered with canvas. It was located on the edge of a drop-off. The waste drained into a pit below that would be sprinkled with lye and covered with dirt every few days. The first night in the cave, they had all skipped cooking and satisfied their hunger by chewing on jerky and anything else worth the effort.

The weary souls collapsed from utter exhaustion thankful to be out of the extreme cold. Sleeping with hot rocks was a thing of the past. What a luxury!

For the rest of her life Lorna would recall what happened on the second night in the cave. It was forever be etched into her memory. Outside, the weather had turned unusually warm for the end of November and the snow was melting. The "cave dwellers" were in a festive mood. The good fortune of finding the cave was something close to a miracle. Pleasant, relaxed expressions replaced those of anxiety and discomfort. A large fire bathed the inhabitants with warmth and light.

Shelter, heat, and illumination would never be taken for granted, not by these people.

Smiley-face, Bert's new nickname stood, and said, "Hey Tommy, got your juice-harp handy?"

Tommy flashed a mischievous grin and patted his chest. He quipped, "Just happens that it is rite-cheer in my pocket." Tommy never had to be asked twice to play a tune. A celebration seemed appropriate so Tommy started the party by playing a lively tune. The jovial clapping and foot tapping kept time with the music. Old Tommy had done it again, lifted the spirits, just what the doctor ordered. The younger ones of the group commenced to stomp out a jig. When the party atmosphere was at its height, the women began preparing a meal, keeping time to the music by tapping their feet.

Lorna, busy peeling rubbery and shriveled turnips and potatoes, found her gaze seeking out Jack. She was thinking about him, *his collapse in the snow and how he had surprised me with the crutches. The way he volunteered to care for both me and Dora at our time of greatest need. He is conscious of the little things that makes life more comfortable, things that most men would never think to do for a woman.* She loved looking at him; she couldn't help herself. The word 'handsome' would pop into her mind every time she looked. Lorna continued thinking and risked another look. *Handsome, but not 'pretty boy' handsome, but rather rugged, strong and intelligent handsome. By far his most attractive feature was his self-assured manner.* The combination of looks, precisely his tall, strongly muscled frame and confident, authoritative persona made him the most attractive man she had ever known. What would he think of her if he knew what she was thinking? It was unsettling to notice that each time she looked his way, his eyes were trained on her. *Is it possible that he is attracted to me?* She lowered her eyes and pretended to concentrate on peeling the vegetables.

Across the room Jack was thinking, *Lorna is sure paying a lot of attention to me, likely just appreciates all we do for her.* But the next time Jack looked in Lorna's direction he caught her staring at him. *Maybe she needs to speak with me, or is it even remotely possible that she is having feelings for me?* Jack's internal dialogue continued: *here I am, a single, healthy male, and she is a single woman, and a beautiful one at that.* The voice that started with a whisper was now shouting, *Old boy, are you gonna do som'thin about how you feel or are you gonna let the moment git away from you?*

During the next harmonica song, Jack walked over to Lorna and removed the paring knife from her hands. He lifted Dora from her sling and playfully spun around holding the baby in front of his face. Next, he tickled her slobbery chin. She burst forth with a precious giggle. Dora's shrill little laugh was heard over the harmonica, and everyone smiled. Jack kissed the irresistible cherub on the top of her head, and handed her to Jane.

Jack held out his right hand to Lorna. She wiped her hands on her apron, reached for a crutch, and slowly stood. With questioning eyes, she reached out and took his hand. An observant Tommy had abruptly stopped playing mid tune. In one fluid movement, Jack placed one arm around Lorna's waist and the other under her knees. Her crutch dropped to the floor with a thud. Jack smiled and then nodded for Tommy to resume the music. Jack focused his attention on Lorna's surprised face and began waltzing around the fire in time to the music. Jack yelled, "Come on everbody, time to kick up your heels. Act lively!" The next song had a faster tempo, and Jack danced on, dipping and swaying with big sweeping steps. Lorna wadded up Dora's carrying scarf and pitched it to Lyla who had flour up to her elbows making biscuits. Lorna felt Jack's mood and relaxed, returning his smile. She placed an arm around Jack's neck and planted a kiss on his cheek.

Known to his fellow travelers as a serious fellow, Jack's sudden playfulness was infectious. Jane and Jon began waltzing around the circle, joined by Lucy and Abe with a lively polka. The children joined in and were having a grand time.

> *Uncle Sam came there to change*
> *Some pancakes and some onions,*
> *For' lasses cake to carry home*
> *To give his wife and young ones.*
> *Yankee doodle, keep it up,*
> *Yankee doodle dandy;*
> *Mind the music and the step,*
> *And with the girls be handy*

Jane and Jon stood side by side and performed an Irish jig. Lyla asked Kingston to hang the heavy Dutch-oven over the coals and then asked him to take her for a turn around the fire. Never one for dancing, he declined, pointing to his gimpy leg. Lyla put her hands on her hips and stretched to whisper something in his ear. He flashed a look of disappointment and shrugged his shoulders. He grabbed her by the waist and whirled her around before embarking on a comical looking, stiff-legged two-step. It reminded everyone to be thankful that the arrow wound was healing as fast as it was. There was no doubt that Lyla knew how to motivate her man. Later Lyla shared her incentive with the other women and they all raised their eyebrows and had a good snicker.

Jon won a round of spirited applause when he did a lively highlander fling. Jane, not to be outdone, demonstrated her early childhood ballet training by doing a graceful pirouette on her tip-toes. Dizzy, oxygen starved Lorna basked in the light-hearted mood, swinging her head to the beat. The movement loosened her hair pins causing her mane of chestnut hair to fall the length of her back, splaying out with each turn. Jack, with blue eyes flashing, was in a splendid mood; he briefly set Lorna on a box long enough to fetch a cup of water for each of them.

Before resuming the dancing, Jack taunted the men to an arm-wrestling contest but had no takers. Next, he surprised the kids by pulling a coin from their ears. This new dimension to his personality inspired all kinds of tomfoolery. Jack, playing practical jokes and clowning at his own expense? What had gotten into him? Jack shouted, "Music please!" and continued dancing. Lorna was in awe of the effortless way Jack supported her weight.

Chapter 7

HEART SONG & OLD TOMMY

L orna was suddenly aware of every point that Jack's body touched hers. The contact aroused certain sensations, very hard to ignore sensations. She spoke to herself, *silly woman, control yourself, lest he think of you as a wanton hussy.* Warning herself to maintain control didn't seem to work, her heart had a mind of its own. She was so overwhelmed no degree of decorum could possibly restrain her. Jack locked Lorna into a questioning gaze and abruptly carried her from the cave.

Outside, cloaked in privacy, Jack slowly lifted Lorna until her face was almost touching his face. He gave her ample time to reflect his passion before continuing. Lorna closed her eyes and tried to relax. Jack tightened his embrace. Lorna could feel his powerful throbbing heart through his vest. Just as she was about to open her eyes, he placed a hand behind her head and brought her mouth to his. The kiss was awkwardly placed, and he withdrew his mouth. They both laughed, and Jack said, "Shall we try again?"

Lorna nodded and waited. The second kiss was blissful, full of trembling sensuous contact and conveyed what they both felt. They searched each other's eyes. Something mysterious was happening. A current of energy had come forth and fused them into one pulsing being, causing them to gasp. They had suffered from a heart palpitation that effectively reset their hearts to beat in unison. Jack shook his head and asked, "What just happened; did you feel that surge of energy?"

"Yes, I felt —." Jack smothered her unfinished sentence with his mouth.

Jack held back nothing. He laid bare his obsession with Lorna. Since the moment he had assumed responsibility for her care he had been hiding the cavernous loneliness she created within him. Finally, he had taken the initiative and left himself emotionally exposed. Lorna responded to his raw emotion with a craving that equaled his own. They had both been concealing the way they felt due to societal pressure and situational ethics. That John Silas had died at his own hand had weighed heavily upon Jack. Lorna was bearing her own guilt and feelings of unworthiness for hiding John Silas' criminal past.

Lorna felt Jack's muscles tense as he waited to see what she would do next. She wasn't ready for the caressing to end, not so soon. She raised one hand to the crown of his head and placed the other behind his neck and pulled his face to hers. She kissed him with tenderness, starting with his forehead, his closed eyes, and on to his waiting mouth, all the while caressing his neck and shoulders with trembling fingers. The kisses intensified, becoming insatiable. Jack's entire body was racked with a crescendo of sensation!

Dusk had turned to darkness in the Clinch River gorge. Jack looked around and found a flat topped bolder to sit upon. Holding Lorna on his lap, they continued kissing. Their individual dams-of-loneliness had burst, sending a torrent that washed away self-imposed barriers. The recent circumstances that subjected Jack and Lorna to the emotional extremes of eminent peril, physical pain, constant discomfort, and grief had expanded their capacity to experience the pinnacle of romantic love uniquely reserved for a man and woman.

This brief interlude set in motion a process that would eventually fuse them in the eyes of God as "one flesh." They had glimpsed what awaited them: their melding into an indescribably fervent love, better expressed in the Greek language as sensual desire, physical passion, and emotional longing.

A faint call sounded: "Time to eat." Jack steadied Lorna on her good leg, and helped her straighten her dress and smooth her hair. "I guess we better git back in there before they put out a search party."

He carried her back into the cave. The others were seemingly engrossed with what they were doing and hardly noticed that Jack and Lorna had returned.

When the meal was finished, Jack helped Lorna settle down for the night. The events of the evening would forever divide the chronology of their lives into before and after.

Over the next few days Lorna and Jack failed at faking normal behavior. They were captive to the buttery, sensual urges that afflict those who suddenly find a love that most people hope for and dream of experiencing. Lorna went through the motions of her daily chores, but her heart was beating a little faster, her breathing was deeper, all the while punctuated with wistful sighs. What the others saw was a woman living in a different dimension, distracted and absent minded, awash in hormones.

In like manner, Jack's burgeoning dopamine and serotonin levels commandeered his thought processes. His ability to focus on the practical tasks of daily living was hit and miss. Circular thoughts were cycling through his mind. *Could a beautiful young woman like Lorna really be in love with the likes of me? Please, God, let it be so. After what I have experienced with Lorna, the thought of resuming my prior life is too painful to consider. Flesh and bone I am, created to need a woman. Lord, please do what you can on my behalf.*

Could a beautiful young woman like Lorna really ————.

Tommy shouts, "Jack, you just put your jacket on wrong side out."

Jackson Long, the former consummate alpha male, a confident, decisive, analytical trail boss is suddenly reduced to a befuddled, distracted, and absent-minded wayfaring alien, relegated to existing in a dreamlike dimension. The other men, aware of Jack's malady of the heart, smiled behind his back and took care of the business at hand. They set priorities and worked long and hard at the important tasks. They enforced the stock corral, built an elevated guard shelter in a massive tree next to the stock pen, built a shower shack near to the privy. Load after load of firewood was cut and transported up to the cave on the mule drawn sledge. The entrance to the cave was closed off with a curtain of canvas with weights sewn into the hem. The stacked firewood helped close in a special pen for the milk cow that was partly sheltered by the jutting rock overhang. Everyone attributed the fact that the cow was still fresh to Tommy's special efforts. He kept the marvelous bovine's nutrition up by hand gathering grass and herbs along the Clinch.

Pairs of men formed hunting parties. Good fortune provided a white tail deer and two turkey hens the first day out. The game would furnish enough meat for several days. As more meat was brought in, the women set about preserving the meat on drying racks. They used bird feathers and down to stuff comforters and saved tallow from rendering animal carcasses for making soap and candles. A rope clothesline was strung outside the cave and soiled clothing and bedding was boiled in a large iron pot of sudsy water. Surprisingly life at the Clinch River cave took on a degree of normalcy in spite of the primitive, even pre-historic setting.

For Lorna and Jack, life was anything but normal. With each passing day the love-stricken couple became more desperate for closeness. Finally, Jack decided that it was time to act upon his impulses and plan some time to be alone with Lorna. They had a lot to discuss. When he approached Lorna, she gazed at him with stars in her eyes. Jack took her by the shoulders and said, "Lorna, let's go on an outing, take some food and spend some time alone. Want to?"

Lorna's expression gave him his answer.

Jack looked at Dora and said, "How about a picnic?" He saddled Bones and packed some strips of jerky and a canteen of water into the saddlebag. The sun was bright, but the wind had a chill. Lorna bundled Dora in her warmest bunting, sewn from a blanket. Jack cleaned and loaded his muzzle-loader and carried it slung on his back. Both of his matching pistols were primed and fitted into his belt. He boosted Lorna onto the saddle and then handed Dora up. Jack chose to walk leading Bones rather than ride double. Considering the rough terrain, it would be safer.

They followed the western side of the riverbed upstream, but found the going difficult. After a couple of miles, Jack found a curve in the stream and stopped to rest. A row of small trees and brush sheltered the area from the wind. "Lorna, don't you think this is a good place for our picnic?" She nodded, and Jack spread a blanket on a sun-warmed slab of rock near the water's edge. As Jack carried Lorna and Dora to the blanket, Dora giggled and kicked her feet. The heat from the sunlight felt so good. Seated facing the river, Lorna put Dora down to play. She reached out a chubby little hand and picked up a pebble. She rolled over to her back and curiously investigated the object. Then she decided to see how it tasted. Lorna said, "Oh no you don't, you must be hungry, come here." Lorna placed the squirming baby on her lap and began feeding her. Jack noticed the glow on Lorna's face as she gazed behind the blanket that covered Dora's head. She was radiant with tenderness.

Finally, just being alone with Jack, being able to touch him and hear his voice made Lorna's heart soar. She felt deliriously happy. Lorna watched as Jack unscrewed the cap from the canteen of water and handed it to her. She downed the water with a nursing mother's thirst. Jack opened the pouch of jerky, unwrapped some crackers, and placed them on the blanket. He sat down on the blanket and handed Lorna a piece of deer jerky.

The time had arrived. Lorna knew that she must tell Jack what John Silas had done. Lorna glanced under the modesty blanket covering her bosom. Dora had fallen asleep, but was still nursing. Lorna started by saying, "There are some things about me you should know. She gently placed the sleeping baby on a corner of the blanket, shading her face from the sunlight with a fold of the blanket.

"Jack, I'm not sure where to start. When you hear —what I have to—tell you—. You need to know that John Silas was a common criminal. We were fleeing out home because he resisted arrest and accidentally killed the Constable. All over a liquor still." Jack grabbed both of Lorna's hands and peered into her eyes. Lorna continued, "I'm sorry I didn't tell you sooner." Welling tears made Lorna's eyes glassy. Jack, recognizing her pain, pulled Lorna's face to his chest.

Jack rocked back and forth, patting her back, and said, "Lorna, you don't have to do this. My love for you has nothing to do with John Silas. Remember that I know what he was like. You are not like him. You are fine and good."

Lorna dried her eyes and continued, "When he rushed into our house and told me what he had done, I did not go to the authorities. I told him to leave without us, but he threatened to take Dora if I refused to go. I was too weak to stand up to him. That makes me guilty too, doesn't it?"

Then Jack said, "I hate to think what would have happened if you had stood up to John Silas; Enough of blaming yourself."

Lorna continued, "The Constable accused John Silas of selling tainted whiskey and was in the process of arresting him. I suspect some of those who were poisoned may have died. John Silas resisted arrest, and the lawman fell backwards and struck his head, according to John Silas. When John Silas saw that he was dead, he panicked, and ran home. I asked if he had hidden the body, and he said no and went back and dumped it into an abandoned well."

"We packed up a stolen wagon and left our home within a few hours. I didn't have the option of returning to live with my parents. They were barely getting by, and they didn't need two more mouths to feed. So, we headed west before the body of the Constable was discovered. Jack, John Silas picked Jones for a last name but it is really Maxwell. In spite of your rule about drinking, John Silas had a keg of liquor along and stayed drunk most of the time. He always got mean when he was drinking."

Then Jack said, "Lorna, why didn't he stay and explain that the scuffle had ended in an accident?" Lorna replied, "John Silas was certain that no one would believe him. And I think he was right. John Silas had been in trouble so many times before. I was glad to leave the stolen wagon behind."

"Lorna," Jack suddenly grabbed Lorna by the shoulders, "Maybe the Constable was right, I mean about the whiskey poisoning his customers; Lorna, is it possible he was poisoning himself! That would account for his bizarre behavior?"

Lorna said, "Yes, you may be right. He complained of a headache and stomach pains constantly. I didn't think about the whiskey making him sick."

"Lorna, the stolen wagon was left on the trail, beside John Silas' grave. Now you need to leave it all behind. You and Dora deserve a new start." Jack took Lorna in his arms, and they laid back on the blanket. Jack began running his hands over Lorna's hair and back. She buried her face in his powerful chest. The sound of his beating heart soothed her painful memories.

Lorna was relieved for Jack to know her secret. She desperately wanted to spend the rest of her life with Jack, and that was the only barrier. Lorna said. "Jack, hold me close." Just as they were settling down to enjoy the sound of the flowing stream and the warmth of the sun, Jack had something nagging at him and decided to throw it out for discussion. Minutes passed before Jack spoke softly into Lorna's ear, "Some folks might say I'm too old for you?"

Lorna responded with surprise, "Too old, you are not old; you are in your prime. Anyway, what does that have to do with the way we feel about each other? I can't imagine any of our friends even thinking such a thing."

Jack looked at Lorna with a vulnerable and tender expression on his face, and said, "That's what I was hoping you would say." Jack was silent for a while and then said, "You know, I've been a "lone wolf" for a long time. I was married. Her name was Martha. I loved her very much, and I was thrilled when we were expecting a child. Martha worked hard preparing for the baby. The night she started to labor with the baby, a blizzard had blown in. She begged me not to leave her to go after the mid-wife. When she was ready to deliver, a large bloody mass came out first, and when the baby followed, she was gushing blood. Our little boy was stillborn. Later, the mid-wife told me that the womb came out first, and that was what killed them both. Martha bled to death, right in front of my eyes. I didn't know what to do. Jack's glassy eyes stared into space.

Lorna said, "I'm so sorry, I didn't know."

Jack continued, "I guess after that I didn't want to go on. I pushed friends away. Work became my life. I have felt no joy in living since, not really, that is until the night I carried you out of the cave. Lorna, having you in my life has saved me from the black hole I had been living in for so long."

Then Jack began kissing Lorna, slowly and tenderly at first. A mutual surge of fervor possessed them. Jack paused and took Lorna's face in his hands and said, "Marry me!"

Lorna pressed her face to his and between kisses moaned, "Yes, yes, my answer is yes." A thought popped into his mind. Jack tilted his head and said, "Abe is a religious man, maybe he can marry us. We'll make it legal as soon as we reach civilization. I'll ask him when we get back, if you agree."

Jack and Lorna had resumed kissing when a rock tumbled down the steep embankment on the east side of the stream. Jack, under the guise of needing a breath and to avoid alarming Lorna, searched the direction of the sound, but saw nothing. Then Bones snorted and pawed the ground, confirming Jack's alert to a presence. The gelding had never given a false alarm. Jack stiffened as soon as he realized they were not alone and in plain view. He whispered to Lorna, "Do not let on, but there is someone across the stream. I can't see them clearly. Lorna, when I tell you, can you walk well enough to get Dora and take cover behind that bolder just behind us?" She nodded, and he continued the embrace as his eyes searched the far bank.

Then he saw movement. He said, "Go now." Lorna gathered Dora under one arm and limped to the cover of the bolder. Their scramble for cover brought a gunshot that ricocheted off the rock that Lorna had gone behind. Springing into action, Jack gathered Bones' reigns and pulled him behind the bolder. Jack quickly removed his powder horn and bag of shot from the saddlebag and hung them around his neck. Lorna noticed Jack's heaving chest, visible beneath his linsey-woolsey shirt. Lorna tasted fear as her heart moved up into her throat, wildly pounding. Jack stopped to listen and heard hooves splashing in the stream. He climbed to the top of the bolder and peeked over. Then he yelled, "Hold it right there, boys. Come no closer if you value your lives."

The two men stopped mid-stream and yelled back, "We thought chu wuz Injuns. We don't mean no harm. We be looking for our partners, you seen any trappers in these parts? Sposed to be hole'd up in a cave a little ways from chere."

Jack replied, "A few days back we found two dead men. We buried them. Might have been your friends. You fellars seen any Indian sign? We had a run in with a war party a few days back."

The two men looked at each other and mumbled softly. They seemed confused and after a pause the one on the gray mare spoke. "Guess we will be heading on then. Sounds like Injuns done our friends in. Too bad 'bout the boys, and thanks for the warning bout ta'injuns. What tribe ye reckon?"

Jack said, "Judging from the arrows, most likely Creek, probably Red Stick, or maybe Cherokee." The men turned their horses around and climbed out of the river bottom. Jack watched them until they were out of sight and then told Lorna to get ready to go back. "We need to get back and tell the boys to post an extra sentry for the next few days. We may not've seen the last of these fellars." And, then with a lop-sided, mischievous smile Jack said, "Besides we have a weddin' to plan." Jack caressed and kissed Lorna as he loaded her and Dora on to the horse. Lorna noticed that Jack took extra precautions on the trip back to the cave. He would stop and listen and kept to the cover of trees when possible.

When they arrived, the sun was about to go down, and supper was almost over. Jack and Lorna were both given a plate of food and a cup of soup for Dora. Almost 8 months old, Dora was learning to eat soft, bland solids. While playing on a blanket, she would try to rise on all fours, but she was a long way from crawling. It was apparent that her injured hip had mended in an abnormal way, though it no longer pained her. Lorna's ankle was mostly healed. Most of the swelling was gone, and she was starting to put some weight on it. Other than a knot on the bone, it appeared to have mended well, and with time she had reason to expect near normal motion of the joint.

The day after returning from the interrupted picnic, Jack asked Abe to walk with him. Jack asked, "Abe, I reckon you are the closest thing we have to a preacher man. Do you feel that you could say a ceremony for Miss Lorna and me? See'n you have your Good Book along and all."

Abe placed his hand on Jack's shoulder and responded by saying, "Ya, zee kinda figured idt vas comin' to zhis. Z'd be happy, Ze mean gladt to, that. Ze never tolt you but Ze did some preachin' bact east. Z'm purty sure zee Lord voo'd approvt. Vhen ya vant to do zis, that?"

Jack spoke up, "Ah heck, Abe. The sooner the better. I been alone too long, hard on a man. You know what I mean?"

The following day winter returned with a vengeance. The blizzard dumped at least three feet of snow. December was living up to its reputation. The men had built a plank barrier at the cave entrance. Wind gusts created a snow drift against the wood effectively insulating the cave's interior from the extreme cold. Hauling in firewood suddenly took priority. Working in teams the men used mules to pull the wood up the incline to the cave. The limbs were then cut into useable lengths and stacked inside the cave.

All of the food stuffs were almost exhausted. It became harder to gather grass from under the snow for the cow. Keeping the old girl well fed was the only way to keep her fresh. Old Tommy stepped up once again. He said, "Nothin' but meat jerky is gittin' tiresome, and we all need some herbs in our soup. Think I will go out and dig up some plants, and while I'm at it gather grass for the cow. "Hey, Ian, Bert, you boys want to come along?" They jumped at the chance to escape the confinement of the cave, so Tommy helped them make some snow shoes like the ones Tommy would be wearing. "Wrap up in your warmest clothes and bring a canteen that can stay under your clothes to keep the water from freezin'."

"Bring your blunderbuss, pistol, and plenty extra balls and powder. We might run acrost a big fat turkey or a whitetail. I figger to be gone about six hours but we might need to bivouac overnight. You boys up for that?" Bert and Ian looked at each other and grinned. They were thinking it would be an adventure and as it turned out, not just an ordinary adventure but one they would never forget. "We can pull the little sled with our gear and have it to bring back any game we kill." Tommy placed a large sheet of canvas on the ground and piled on a buffalo robe and some dry kindling. Other gear that fell in the just-in-case category was a coil of rope, small wood saw, small cooking pot, a candle, a hatchet, extra shovel, and a bag of jerky. Bert helped Tommy fold the canvas over and tie it on the sled with more rope. At the front of the sled, Tommy fastened a ceramic pot full of hot coals.

The two happy boys crunched through the deep snow behind Tommy, anticipating some adventure hinted at by Tommy. He stopped and grinned at them trying to get the hang of walking in show shoes. After a few chuckles he gave them a demonstration, lifting the toe well above the snow before moving the shoe forward. The first find came from under the snow at the Clinch River bank. They gathered watercress and bitter cress herbs. They gathered more than a quart. Tommy was careful to leave the root system in place. Upstream on the opposite side was a large stand of cattails. The three of them filled a satchel with about two gallons of cattail roots.

Tommy, asked, "How's yore toes and fingers? We can stop and build a fire when we need to." At that moment Ian saw a rabbit dart into a brush covered hole in the side of a bank and took after it. Just as Tommy was about to say let it go, there was a ferocious growl. The rabbit had gone into an animal den. Tommy bent down to see what was in the cave. He saw the reflection of two eyes glistening back at him and from the size guessed it to be a badger. Tommy started backing up very slowly and sniffed the air. He said, "Wheu, this ain't no badger, we got us a Wolver—!" Before Tommy could get the word wolverine out of his mouth, the attack was on. A cinnamon-colored ball of fur charged from the cave and sprang at Tommy. The three of them froze with fear at the sound of growling and snapping teeth. Tommy yelled "Look out boys." The wolverine was moving so fast it was a blur. Ian and Bert looked at each other trying to decide if they should try to help Tommy.

The wolverine jumped high enough to attach its claws to Tommy's overcoat and then moved up to his head. Tommy was yelling like a mad man and trying to get at his knife. He found his pistol and wounded the critter. It jumped to the ground, trying to escape but inadvertently ran in Bert's direction. Bert tripped over his snow shoes and fell with his face buried in the snow. The wolverine attacked one of his legs. Ian tried to go to his aid but moved awkwardly. Ian pulled his pistol and cocked it. He shuffled over to where the large male was ripping at Bert's leather britches and fired at the wolverine point blank. The shot struck the animal in the chest, and it made a high-pitched scream but stayed attached to Bert's leg. Ian began beating the animal with the butt of the pistol, scared out of his mind.

The wolverine eventually loosened its grip and fell to the snow-covered ground. Tommy, supposing it to be dead, went to look it over. When he kicked at the beast, it revived and attacked Tommy's foot. After a brief flurry of kicking, growling, chomping teeth, and Tommy's screaming, the brown and grey wolverine loosened its grip on Tommy's foot and fell in a heap. Tommy backed up and waited. The three of them were in shock. Then Tommy pointed his pistol at the animal before he summoned the courage to poke it with a stick. He looked at the boys and said, "Looks like we kilt him this time." Bert and Ian nodded their heads but had not yet found their voices.

Tommy and the two boys were so unnerved that they sat down in the snow and starred at each other in disbelief. It didn't take long for Tommy to recover his sense of humor and said, "What say we build a fire and cook us up some wolverine?" The boys had a green tint to their faces and responded to the suggestion with disgust. All three of them had been smeared with foul smelling scent gland oil, and the thought of food much less the source of the foul smell made them feel like upchucking. Tommy felt bad that the boys' first wild encounter had been so terrifying, but he figured it had instilled some lessons they would never forget. Some day they would have a great fireside story to tell to their grandchildren. In the meantime, Tommy would add it to his repertoire of nail-biting stories. From the look on the two boys' faces, they needed a change of underpants.

"Ah-right, guess you boys ain't hungry yet. First off, we reload our weapons; then how 'bout we move a ways off and build a nice fire? Once we have the fire burning, we can warm up while I sew up the holes in my jacket. Not much light left so step lively. Don't ever forgit to reload, got it? I'm bumfuzzled over finding a wolverine this far south. I guess the extra cold winter drew him out of his normal range. Ian, look for some dry kindling, and Bert you can clear a circle in the snow and bring some rocks to ring the fire pit."

"Looks like I am the only wounded member of the team, right? Glad for that! Bert, how much damage ya got to your leather britches? Not too bad, looks like only one place needs sewing. Ian, ya wanna come over here and put some of this salve on my bites. They's mostly on my ears and chin. Those claws did some damage to my neck too." Tommy told the boys about some of his run-ins with animals over the years while he threaded his needle.

Tommy lapsing into his most gregarious self-continued the monologue, "Most folks say that the wolverine is the most vicious of all of the animals of North America. They been known to attack animals 3-4 times bigger and win the battle. Timber wolves, pumas and bears don't want no part of'em. Bert, see how I am sewing the slits in my buckskins? Wonna try sewing your britches? This is called a slip stich and will get the opening closed until your mother er I mean your pappy patches them. Don't we wish our dear Sally could be with us to hear your adventure with a wolverine?"

After finishing the sewing, doctoring, and thawing of their extremities, Tommy struck out in the general direction of the cave. On the way back twilight forced them to light the oil lantern. Along the banks of the Clinch, they were able to rake back the show and chip away the ice to gather a nice variety of herbs. Tommy knew from memory the location of the plants. Once again, he stressed the importance of harvesting herbs without disturbing the root system.

Their bounty of Day Lilly shoots, Wild Onion bulbs, Ramp shoots, and some Chicory would make their bland diet more appetizing. With herb foraging a success and the lessons on defending against wild animal attack well learned, Tommy was feeling good about imparting his home grown "wisdom." As they trudged through the crunching snow, Tommy said, "Now sometimes you can avoid gettin' attacked and sometimes like this case you just happen to be in the wrong place at the wrong time. Then you have to defend best you can. Scary things happen, and they are hard while they are happening, but afterwards you git to tell the story and even become a hero of sorts. Course you don't want to overdo your bravery or folks will think you made the whole thing up." After the moon came up, they blew out the lantern. The reflection of the moon on the snow made for easy going.

Bert and Ian had advanced a step toward manhood. They were a little wiser and trail hardened. How many boys their age had gone hand to claw with a wolverine and lived to tell the story? Upon arrival back at the cave the teenagers were eager to relate the adventure. It was all they spoke of for the next week.

Tommy had an unorthodox brand of storytelling. He could entertain small children hours on end especially around Christmas time. Helga asked if Tommy had a story about Christmas, and Tommy smiled and said, "I reckon I do." The following day Tommy went out and cut an evergreen tree that was a twisted and lop-sided juniper bush. For decorations everyone contributed to the project with bits of broken jewelry, toys, and ribbons. The final result was certainly a very memorable Christmas tree. In civilized communities it would have been scorned as ugly, but the circumstances called for a different standard. What mattered was that Rolf and Helga had fun decorating the bush.

After the evening meal, and to the delight of Rolf and Helga, Tommy took a seat by the fire and seated a child on each knee. Tommy had always liked telling tall tales, almost as much as playing his harmonica. The tale he told that evening was a long one, full of offbeat humor that appealed to the adults as well.

"One year at Christmas time St. Nick overslept and was running late leaving to deliver toys to all of the good boys and girls. He jumped out of bed, and yelled "help" at Mrs. Nicholas. He got his black boots on the wrong feet and forgot to wear his red stocking cap, the one with a white tassel. Christmas was getting off to a bad start. All but one of the reindeer was feeling poorly, and he would have to find replacements. Santa hooked up the one healthy reindeer to a small toboggan and went in search of fill-in sleigh animals. First, he tried to sign up a bull moose until he realized that the harness would not fit over its antlers.

Misses Nickolas decided to help out and sent St. Nick to pick up a pair of magic camels in Arabia. Next, he flew over to Africa, and recruited a pair of zebras. These ones could fly, though most cain't. In South America he found a pair of llamas eager to help. Then jolly St. Nick took the new crew back to the artic workshop and told the elves to load the big red sleigh. By then it was December 26th, 1811, and there were disappointed children all over the world. For the first time ever, St. Nick had let down the ones he had spent a lifetime pleasing. He decided to make it up to the boys and girls for being so patient.

This had to be the Christmas of all Christmases. Out of the clear blue, an idea came to the jolly old man. Ya see, he decided to give sleigh rides to all of the helpful and kind-hearted boys and girls. And as an afterthought he told the elves to pile in for the ride. Once he was airborne, he thought of Mrs. Nicklaus and went back for her. At each stop on his route the first order of business was to pass out the gifts.

Next it was time for the big surprise! When the children looked out, they couldn't believe their eyes. Tied behind the big sled was a long string of smaller sleighs. The tags along sleighs were partly held aloft with giant red and green balloons filled with helium. St. Nick told the children to climb aboard the sleighs and hold on. At the last minute some of the children that had been especially good were allowed to bring along their favorite pet whether rabbit, bird, cat, or dog. The jolly old man understood the love boys and girls have for their pets.

St Nick hurried the sleigh animals along by dangling a long whip with a rope of black licorice at the end hanging just out of reach of the sleigh animals. They sped to the South Pole, and then to Germany, back to Tennessee, and on to England. Next, they went to Greenland and Iceland and lastly to the cave at the Clinch River Gorge. By the time he landed at the Clinch River Cave, there was no more room on the sleighs, but St. Nick promised to come back and treat Helga and Rolf to a private trip to see the world from the skies, and they could invite any and all. The magical train of red sleds went to country after country, loading up more kids. For hours the string of sleds circled the earth, giving the children the most wondrous time of their lives. As they swooped around the heavens, the children took to singing Christmas carols. The children had so much fun they didn't care if St. Nick was a day late.

When the tired but happy St. Nick landed back at his compound, he was all smiles. All of the elves cheered and gave him a big cup of hot apple cider and a piece of peppermint candy. The recovering reindeer were relieved that St. Nick had used his imagination and saved Christmas for the children of the world. Christmas that year was one for the history books. The old sayin' where there is the will, there is a way, sure came true that Christmas, right kidos?"

Jack looked at Tommy, turned his head to the side, and said, "Tom, old man, there's no end to your talents." Before turning in, Jack stood and said, "I have an announcement. I am a very happy man tonight. Miss Lorna has agreed to be my wife. Abe thinks he can do the honors in a hitchin' ceremony." Jack walked over to where Lorna was seated. He lifted her into his arms and kissed her. The entire group converged upon the happy couple. For at least half an hour, the little Clinch Creek Cave rang out with the most sincere and spirited congratulations.

Chapter 8

THE TREE HOUSE

It was still fifteen days till Christmas, but the wedding was planned for the following day. The cave inhabitants were energized and happy, almost giddy. Everyone got busy helping with the wedding. Jane pulled Lorna aside and said, "Lorna, my wedding dress is packed away in my trunk. I think it would fit if you want to wear it?

Lorna literally pounced on Jane with a bear hug. "Thank you! I would be honored to wear your dress. Quick, let me see it. We can't let Jack see us. I want to surprise him." Jane went behind hers and Jon's sleeping area and opened her trunk. At the very bottom, was the cheesecloth wrapped dress.

Lorna caught her breath when she saw it. "Jane, it's so beautiful. Are you sure you don't mind me wearing it?"

Jane said, "I will be delighted for you to wear it." The two women held it up between them and smoothed the wrinkles from the folds. The white satin dress had long lace sleeves and a sweetheart neckline with tiny covered buttons that closed the bodice of the princess style formal gown. A long, full skirt that reached the floor was generously gathered onto the waist. Next, Jane pulled out her lace veil with pearl encrusted hair combs.

Jane placed it on Lorna's head, and smiled. "You will take Jack's breath away." Jane devised a way to hang the dress, well hidden under a muslin bed sheet. Most of the wrinkles were gone by wedding time.

Lyla offered to bake a wedding cake. There was very little flour or sugar left, but what there was, along with some cornmeal and honey and fresh butter, resulted in a sweetish crumbly loaf that would serve the occasion as a wedding cake. The finishing touch to the cake was a few pieces of crushed hard candy, some stirred into the batter and the rest sprinkled on top. A large venison roast was cooking on a spit over the fire. Two small trout from the stream, caught the day before by Bert, were made into a soup containing wild onion tops, ramps, dried chickweed, and the last of the shriveled carrots. The last box of soda crackers would round out the special wedding feast.

That night sleep was illusive. Lorna's mind was too busy to settle down. She thought, "A man like Jack could have any woman, and it's me he wants; thank you God for sending Jack Long into my life."

Jack too, was having trouble falling asleep. He was occupied with a more practical concern, the matter of finding privacy for the wedding night. Suddenly, he thought of the tree platform down at the stock pen. Tomorrow he could close in the sides and make a little bed on the floor. A fire at the bottom of the tree would heat rocks for the bed. Once Jack had his preparations planned and a prayer of gratitude sent heavenward, he was able to sleep soundly.

As first light Jack arose and began work on the surprise honeymoon nest. First, he nailed wider steps to the tree trunk. He would be carrying Lorna up the steps, and he wanted to be sure they would support the weight. Next, he gathered firewood and piled a mound of rocks, collected from higher ground, around the fire. He didn't want any exploding rocks to mar the honeymoon. Jack wove together sticks for the wall panels and wrapped them with canvas. Inside the canvas he stuffed grass and leaves for insulation. Next, he lashed two blankets together and stuffed them with some of the dried grass collected for stock food. That will make a fine mattress, he thought. Jack took a moment to admire the tree house. "Too bad the weather has to be so cold."

Each time Jack went back to the cave to get items for the tree house, the women giggled and whispered among themselves. He realized that they must be hiding Lorna from him. The second trip back to the cave, the smell of food reminded him that he had forgotten to eat or drink anything. He stopped long enough to drink a cup of hot broth and stuff a couple of pieces of jerky into his pocket. Jack stuck a candle in his other pocket and grabbed his spare set of clothing and old blanket. Instead of using the shower outside the cave entrance, he decided to take a bar of soap and jump into the stream. While Jack walked to the creek, he was thinking about how lonely he had been since he lost his wife. Jack had to admit that he was nervous about being with Lorna for the first time.

Getting washed up in the stream would test his willpower. By mid-afternoon the ice was gone from the stream, and he jumped into a waist-deep pool hidden around a sharp bend. He knew to jump in all at once, lest he lose his nerve. He yipped and hollered a little at the shock before he climbed out on the bank and soaped up his head and body. The water was just as cold the second time when he had to rinse off.

Back on the bank, Jack pranced around on the still icy creek bank, chilled to the bone. He was in the middle of imitating a wet hound dog when he heard the boys laughing. Behind him stood Tommy, Jon, Abe, Trenton, and Kingston all spying on him. "Git out'a here, you scallywags!" yelled Jack. Jon yelled back, "The women drove us away, said to stay away for a while." Jack fastened the blanket he was using as a towel around his waist and took out after Jon. Around and around he chased him, but Jon was too fast, so he went after gangly Abe. Jack half carried Abe to the bank of the creek and was about to pitch him into the water when he reckoned that Abe would be performing the ceremony, so he put him down opting to stay on his good side. Then Jack took out after a suddenly swift footed Tommy, considering his bum leg. Calls from the women back up at the cave saved Tommy by a yard or two. We need you to hurry back with the buckets of water and bring Jack with you. Abe, feeling lucky, was shivering from the thought of being in that icy water. Jack quickly dressed in his suit of clean clothes. On the walk up to the cave, Jack insisted on carrying one of the buckets of water. Just before reaching the cave entrance, Jack said, "Oh, I plumb forgot to comb my hair. I may need you boys' help." He stopped, put down the bucket, and in an exaggerated pantomime, ran his fingers over the bald spot on top of his head as though he still had hair in the spot and then asked if his hair looked better. The men all shook their heads at Jack and thought, that is a happy man.

Jack was grateful for the close relationship he had formed with these fine, generous men. Of late he felt comfortable with being self-deprecating at times. Then he asked the men how he looked? Tommy said, "I cain't see no difference, but you shore smell better." The laughter was interrupted when Lyla and Jane came running down the path and shouted for Jack to stop walking. Jane said, "It will bring bad luck if you see Lorna before the wedding." She stood on tiptoes and tied a blindfold around Jack's face. One of the men took Jack's hand and led him the rest of the way back to the cave. Cooperating with the ruse, Jack pled with his captors and called out for Lorna to rescue him.

Jane had planned the wedding in advance. The ceremony would come first and then the meal. After that, the celebrants would dance to Tommy's harmonica music. While a pitiful Jack sat blindfolded, Lindsey and Bert leaned over him and placed an object in his hand. Jack, peeking from under the blindfold, saw a gold wedding band.

Lindsey whispered, "I know that my Sally, Lord-rest-her-soul, would want Miss Lorna to have her gold band. She wasn't able to wear it for the last few years because her hands had begun to swell some; I think it might fit Lorna."

"We can give it back when I get to where I can buy one," assured Jack.

Lindsey replied, "Consider it a gift."

Lorna spent the wedding day being fussed-over by the women. First, they helped her shampoo and curl her waist length hair. Lucy gave Lorna a cake of soap perfumed with rose water for her shower and a jar of heavenly smelling Lavender lotion that she had been saving. Minutes before the wedding, Jane applied rouge to Lorna's cheeks and lips. Jane hugged Lorna and said, "Oh, Lorna, look at you, you're stunning." Lorna was bursting with excitement. Lyla put the finishing touches on Lorna's hair by pulling wisps of hair at the temples and braided them together at the nape of Lorna's neck. Lucy, Jane, and Lyla all helped Lorna on with the wedding gown.

Lyla handed Lorna her gold cameo locket and said, "Lorna I would love for you to wear my locket."

Lorna's eyes sparkled when she saw the exquisite necklace. She gave Lyla a big hug and said, "Lyla it's beautiful, I will be honored to wear it, thank you!" Lyla took it from Lorna and fastened it around her neck and then brushed Lorna's hair back into place. Lorna spun around, and held out her arms to her friends. "Thanks for making me look and feel like a bride. You make me feel special and really pretty! Lorna was moved to tears, happy tears as she hugged and kissed the three women on the cheek."

Abe, wanting to lend pomp to the ceremony, wished for some dress clothes but had none of his own. Just in the nick of time Tommy remembered a pair of black woolen trousers he had stashed in the bottom of his trunk and offered to loan them to him. Kingston offered a cream-colored linen shirt and Jon handed Abe a black neck tie. Now he looked the part, officially a preacher man!

Jane dressed for the occasion by wearing her best two piece grey and pink damask dress with matching bonnet. She had the perfect wedding song to sing. It was an old English Ballad titled, "The Young Man's Dream."

The ceremony began with hushed anticipation. Tommy removed Jack's blindfold and stood him in front of Abe. Lindsey with dignified formality escorted Lorna from behind the stack of boxes at the back of the cave. Jack drew a deep breath when he saw Lorna floating toward him, a heavenly vision of ivory satin and lace. Her smiling face was radiant beneath the veil. The expression on Jack's face quickly brightened the interior of the primitive colorless cave. Jack whispered, "Lorna, you're beautiful" and placed an arm around her shoulders.

Jack and Lorna turned to face Jane as she sang "The Young Man's Dream" with a clear soprano voice that filled the cave. Her Irish brogue added to the charm of the song. Lyla leaned toward Kingston and whispered, "The voice of an angel." The lyrics of the 17th century Celtic folk song were a perfect fit for the occasion.

THE YOUNG MAN'S DREAM
(Aisling an Óigfhir)

Oh peerless perfection! how canst thou believe,
That I could such innocence hurt or deceive?
I implore the Great Fountain of glory and love,
And all the blessed saints in their synod above;

That connubial affections our souls may combine,
And the pearl of her sex be immutably mine.

The green grass shall not grow, nor the sun shed his light,
Nor the fair moon and stars gem the forehead of night;

The stream shall flow upward, the fish quit the sea,
Ere I shall prove faithless, dear angel to thee."
Her ripe lip and soft bosom then gently I prest,
And clasped her half-blushing consent to my breast."

With an air of importance, Abe cleared his throat and waited for Jane to quiet Dora, who was holding out her hands to Lorna. Jane produced a soda cracker from her pocket with instant success.

Abe pulled a written note from his pocket. "Ya, Upzon zhis day of December 15th, in zee year of 1811, zhis group of friends gatder to vitness zee marriage of Lorna Maxwell to Jackson Long, that. Vee stant here before Godt," —. Abe's trembling hands dropped his note, and he bent at the waist to retrieve it. What happened next changed the tenor of the solemn occasion. A loud ripping noise signaled a division of the back seam of Tommy's woolen britches. Abe quickly stood and checked the damage with his left hand. Abe's expression changed to one of horror. That is when Walter, Bert, Ian, and Rolf all in unison made strange choking noises in an effort to suppress the laughter that was trying to escape. Boys of that age are not known for controlling their emotions, and when Ian burst forth with a loud guffaw, all restraint was lost. The chorus of boyish cackling permeated the atmosphere.

The humor of the mishap infected the adults who threw composure to the wind and indulged in a session of unabashed laughter. Jack succumbed to the hilarity and grabbed Lorna by the shoulders and bear-hugged her. The entire group of celebrants laughed until tears ran from their eyes. Just as the delirium abated, Dora decided to mimic the laughter. The sound of her high-pitched laugh brought on more giggles and further delayed the ceremony. The final straw was when Dora clapped her hands. The entire crowd started clapping, and the laughter began all over.

Lucy the dutiful wife, stifling a belly laugh, walked to Abe and peeked around at his backside. She spun Abe around so that everyone could see the bright red patch of flannel long johns back-lighting the foot long rip. Abe suddenly saw the humor in the situation and bowed with his backside toward the spectators. "Zat zis vhat I gidt for borrowing za smaller man's breetches."

Tommy spoke up and announced that he had a fix and untied his red neck-kerchief. He ceremoniously shook out the scarf and tucked it into Abe's waistband so that it totally covered the split in the trousers. Tommy then picked up Abe's note and handed it to him. Next Tommy spread his hands palms down and said, "Quiet everyone, let the nuptials continue." A flustered Abe stuttered, "Zah, vhere vas Zi?"

Jack spoke up and said, "The part about, and now I pronounce you man and wife?" And then a mischievous Jack grabbed Lorna and planted a long passionate kiss on her. Pandemonium revived and Abe, unsure how to handle the situation, yelled over the noise, "Vhat Got hast jant togeter—ah— zet no mant—parst—asunder. Vit zhis ring—gote ahead and pud zit on her finkger. You may kiss zee bride—againt. Ament."

The merriest wedding celebration in memory broke out. The partiers' smiles reflected the depth of affection they felt for the bride and groom. The relationship among the group of sojourners had gradually changed from neighborliness to that of an extended family. Any formality and reserve had been replaced with sacrificial love.

The remainder of the shindig only had one serious time, and that was when the hungry souls were eating the prepared food. They chewed very slowly, savoring each bite. The last of the flour, cornmeal, and sugar had gone into the wedding feast, and everyone was aware that their diet was about to become monotonous to the extreme.

The group began dancing to Tommy's lively tunes, waltzing counterclockwise around the fire pit. Happiness permeated the dwelling and its inhabitants. The two-step and waltzing quickly devolved into more innovative dancing with the juveniles competing for the best summersault and handstand.

Jack couldn't take his eyes off Lorna. Her countenance was glowing. Jack lifted her into his arms and joined the circle of loved ones dipping and swaying in time to the music. Both Jack and Lorna looked contemplative as they stored memories. Jack seated Lorna upon a box to prevent over stressing her injured ankle and stood behind her, all the while keeping time to Tommy's harmonica music with clapping hands.

Lorna took Dora to her sleeping area and nursed her while Jack stepped outside to visit the privy. Before returning, he paused to savor the fresh cold night air and admire the beauty of the night sky. The sparkling canopy had never looked so near or so bright. Just as he was about to re-enter the cave, a huge meteor streaked across the sky. For a moment the area was bathed in bright light. Then Jack heard the distant noise of an impact. *We got us a good omen*, he thought. Jack was eager to tell Lorna about the shooting star and walked inside.

Back in the cave the dancing had degraded to a rowdy game of keep-away using Tommy's kerchief. The person with the kerchief had to dance around in such a manner that the others could not remove it from his waistband. The women, nodding their disapproval, withdrew from the dance floor and prepared to serve the wedding cake.

Jack gently lifted Lorna, a bundle of creamy satin and lace, and carried her outside the cave into the freezing air. He stood her on her feet and stepped behind her. Jack unbuttoned his coat and pulled her to him and buttoned the coat around her. He pulled her even closer and nuzzled her neck. Then he whispered into her ear, "We got a special weddin' gift tonight, our marriage was blessed by a shooting star. It lit up the whole sky when it flew by. I ain't ever seen one that bright before. When it struck the ground, it sounded like a distant thunder jolt." Jack traced the arc with his hand and said, "It was right up there, just a few minutes ago. I wish you could have seen it." Then he turned her, still buttoned inside the coat, to face him and kissed her quivering lips. Jack whispered, "I have a place ready for us to go tonight." Let's go back in and eat some wedding cake, and then we will get ready to leave the party. I'll be gone for a few minutes. After the cake, be sure to change into your warmest clothes. It's cold where we're going. You think the women can care for Dora until morning?

"Yes, sure, Jane volunteered, she is wonderful with Dora," answered Lorna.

Jack pulled on his warmest coat and boots. He stuffed his matching pistols into his waistband, and slung the muzzle loader over his shoulder. It took Jack about a quarter hour to hike the trail to the tree house and ignite the prepared fire. He trotted back to the cave with his thoughts fast-tracking, his heart doing flip flops, and inside his gloves, his palms were sweating. He entered the cave wearing ice crystals on his beard.

For North America, the wedding of Jack and Lorna was an irrelevant event on the world stage, but the geological convulsion that coincided with their wedding night remains of much import more than 200 years later. December 16, 1811 is the date of the New Madrid earthquake. Some believe, including a respected historian, that the seismic event was sent to sanction Shawnee Shaman Tecumseh's warning to defend the tribal lands with war. The charismatic Tecumseh was believed to possess extra sensory perception and clairvoyance. The Shawnee Shaman traveled among the indigenous North American tribes predicting the date of a coming sign would verify his message.

The earthquake represented the stamping of Tecumseh's foot, a signal that the gods supported Tecumseh's effort to organize a great confederacy of war parties that would rid the continent of all white men and restore the land to The People, its rightful owners.

Previous to the earthquake, Tecumseh traveled about the eastern half of North America speaking to the many tribes. He revealed an elaborate plan to rise up against the Europeans. Tecumseh's earnest love for his people was unquestioned. His dignified formality and spellbinding oratory was hypnotic as he presented a logical case for his war. Just hours before the temblor struck the North American continent, a second meteor streaked across the shy, a repeat of the meteor that appeared the moment Tecumseh was being born. The name Tecumseh is purported to mean 'Panther Across the Sky' in the Shawnee language. The prediction that would be manifest as a demonic, spring-loaded cataclysm was to coincide with the burning of the final stick previously distributed to the various tribes by Tecumseh.

The New Madrid Seismic Fault is a present-day threat and sits like a crouching puma, ready without warning to strike our modern infrastructure. Now in the 21st century, the New Madrid Fault Zone is increasingly active and is believed to have built up dangerous levels of kinetic energy. The 1811 North American population was sparse and the infrastructure primitive. If a present-day temblor along the New Madrid fault line were to strike with an equal magnitude as the 1811-1812 series of temblors the majority of the tillable farmland known as the nation's bread basket would be left desolate. It is possible that millions would be killed or eventually die of starvation and sickness. Such an event would disrupt American civilization for decades.

Lorna sat on a box while she cut the cake. Jack stood beside her, but as soon as she finished slicing the cake, he picked her up and sat down holding Lorna on his lap. The group of well-wishers gathered around while Lorna fed cake to Jack. When some crumbs fell from the fork to the plate, Jack made a show of picking them up. "Can't waste any of this, best cake I ever tasted." Next, he stuffed a mouthful of cake into Lorna's mouth, and then before she could swallow it, he fed her more. Then he said, "Tell me when to stop," and shoved more cake into her mouth. "You didn't say stop yet!" Her big eyes signaled alarm at trying to swallow such a big mouth full. The picture of Lorna with her cheeks puffed out brought forth a burst of laughter and created a lasting image of the happy couple. The cake was savored, consumed purposely, to the point of memorializing its sweetness. Any crumbs were trapped by a moist finger and brought to one's mouth carefully to avoid any possibility they might fall to the sandy floor.

The prospect of starvation was getting ominous. The diversion of the wedding celebration helped to blunt such worries. The post-wedding larder consisted of meat, most of which was in the form of unsalted jerky. Meat from turkey, venison, bear, squirrel, and rabbit were the most desirable but didn't totally eliminate more exotic animals, with some notable exceptions like skunk and wolverine. The other source of sustenance was the milk and butter from the cow. Walter, Bert, and Ian were developing hunting skills and regularly contributed to the food supplies. Tommy had proved to be a good instructor.

The good people taking refuge in the Clinch River Cave had been toughened and honed by life on the westward trail. These people were God fearing, honest, and loved their fellow man. They had withstood Indian attack, blizzard conditions, and the rampage of a mad man. But one must ask if they were prepared to survive what is about to be visited upon them? The cataclysmic event about to inundate them will be the supreme challenge, one that will comparatively trivialize their prior Challenge.

Jack pulled Tommy aside and told him that he would be taking Lorna away in a few minutes, and that he was placing him in charge of posting guards for the rest of the night. "I'll keep watch over the stock," Jack mused with a wink at Tommy.

Tommy nodded with a knowing grin. "You betcha, we cain't afford to lower our guard none. Those fellars you run acrost are still out there somewhere." Then Lorna walked out from behind the divider so bundled up she looked like a gingerbread man. Jack lifted the bundle of clothing off the floor and thrust his hand under the layers to tickle Lorna. "Just want to make sure that my bride is in there somewhere." Next Jack picked up a lantern and walked toward the entrance of the cave. Before walking into the night, the newly-weds turned and thanked everyone for making the occasion so memorable. Jack hefted Lorna into his arms and said, "We love you all."

Looking back over Jack's shoulder Lorna blew kisses to the smiling well-wishers. "Good night, everyone, we love you, thank you all."

Whether it came from Mother Nature, Tecumseh, Kanati, or was just a random geological event, what happened next was nothing less than widespread devastation on an apocalyptic scale.

As Jack walked down the steep path from the cave, he said, "let me know if you git too cold." Lorna reached up to his ear and whispered, "Being near you keeps me warm." The walk down to the tree house was tedious in the dark, especially when traversing the icy patches.

Lorna asked, "Where are we going?"

Jack answered, "See that fire ahead? We're almost there." When the honeymooners reached the corral, the stock reacted to their presence by snorting and stomping their hooves. Jack told Lorna to hang on as he carried her up the steps to the tree house. "This, my duly wedded wife is our honeymoon palace, finally we can be alone." Lorna cupped Jack's face in her hands and repeatedly kissed him. Jack said, "Hold on, you better wait 'til we get to the top, or we may be the first couple to consummate a marriage while climbing a tree."

Jack placed Lorna on the mattress and covered her up with a mountain of quilts and blankets, head and all. Then he used the lantern to light the candle. Before leaving, Jack peeled back the covers to expose Lorna's head and said, "Soon!" He took the lantern back down the tree and built up the fire. A dozen of the hot rocks were loaded into an oversize leather satchel. Jack's heart was beating rapidly as he started back up the tree ladder.

Chapter 9

MIRACULOUS SURVIVAL

Jack stopped the climb to listen to the sound of howling of wolves. The mournful noise was coming from three different directions at once; three separate packs howling simultaneously? The sound they made was different from normal howling; it almost sounded as though they were in pain. Jack took the next step, and a different sound drew Jack's sight to a herd of frightened deer running directly at the tree he was climbing. When they reached the tree, they divided and charged past without even noticing him. He thought, *something unnatural has frightened those deer*. He took another step and noticed that the mules and horses were frightened too. They were snorting and running in circles. Just as Jack reached the top step, he noticed that thousands of roosting birds had taken flight and were squawking and screeching in the darkness as they circled overhead. The frantic birds were colliding in flight and made a thumping sound as they pelted the ground. Jack realized that the animal world was reacting to something more threatening than predators on the prowl. The phenomenon puzzled Jack, but he decided that identifying the cause could and must wait.

It would have never occurred to Jack that the strange wildlife behavior was due to seismic activity. The continental tectonic plates were releasing stored energy due to slow distorting encroachment. The more sensitive hearing and ability to detect vibrations from under the surface of the earth had driven the wildlife into the state of frenzy he was witnessing.

Jack carefully placed the hot stones underneath the bottom blanket that Lorna lay upon. Lorna squealed, "Ouch, not so close. Are you planning to make love to me or cook me?" As Jack and Lorna spoke, their breath condensed into streams of smoke.

"Sounds pretty good either way." Jack said. Seated on the edge of the mattress, he began removing his boots. It was so cold Jack began to shiver. Next to the wall Jack noticed the neatly folded stack of Lorna's clothing, with her underclothes on top. Jack had controlled his passion for so long, too long. As he removed his outer garments, he heard the covers rustle. When he looked in Lorna's direction he was overcome with urgency, "Oh, Lorna!" and she rose to knees and began undressing him. The sight of her caused him to shutter. As Jack leaned toward her, she removed his coat. Lorna looked into Jack's eyes while she removed his shirt and undid his belt buckle. Next, he stood and allowed her to pull his trousers to his ankles. Then he sank to his knees and folded back the thick stack of covers. They slid into the envelope of bedding simultaneously, never losing eye contact. He held his breath as she continued undressing him under the covers. He ran his hands over her body, and asked, "Cold?"

"I don't feel—" but he stopped her words with a kiss. Suddenly being cold was the last thing on their minds. What a wonderful gift, this woman that God made. Jack knew how Adam must have felt with Eve the first time they became one flesh.

Well after midnight, Lorna awoke. She was hearing strange sounds. The candle was still burning. Lorna lay with her head on Jack's shoulder. He was sleeping soundly. She wanted him to rest and kept perfectly still. She was enjoying watching his peaceful expression. Then, Lorna heard the livestock, snorting and stamping as they had been on and off for the last few hours. She wondered what could be upsetting them.

She considered waking Jack. Then something jolted the tree house and made it sway. Jack's eyes popped open. Lorna whispered, "Something is happening down there." Jack sat up and started dressing. After a few seconds there was an ear shattering crash followed by groaning sounds accompanied by more shaking. Then there was a strong jolt that caused two of the walls of the tree house to break loose and fall to the ground. The candle ignited the fiber wall on the way to the ground and started a debris fire. The fire illuminated the chaotic ground movement. The tree continued to sway. "Lorna, get dressed! Hurry and then ride on my back to the ground. We must take blankets with us." Jack grabbed his muzzle loader, shot bag, and powder horn. He inched his way to where the tree house door had been, hoping the shaking was the mischievous boys meeting out some sort of shivaree.

When he looked down, he realized the fire was extinguished by dirt and gravel. Jack could see the stock trying to jump from the corral. Jack surmised the shaking was the result of an earthquake. Lorna screamed and asked, "Jack, what is happening?"

Jack had never heard of an earthquake east of the Mississippi. He personally had never experienced one. Jack knew from the subterranean groaning and sound of cave-offs this was an unusually strong and destructive event. Jack decided to keep that bit of knowledge to himself since Lorna was frightened enough already. On the way down the tree's steps, there was a terrible jolt, and they both fell to the undulating ground at the base of the tree. It was impossible to stand until the tremor ended.

Jack walked to the fire started by the candle and wrapped a bed sheet around a limb to use as a torch. He gathered Lorna in his arms and started toward the river bottom. Following the bank would help him go toward the cave. The rumbling sounds kept changing character and at times resembled thunder. South of the corral, the riverside cliff gave way to a rockslide. Hideous grinding and roaring sounds were coming from below the ground. Jack had noted that the tree that held the demolished tree house was buried to the halfway mark with boulders and gravel, and the tree was actually listing toward the river.

The corral was obliterated. He feared that many of the animals were buried under the slide. The surviving animals were making terrible sounds. In the dust laden darkness, Jack thought he could see Bones. Jack waited for a lull between convulsions. When the angry grinding stopped, he whistled to Bones and was answered with a whinny. "I'm coming, Boy? Jack sat Lorna on a flat stone and said, "Stay where you are. I'll be back soon."

Jack had to climb and jump over trees and boulders to get to Bones. The torch was about to go out. Jack saw a split pine tree with pitch on its trunk. Jack pulled away some of the pitch coated bark and added it to his torch. It ignited to burn brighter. Jack filled his pockets with flakes of bark smeared with pitch that could be added as needed. Jack whistled again to get his bearings for finding Bones.

Finally, after about fifty yards, Jack was zeroing in on Bones by sound. Finally, Jack could see the gelding straddling a large bolder. He was supported by three legs and the fourth his front left leg was dangling and bleeding. As Jack approached the horse, an aftershock caused Bones to start kicking with his hind legs. The bolder lodged under his belly kept his upright. It was obvious that the leg was shattered. Jack climbed over the last few feet of debris to where the wild-eyed horse stood. Jack rubbed his nose. The sight of Jack calmed Bones, and he approached without danger of being struck by the flailing hooves. Seeing the nature of Bone's injury stabbed Jack in the heart. "Sorry, boy, but I can't let you suffer; you've been a good one." Jack pointed the muzzle loader between Bones eyes. He paused for a moment and gritted his teeth as he pulled the trigger. The horse dropped without a struggle. Jack was glad that it only took one shot. Jack ran his hand over Bone's neck and shoulder and then paused long enough to place a couple of blobs of pine pitch on the torch and to reload the long gun before hurrying back to Lorna.

An aftershock rearranged the ground under Jack's feet as he stumbled along, and one large boulder almost pinned Jack's right foot as it came rolling directly at him. When Jack finally reached Lorna, she had a quizzical expression on her face as Jack enveloped her in his arms. "I had to shoot Bones." Lorna gripped Jack's shoulders as he picked her up and started toward the cave. There was another jolt, and more falling rock caused Jack to take refuge behind a huge bolder that had rolled to the streams edge. The footing was treacherous even with the faint light of the torch. Jack stopped to gather more pine pitch from an uprooted tree. When they finally found the place that must have been where the path to the cave entrance had been, there were piles of rock, mixed with tree trunks and brush. There was no path.

Lorna began screaming incoherently, "Jack, the cave, it fell in, I left Dora behind, my baby, they are all buried!"

Jack held Lorna to his pumping chest and murmured, "Here now, we really can't see. It will be getting daylight soon. I'm thinking they all may be safe from the landslide inside the cave. Lorna, Lorna, listen, calm down, we are in a position to rescue them, I promise." That was one promise Jack wasn't sure he would be able to keep.

Jack wasn't sure how long it was until daybreak. Jack's worst fear was that the giant rock ledge that had sheltered the cave's entrance had fractured and fallen to shut off access. Lorna, terrified by what she could not see, tore away from Jack's embrace and started to climb over the loose rock.

Jack said, "Wait, you stay here, and I will go up to see if I can find a way into the cave." He had to forcibly restrain her.

"No, Jack, I'm going too, don't try to stop me."

Then Jack said, "Okay, we'll go together. I think we should find a place to climb to the top of the cliff and then try to work our way down to the ledge over the cave opening."

While Jack considered their options, he noticed that Lorna was shivering from the cold. Neither of them was sufficiently clothed for such extreme cold. Jack said, "Lorna, I want you to stand behind this boulder for a wind break while I go back to the tree house and bring more of the covers, and I left my pistols behind. After an hour, Jack returned with a bundle of blankets and his and Lorna's outerwear and Lorna's boots. Jack had found his extra powder horn and larger bag of shot but only one of his pistols. Jack spread the blanket and started wrapping Lorna in her clothing and then tied a thick wool blanket about her head and shoulders Indian style. Next, he carefully buttoned his own jacket and then tied a blanket about himself. The remaining three blankets and a padded quilt he tied into a bundle and began traversing the creek bank toward the ford. Jack was thrown off balance with Lorna in his arms and asked Lorna to ride upon his back. At the ford, the creek was frozen solid. The natural break in the cliff appeared to be mostly free of debris to the top of the ridge. From there Jack and Lorna trudged north along the high ground above the cliff. There were deep cracks in the ground. Once Jack fell into a crack and Lorna had to step on his shoulders and climb out of the crevice and then help him to the surface. There were more fissures as they continued. One was so wide that Jack had to build a bridge by dragging up fallen timber. They both crawled across on their knees. The torch was lost when it fell to the bottom of a fissure.

A slight pinkness appeared in the eastern sky by the time they got to a position above where they supposed the cave to be. Jack decided to rest and wait for more light. Jack folded one of the extra blankets and seated Lorna on a rock and sat down beside her. Jack moved Lorna to sit on his lap and wrapped his blanket around her. The bodily contact helped to calm their nerves and to ward off the cold. After a half hour, Jack sat Lorna on the blanket and said, "Stay here and stay covered up with the blankets. I will see if there are any openings around the ledge." Lorna, shivering from shock, nodded and sat facing the drop-off that had supported the top of the cave.

First light revealed a heavy frost that covered everything. It was dangerously cold. As Jack walked away, he spoke over his shoulder, "Wish I could build a fire for you, maybe I can when I return." After Jack left to climb down to the rock shelf, Lorna repositioned the blankets about her shoulders and paced back and forth trying to see Jack as he descended the rockslide area.

There are times when actual historical events surpass the most imaginative fiction, especially when it comes to bizarre coincidence. The morning after Lorna and Jack's wedding was one of those times. On the morning of December 16, 1811, at about 2:00 A. M. in the morning, the first of three devastating earthquakes struck the central Mississippi Valley of North America. All three of the major "New Madrid Earthquakes" would have measured more than 8 on the Richter scale, though that method for measuring earthquakes did not exist in 1811. Please consider the following quotes from an article published by the United States Geological Survey.

THE MISSISSIPPI VALLEY- "WHOLE LOTTA SHAKIN' GOIN ON"

"In the winter of 1811-12, the central Mississippi Valley was struck by three of the most powerful earthquakes in U.S. history. Even today, this region has more earthquakes than any other part of the United States east of the Rocky Mountains."

"The 400 terrified residents in the town of New Madrid, Missouri were abruptly awakened by violent shaking and a tremendous roar. Survivors reported that the earthquakes caused cracks to open in the earth's surface, the ground to roll in visible waves, and large areas of land to sink or rise. The crew of the New Orleans (the first steamboat on the Mississippi, which was on her maiden voyage) reported mooring to an island only to awake in the morning and find that the island had disappeared below the waters of the Mississippi River. Damage was reported as far away as Charleston, South Carolina, and Washington, D.C. The New Madrid earthquake of December 1811 rang church bells in Boston, Massachusetts, 1,000 miles away."

(Coincidentally, it was 106 years later to the day that Cornelia Fannie, Cheatiebo Wainwright was born in McCurtain County, Oklahoma.)

Jack crawled part of the way down the rockslide and lost his footing. He slid and tumbled the last twenty feet. All of the slide area was unstable and dangerous. About halfway between the top and the riverbed, Jack surmised that he stood on the surface of the fractured shelf. He squatted on his haunches and listened for sound. All was quiet. He moved a few feet and listened again. Then he smelled smoke. It was seeping through the rocks. Jack prostrated himself over the area where he saw small whiffs of smoke rising and noticed that the places that emitted smoke lay in a straight line. Jack found a limb and stripped it of foliage. He used it to probe along the line of smoke. It appeared that there was a crack in the roof of the cave, a disturbing discovery.

Then Jack knelt and called out, "Hello, can anyone hear me?" And then even louder, "Anyone there, hello down there, can anyone hear me?

Then came the far away sound of Tommy calling out, "That you, Jack?"

Jack jumped to a standing position and cupped his hands over his mouth, "Lorna, I can hear Tommy, stay where you are, we don't want to cause rock slides." Suddenly Lorna had reason to hope. She rose from her seat on a boulder and resumed pacing back and forth near the drop off while straining to see and hear Jack.

Jack started carefully moving rock from where the largest plume of smoke rose. After each stone, he waited before moving another. Then a stone fell into the cave, and he heard it hit bottom. Tommy called out, "Careful, Jack, this whole ceiling is likely to cave in, from the light filtering in it is a large section that broke off." Jack asked,

"Tom, everyone safe?" "Yep, bunged up some by falling rock, noth'n serious, but its smell'n like rotten eggs down here, and the air is full of dust, hard to breathe; we need to get out of here."

Jack could hear coughing. "Tommy, tell everyone to tie a wet cloth over their noses." The sound of pebbles falling from above and striking the cave bottom troubled Jack. He continued enlarging the hole until he could see Tommy below. "Tommy, what do you think, should I lower a rope?" Then Jack thought "what rope?" Jack thought of the blanket around his shoulders. He used his knife, and tore it into strips, and then knotted them together. Jack told Tommy to get a rope and see if he could reach the makeshift rope. Tommy called back and said, "Got it, now what?" Jack said, "Tie them together and I will bring the rope up and tie it off up here."

With the rope in hand, Jack looked around to find a stable anchor. There was an uprooted tree resting up the incline. It took all of his strength to move the tree trunk until it was held in place by two fairly stable boulders. Jack tied the rope to the tree trunk and went back to the opening. "Tommy, the rope is tied off; find all of the rope you have down there. I figure we should make a rope ladder. First, can you send Dora up in a container of some kind? Lorna is beside herself. Also, we need to build a fire up here. Can you send up some coals from the fire pit?"

Tommy, elated with the turn of events, cheerfully yelled, "Com'in right up, Jack."

Soon Tommy tugged on the rope, and Jack pulled a can of hot coals to the surface. Jack yelled back to Tom, "Get Dora ready, I'm gonna take the coals to the top and start a fire." As soon as Jack's head appeared above the ridge, Lorna was there.

"Jack, did you say they are alive, safe, all of —?"

Jack interrupted, "Yes, good news, help me, we have to get a fire started with these coals. First, I'll scrape away the snow, and then you can work on building up the fire while I go back down and start bringing folks out." Jack stripped a limb of branches and used it to clear a six-foot square area, best he could. The ground was frozen underneath, and would get muddy as soon as the heat from the fire thawed it. "Lorna, look for some flat rocks to surround the fire pit and then gather dry leaves and pine needles to cover the ground. We men will bring in larger rocks to surround the fire." Lorna was cold and hungry but gave no indication, not even a groan. She immediately went to work. As she worked, she was smiling. Jack used his considerable strength to quickly drag up a few dead logs. The others could get the smaller kindling. Lorna helped to ignite a handful of tender and started feeding it the driest kindling she could find. The importance of having a robust fire burning did not escape Lorna. But what she really wanted was Dora safely in her arms.

"Lorna, the next chore is to create a windbreak. A teepee would be fast and easy. I will get the frame ready, and you and the others can work on it. He gathered up a pile of limbs and chose six to tie together at the apex. He and Lorna spread the bottom end of the limbs far apart and pushed them into the frozen ground. He placed the structure a few feet from the fire with the covered back facing northwest. There, that should help with the wind. Jack told Lorna to put some green branches in the bottom of the teepee and to add others to the teepee's upright poles. Lorna knew to cover the sides of the teepee with branches once the fire was established. She gathered flat stones and slabs of sandstone to outline the fire pit. Jack had never seen Lorna move so fast. She was making each minute count.

"Good job Lorna, I'm goin' back and start bringing people out." Jack embraced Lorna and gave her a tender kiss. "Pray that the temblors stop and the rock slides end." Lorna paused just a moment and watched Jack start the descent. "Be careful Jack, I love you!"

After almost an hour topside Jack called into the cave and asked, "Tom, how is the rope ladder coming? Got Dora ready? We got a fire going up here."

Tom called out, "Don't need no ladder; we piled up some crates to climb on. Jack, Dora is ready. We packed her into a drawer and then tied her in real good." Jack started pulling the rope slowly, hand over hand. The frightened baby drowned out further communication with Tommy. The high-pitched crying was interspersed with gagging coughs. When Jack got Dora to the surface, he used his sleeve to wipe some of the soot and dust from her filthy face. He bent to kiss and soothe the baby. She immediately stopped crying and with a big-eyed stare returned Jack's smile. He said, "Hi there, little one, sure glad to see you. Let's go see your Momma." Dora was coughing and then sneezed. She smiled at Jack all the way to the top of the slide area. By the time they reached the top of the slide area, Dora was a mess. It was obvious that she had soiled her diaper, and her face was smeared with slimy dust encrusted mucus. As Jack handed the baby to Lorna, he exclaimed, "Whew, this one needs the attention of her mother."

When Dora saw Lorna, she started crying again. Lorna took Dora from Jack, and said, "Thank you, Lord." Lorna soothed Dora with soft murmurings as she untied her bindings. Jack was surprised at how much Lorna had accomplished in his absence. The brush teepee was padded and had more branches woven into the walls. The fire was burning well, and she had even carried some flat rocks to cover the mud at the fire's edge. All that ended as soon as Lorna had Dora in her arms. She was overwhelmed with relief and thankfulness. As Lorna removed Dora from the drawer, she noticed that there were diapers and blankets packed around the baby. Lorna wet one of the diapers with melted snow and cleaned Dora's face and then wiped up her messy little bottom and pinned on a clean diaper.

Jack said, "Take her into the tepee and both of you try to stay warm. It is going to be a long process getting everyone out." Jack wrapped Lorna and Dora in a wool blanket and then quickly piled more wood on the fire. He placed some short sticks close to Lorna that she could pile on the flames as needed. Jack rolled a couple of large stones into the teepee and placed sticks across them to provide a wooden structure that would keep Lorna off the ground. He planned to make it better as soon as he could. Jack spread one of the blankets on the outside of the teepee and covered it with more brush to make a wind break.

Lorna crawled into the tepee and placed Lorna on her lap. Dora started pulling at Lorna's clothes, wanting to nurse. Lorna gave the baby her breast. Dora almost strangled when Lorna's engorged breast milk began flowing. Dora made gulping noises as she swallowed. Lorna held Dora next to her body and covered her with the padding from the drawer. The sun that shone into the tepee gave a little warmth.

Lorna was primarily consumed with caring for Dora but would occasionally walk to the cliff edge to check on Jack. The aftershocks were spread out and less severe, but they didn't stop. Lorna rocked Dora and hummed a soothing song until the baby was sound asleep. Lorna thanked the Lord for saving the baby and the others. On the way back down to the hole, Jack grabbed a handful of snow and ate it. As soon as he stuck his head over the hole, Tommy said, "Jack, we been stackin' up the wooden trunks and securing them with what we can find so they don't shift; sorta like stairs."

"Hey Tom that'll work!"

"We should be able to get close to the top what with holding on to the rope, and then you can help us the rest of the way out. Jack, I got the women packing up our stuff to bring out while we help the kidos out. Jack, the quake killed the cow, she was too close to the cave entrance, and a big slab hit her. We were able to pull her out of the rubble and bled and gutted her. Good thang we have that meat. I have purty much finished skinning and carving the meat."

Jack said, "Right, now wrap up the youngins 'cause it is bitter cold up here. Wrap them in any canvas or heavy quilts we can use to cover the teepee I started to build. Send up a pot and dipper to melt snow for drinking. Why don't Abe come on up so he can take the kids up to the fire. Then I can stay here and help you."

Abe's lanky arms positioned themselves over opposing sides of the opening and raised his bulk from the abyss below. Abe had a bloody cut across the bridge of his nose and was covered in a coat of dust. Jack fished out little Rolf and then Helga and Ian. The children had minor cuts and bruises and were glad to be out of the cave. Jack pointed to where Lorna waited, and Abe started the climb up the incline of rubble. Suddenly a tremor hit, and Abe lost his footing. He was carrying Rolf and holding Helga's hand. He sat down with a jolt and rode the loosened rockslide downward. The two older children slid down headfirst. Abe warned them to stay still. Then Abe crawled to where Helga and Ian lay sprawled on the rocky surface. The big-eyed children both stared at their father with open mouths. As soon as Abe was within reach, the children clung to him out of sheer fright. He had to sit on the rubble and take a moment to reassure them.

Lucy screamed from inside the cave, "Abe, where are you, the kids?" The after-shock had showered rocks down on the folks that remained in the cave below, but Tommy said they were all okay. Next, Bert climbed out of the hole. After him was Lucy followed by Jane. Lyla appeared with a satchel filled with jerky, hung around her neck. At the surface, Lyla handed Jack a piece of jerky. "Here Jack, keep up your energy." "Thanks Lyla, I'm starved. The rest are straight up that-a-way. Watch your step." Lyla's dust covered face would've been unrecognizable if not for the familiar smile creases.

Back at the tepee, the women gathered more firewood and worked to fortify and enlarge the windbreak. The blustery wind seemed determined to defeat their efforts. Lindsay and Kingston climbed out on top and helped Jack enlarge the hole. Then the men began hoisting up the most important items from below. Lucy and Jane slid down on the loose gravel to help carry the retrieved items up to the camp. The women had a pot of melted snow ready for the thirsty. Lyla set a second soup cauldron over the coals and made gruel of finely chopped deer jerky, some chunks of fatty stew meat and a large leg bone from the cow. She thickened the mixture with arrowroot and added wild onion, watercress, and any other fresh greens Tommy had scavenged on his recent foraging trips. The soup was lacking salt and black pepper but would be filling and nutritious. As it was consumed more ingredients and snow was added to the pot.

The hours sped by as the removal progressed. Lyla checked for injuries from falling rocks. Dora had a black eye. Jane appeared to have a bruised or fractured rib and was having a lot of pain. Kingston had tripped and stubbed his big toe when he jumped up from his pallet when the quake hit.

The daylight was fading quickly. The sky was clear and air was already getting colder. Now if only the wind would lay down. The men managed to haul many of the bulkier items from the cave opening, including the rest of the butchered cow. Tommy climbed to the top. He chose a tree about a hundred feet from the fire and threw a rope over a limb. He tied the bags of beef to the rope and raised them well off the ground. Then he went to make sure that the women and children were as warm as the conditions allowed. Lucy stood next to the fire stirring the pot of boiling gruel. Several chunks of jerky floated in the liquid and the aroma got everyone's attention.

Jack had reclaimed his leadership role, and said, "Hey, boys, it's time to rest and eat something. Let's go up and see how the women and kids are doin'. Then I want to go down to the corral and see if any of the mules or horses survived. Bones didn't make it. I had to shoot him. I'm gonna miss that horse. Glad it was dark, and I couldn't see his eyes when I pulled the trigger. I think some of the mules might still be alive. Tomorrow we need to work on a shelter that can keep us dry. We have considerable winter weather ahead. I figure we can use the wagon beds if we can dig them out. Maybe cave livin' weren't that good-a idea." Jack's rhetorical statement required no response, and none was given.

During the lunch break, Lyla passed jerky to each of the men and then carried them cups filled with the steaming soup. Jane ripped some sections from her petticoat and moistened them for everyone to wash the dirt from their faces. The radiant heat of the fire helped warm numb fingers and toes. The seemingly miraculous survival from the death trap of the cave generated a great swelling of gratitude for each adult member of the Long Expedition.

The bitter cold day was made more uncomfortable with a brisk wind. The little group of travelers were shivering, lethargic, and their faces revealed feelings of hopelessness. Jack needed to get the dire situation under control to avoid a tragedy. He searched his mind for a way to deal with the exposure incrementally. He broke down the challenges into smaller tasks: firewood, windbreaks, taking inventory of salvaged goods, meal preparation, maximizing the insulating value of clothing by layering, melting snow for drinking water, etc. It was up to him to set the tone of optimism and stay energized.

Jack stood after a short rest and said, I think we should have a prayer and sing a song. Everyone nodded their agreement. Lucy quieted her three children, and Jack asked Abe to lead the prayer. "Ya, ey vill, shalt ve prayt, Dear Godt in hepen, ve are ald tankful zat you'd seed vit to save zus from za earth quate. Lord, ve neet much helpt from da colt and snow. Please kep dez souds safe on da res of our yourney. Ament"

Jack looked to Jane and asked if she had a song everyone knew. Jane said, "how about, GUIDE ME, O THOU GREAT JEHOVAH?" Lucy spoke up and said, "That's a goudt song."

Jack started the hymn with his booming baritone voice:

Guide me, O Thou great Jehovah,
Pilgrim through this barren land.

I am weak, but Thou art mighty;
Hold me with Thy powerful hand.

Bread of Heaven,
Feed me till I want no more;

Bread of Heaven,
Feed me till I want no more.

Open now the crystal fountain,
Whence the healing stream doth flow,
Let the fire and cloudy pillar
Lead me all my journey through.

Strong Deliverer,
Be Thou still my Strength and Shield;
Strong Deliverer,
Be Thou still my Strength and Shield.

When I tread the verge of Jordan,
Bid my anxious fears subside;
Death of deaths, and hell's destruction,
Land me safe on Canaan's side.

Songs of praises,
I will ever give to Thee;
Songs of praises,
I will ever give to Thee.

Lyla threw her arms around Jack's neck and said, "Jack, the Lord saved us, but you sure helped. I don't think we could've dug our way out of that tomb, praise the Lord!"

Jack planted a big kiss on Lyla's cheek and said, "Ladies, keep the fire going and take care of the kiddos. We fellars are gonna get more of our things out of that cave, and then we will come back and figure how to bed down."

Chapter 10

STONE COLD
& THE GRIZZLY

Jack realized that he was not needed and decided to leave the men removing more gear from the cave while he walked down to the stock corral. The sound of growling wolves caused Jack to think of the carcass of the beloved Bag of Bones, poor Bones, reduced to wolf fodder.

As he drew closer, he could see the large wolf pack tearing at the remains of two mangled mules. He jumped behind a boulder and checked the direction of the wind. Confident that the pack would not pick up his scent, he carefully advanced toward the tree that had held the honeymoon shelter. Jack was desperate to recover his missing pistol, likely lost in the rubble below the tree house. He had managed to get one of the matching set before fleeing. Jack picked up a broken branch and started sweeping the rubble aside in search of the gun and any other useful items. Jack could tell that the pack of carnivores had become aware of his presence, but they were ignoring him as long as he kept his distance. The animals had what they wanted, more than they could eat.

Underneath the fallen walls of the tree house, Jack did find the pistol. The firearm thankfully had not discharged when it fell. He wiped the gun down with his shirt and tried to blow away the dust. Jack placed the pistol under his belt not sure if it would fire.

Lying on the rubble beneath the tree house were the walls that he had hastily stuffed with leaves. These will help with the windbreak tonight. Just then Jack heard a noise behind him. As he whirled around, he drew the pistol from his belt. There before him stood a dirt encrusted mule. Jack figured that the poor critter had managed to climb out of the corral by walking upon the fallen rubble. Jack held out his hand and spoke to the mule. It shied at first but then allowed Jack to approach.

The wolf pack had the mule skittish and wild eyed. Since the mule still wore a bridle, Jack decided to rig up a travois. Jack scrounged some pieces of rope from the tree house ruins and loosened some boards from the corral. With the rope he lashed the boards, floor panel and walls to the sledge. Then Jack led the mule with a short piece of rope tied to the bridle back to the camp. He took the long way back to the camp where the going was easier. He didn't want to risk the mule going lame. Finding a live mule was a stroke of good fortune. As he led the mule up to the camp, he found the way difficult enough but much easier than when he had traveled the route in darkness.

When he arrived back at the camp, he told the women that there were wolves around and to keep watch. After gorging on the dead animals, it was unlikely they would pose an immediate threat. "Look, Lorna, I found my missing pistol underneath the tree house." Dora with only her face visible saw Jack and gave him a big smile. He returned her smile and noted how red her nose and cheeks were. Jack knew that survival depended on how fast they could construct adequate shelter. He was thinking ahead on the best way to prepare for even more severe weather.

Jack tied the mule to a tree close to the camp and went down to where the men were still hauling gear out of the cave. He told them about the mule and the wolves. "I think the dead animals might draw some bear and lion as well. We need to post sentries. Bert, you got first watch, keep your gun handy?" The expression on young Bert's face revealed that he relished taking his place among the men of the group. It was a coming-of-age moment.

Jack spoke to the group of men, "Let's start dragging some of the boxes and trunks up to the camp? Hey, hand me that span of rope. I think we can use the mule to bring up the heavier cargo. Where is the crate with the horse tack?"

Tommy said, "the tack is still below in the cave."

Jack responded, "Tom, what horse tack do we need to harness the mule? He is still wearing a bridle."

Tommy scratched his mustache and thought for a few seconds and then said, "For sure a collar and hames, the traces, and ah, reins? Oh yeal, we better put on a hackamore in case he decides to git ornery."

Then Jack said, "Let me go down and fish out just what we need for now."

Tommy said, "Jack, let me go, the light ain't too good, and I know right wher thet box is settin'. We used it for part of the stairs. I will have to do some movin around down ther."

Walter spoke up and said, "Dad, I'll go and help."

Right away Tommy and Walter lowered their bodies into the black hole. Before long there was a tug on the rope, the signal to bring up the tack. Within a few minutes Jack and Walter carried the horse tack up the incline. Bert climbed down from his lookout spot in the tree to help hold the mule's bridle while Jack and Walter outfitted the mule.

Jack chose three sturdy trees side by side to rig as an improvised pulley. He used his knife to smooth away some of the bark to create grooves for the rope. Tommy spread grease into the groves to lessen friction. Rigging the rope around the three trees yielded greater mechanical advantage than only one tree. Jack told Bert to hold on to the mule while he descended back to where the trunks waited. Jack tied a rope harness around a wooden crate. Then Jack warned the men to be ready to get out of the way if something went wrong. Jack placed his hand beside his mouth and yelled for Bert to begin pulling. Jack pushed on the trunk and scurried to remove obstacles all the way to the top, positioning the crate without incident beside the bonfire. Jack untied the rope and went down to start the process over. The second crate contained the remaining cast-iron cooking utensils, and Jack removed a few of the pots and kettles to lighten the load some. "Bert, we're ready, take it easy."

Bert pulled on the mule's reigns, but the stubborn animal just stood there and belched a long string of braying. Bert tugged again, and the mule's body language threatened a bucking fit.

Lorna was watching, and quickly yelled down to Jack, "Hold on Jack, I've got a hunch. Give us a few minutes up here." Lorna recognized the mule as one of Lyla and Kingston's. Lorna called for Lyla to take over with the mule. Lyla smiled when she recognized the animal. She walked over to the mule and rubbed his nose. She patted his withers, and gently placed her arm around his neck, and then told Bert, "Here we go, Jack, ole Rastus is ready to pull." Lyla started pulling on the reigns and the mule, now totally docile behaved like a big pet. Soon the large crate topped the ridge and joined the other crates beside the fire. Jack had been holding his breath that the rope would hold, and it did. There were three more heavy trunks and two wooden crates to bring up the incline. The men were near to exhaustion by the time the heavy items were all topside. With the most critical items resituated, Jack called a rest period. There were still some of the smaller items and a few small wooden boxes, but they could be retrieved later. Jack didn't want to push the men past their endurance limit and risk injury.

Lyla was a take-the-lead type woman, and she got the ladies organized. "We can fix beds for the kids inside some of these crates, ya think? Lucy, time to put some more wood on the fire. Jane, why don't you add more snow to the pot of water. Think I'll add more jerky and chunks of beef to the soup pot."

With most of the gear at the camp, Tommy wiped the dirt and sweat from his forehead and said to Jack, "Pears you got your head back, we missed you while you was gone." Jack flashed Tommy a self-conscious grin when he realized that he referred to his pre-matrimonial state of (hormone induced) insanity.

After sunset, the wind settled down, but the temperature plunged. The night would be long and cold, even life-threatening. Jack noticed that the Olsen children sat on a stack of green branches inside the tepee, staring at the fire, but a closer look revealed that all three were shivering. Jack carried some warm flat rocks for the children to sit upon. Then he gave each one a warm stone to hold in their hands. "We need more rocks heating by the fire, and make sure everyone is drinking water." The sun was getting low in the sky. Several aftershocks kept the group on edge. Jack noticed how pink Dora's little nose was when she poked it out of the neck of Lorna's sweater. Jack felt a shiver come over him more from the gravity of their situation than from the cold. This first night out of the cave would test the group's heartiness.

The aftershocks continued through the night. A strong jolt opened a large crack in the ground that stretched from the edge of the caved off cliff to a rocky place only a stone's throw from the campfire. Jack asked Walter and Bert to construct a barrier beside the opening.

After their meager meal of stewed meat in thickened broth, the women prepared Rolf and Helga a bed. After taking the children behind some dense brush to take care of nature's call, the women bundled up the two youngsters with layers of insulation.

Jack spoke softly out of consideration for the children now tucked into the make shift beds, "Lucy you and Abe need to get up and check on the children during the night. Feel of their feet and hands and that they have plenty of fresh air." Since most of the clothing was sitting by the fire, the women dug through the wardrobes and shared what they had. There was none of the "this is mine" attitude, and they were all looking out for each other; the Long Expedition was functioning as a family unit.

Lucy opened a large wooden box and pulled out a number of newly knitted garments. Abe and all three children wore two hand knitted sweaters underneath their jackets. Lucy dressed the two youngsters in extra stockings and mittens. Lucy's trunk load of two-sided knitted comforters, stuffed with goose down were a godsend. Also stowed away in the trunk were items that Lucy planned to sell or give for gifts. Lucy invited the adults to help themselves to the hoard of caps, mittens, stockings, neck scarfs, sweaters, long john underwear, and some baby blankets and even some infant apparel. Lucy found it hard to convince everyone that she wanted the knitted articles to be used for the immediate emergency and finally opened her large box of yarn and insisted that the items could be replaced. She pulled out a baby's cap and handed it to Lorna. She held up three multicolored Norwegian style caps with earflaps, chin ties, topped with a tassel. One cap was a beard cap that covered the entire head except for the eyes. Lucy called Bert and told him to take the beard cap. She insisted that Lyla take a sweater and matching mittens. Jack gladly accepted a pair of high-top woolen stockings. He sat down and put them on over his other socks. She had enough stockings for each of the men to have pair. Then Lorna noticed that Jack was sporting a colorful neck scarf that he pulled up to meet his hat so that his neck and lower ears were covered.

Jack built a sleeping surface out of the scrounged lumber. It was elevated off the ground using flat rocks. While Jack worked, he was conscious of Lorna watching him. Their gazes caressed each other and communicated their very private emotions. After a brief pause to warm his hands over the fire, Jack walked over to where Lorna sat in the corner of the tepee. He sat down beside her and whispered, "I'm glad you're keeping Dora inside your clothing next to your skin. Here, show me your feet." He removed Lorna's shoes and stockings and just as he suspected her feet were perilously cold. Jack replaced her socks and shoes and told her to get up and walk around while he took over with Dora. Only the top of her little knitted cap peaked out from inside Jack's sweater and coat. Dora immediately began exploring her new environment, pulling at Jack's chest hair. Jack said, "Dora, that tickles. Stop pulling on my chest hair. Ouch, did you bite me?" Jack got some chuckles from folks before admitting he made the part up about being bitten. Lorna used the opportunity to slip into the darkness for a private moment. When she returned, she quickly changed Dora's diaper, and returned her to her bosom.

The men worked non-stop through the early evening piling more rocks around the fire and dragging up firewood. Jack was an effective leader because of his self-assured decisiveness and ability to look beyond the obvious. He was a master at reading body language and detecting veiled and unintended communication.

Jack told everyone to prepare to bed down. "I'll take first watch and work at exchanging the warming rocks. Here's your chance to get some rest." Tommy secured their remaining food supply by suspending it in the branches of the tree that held the packages of butchered beef.

For Jack protecting this group of travelers had changed from a responsibility to an act of love. The mutual affection among the group felt more like a close-knit family. The laborious act of distributing warming rocks was an effective way to ward off frost bite, and he faithfully incorporated that chore into the other tasks of oversight. His routine was exhausting, one that even a man of Jack's strength couldn't continue. By refusing to face his own limitations, he endangered himself and the others too. He didn't feel he had any other option.

He wanted to make sure everyone was insulated from the frozen ground. Lucy lay inside the tepee on an outside end of the board platform. Next to her sat the crate with the two younger children snuggled next to each other. The wooden container was elevated a few inches off the ground. The lid was held open a couple of inches with a ragged towel placed in the track. In the bottom of the trunk was a folded bag of goose down. Ian slept next to his parents on the platform. Lucy smiled and asked Helga and Rolf to pretend to be baby chicks under their mother hen. With that comment they began peeping. Before lowering the lid Lucy listened while the youngsters recited their bedtime prayers. For added safety Lucy added a second thicker rag to hold the lid open. For even greater safety sake, Jack decided to punch some holes in the trunk.

Jack slid a few heated stones into the trunk. Lucy lay down on the wood platform next to Abe. Ian lay next to Abe, and they shared the down comforters. Next Jack checked on Jane and Jon. Their only barrier beneath their bedding was a two-ply wool blanket. Jack asked, "Lucy, did you give away all of your down comforters?" Lucy replied, "There was one left last I looked. Jack carried it to the Macintoshes. Here, let me fix up your pallet some." Jack fished around in his clothing trunk and pulled out a wool shirt, some raggedy bed covers being used as rags, and a pair of clean long handles. He filled a large laundry bag with Lucy's blanket batting and padded the board surface. Then he replaced the blanket and told them to lie down. On top Jack placed the knitted comforter and topped it with his own wool lined rain slicker and surrounded them with heated rocks.

Jane and Jon smiled and thanked him, "That feels much better." Next to Lucy lay Lorna on the platform. Underneath Lorna was one of Bones' saddle blankets. A wool blanket covered Lorna and Dora and on top was Jack's 20-year-old buffalo robe. Jack decided that Lorna needed more cover. Then he remembered a roll of carpet that had been moved to the cave from his wagon. He placed the thick wool rug and horse blanket underneath Lorna and covered her with two other blankets. Jack tenderly tucked the blankets under her body before spreading the buffalo robe on top. Jack delivered two loads of hot rocks. He outlined Lorna's body with heated the stones. He rolled an old wool shirt from his trunk to make a pillow for Lorna's head.

After an hour or so of making the rounds, Jack was satisfied that the group would survive the night. As he piled more wood on the fire and added snow to the pot of water, he was formulating and rejecting ideas for constructing a better shelter on the morrow. He was certain that more lumber could be salvaged from underneath the rockslides once the wolves had cleared out. They would need to construct a privy and take an inventory of supplies. The food on hand was the meat from the cow. There was still some jerky, but that was it. A foraging and hunting party must be dispatched on the morrow.

Jack was fighting total exhaustion but forced himself to keep moving. While Jack stood holding his gloved hands over the fire, Tommy interrupted his thoughts, "My turn, get some rest Jack."

Jack carried several warmed stones in a sling and walked over to where Lorna lay. He slid them under the buffalo robe and returned the cool rocks to the fire. Then he saw that Lorna was awake and was smiling at him. She motioned for him to slide underneath. He removed his boots and crawled under the cover, lying on his side facing Lorna. She moved the rolled shirt so that they could share the little pillow. Lorna removed a mitten and ran her warm hand over Jack's face and ear. His ear was so cold that the warmth of her hand hurt. When he winced, she pulled the cover over his head and pulled his neck scarf up. Then she moved close enough to kiss him. He kissed her back, before lapsing into a near comatose state of sleep. It took Lorna longer to settle her mind. She drifted off while replaying the events of the last 24 hours.

This is a good time to reflect upon the Saga of the Jack Long Expedition. The members were being tested over and over. Will this latest challenge, the New Madrid Earthquake strike the fatal blow? Will their faith in God and their tenacious resourcefulness bring them through this latest trial? Isn't it amazing how quickly the pendulum of fate can swing? The 1811 New Madrid earthquake struck the group less than 6 hours after the enchanting wedding celebration of Lorna and Jack. Once again, the close-knit band was plunged into a life and death struggle for survival.

Jane and Jonathan, like intertwined vines slept bundled under their covering. Tommy had turned the guard duty over to Trenton and now slept slumped against a log by the fire. Jack woke him and said, "Tom, I'm back on duty, better move over to the space on the board platform next to Lorna. You will get too cold out here. Where is your bedroll?" Tommy took Jack's advice but didn't disclose that he had given most of it to others. Tommy groaned when he moved, and Jack remarked that he sounded like an old man. Jack tucked some hot rocks around him and gave him an affectionate pat on the shoulder. Tommy's man-child, a mature 17-year-old, Walter slept on two wooden trunks stationed next to the fire. The kid was too tired to fuss with neatness and buried himself in his pile of covers. Jack came along and tucked him in with some hot rocks. The warmest member of the group was Dora, tucked away in her marsupial pouch.

At daybreak Jack called the group together for a short worship service. He led them in prayer to ask God for providential assistance and wisdom. Under Jack's dynamic leadership, the men got organized and hour by hour improved the sleeping quarters, constructed a covered cooking area, and built a high backside to the fire ring that reflected heat toward the sleeping quarters. A privy was built far enough away to avoid water contamination or odors. Rain proofing the shelters was completed and none too soon. Several days of sporadic rain added to the discomfort. The only bright spot was good old Tommy. Spending the entire day crowded elbow to elbow under the shed while trying to stay dry and somewhat warm would have been torture but for Tommy. He recognized the need for some mood raisin' and blossomed into his most entertaining, gregarious, comedic self. Old Tommy dug deep into his repertoire of tall tales. He varied the activity with hymn singing, lively harmonica music, storytelling and even some humorous poetry. Suddenly Helga started to weep and hid her face. Lucy picked her up and asked, "Helga, vhy ze critin?"

Helga between hiccups said, "Ve mist Christmus and St Nick. I dit'n getz zi toy."

Flabbergasted, Tommy looked at Lucy and Abe and said, "You're right Helga, but we didn't really miss Christmas we just postponed it, you know like in my story when St. Nick delivered the toys one day late. Yes, I hear you too, Rolf; St. Nick has a plan 'cause he sure don't like disappoint'n children, specially extra good ones like you and Helga. Member what happened to our Christmas tree? The earthquake smashed it with those big rocks. With havin' to move out of the cave out here on bare ground, the 25th just got moved to next year." Tommy promised to find a replacement yule tree to decorate for when St. Nick came back on a special trip just for Helga and Rolf. Just as they turned to crawl back under their covers Rolf turned and said, "St. Nick needs to gitz Dora somezin cause zee is big enough to play vith zee toy."

Tommy and his gang of boys managed to provide game and fresh herbs. He even found a dormant bee hive full of honey. Walter, Ian and Bert were becoming excellent marksmen and skilled trackers. It was unusual for them to come back from hunting empty handed.

So far, they were surviving life topside better than expected. The cold was hard to deal with, but the warmed rocks and plenty of firewood kept them alive. Then something terrible happened. It was the darkest part of the night when a sound, a very slight intermittent crunch broke through Jack's slumber. His internal alarms started sounding. Tommy and Walter were on watch and a distance from the fire preparing some brush to be dragged to the wood pile. What Jack was hearing was nearby and not in the direction of the two wood cutters. Jack removed the cover from his head and looked in the direction of the sounds. Only twenty to thirty yards away a pair of eyes reflected the fire light.

Judging from the distance between the eyes, Jack knew it was a large, a very large animal.   Sniffing sounds came from the hidden form, then more crunching in the snow. Jack stiffened and felt tingles moving up and down his spine as every muscle in his powerful body became spring loaded. The unidentified animal was peering from behind a dense evergreen bush. Jack first thought of the wolf pack but decided that this animal was alone, and that narrowed the possibilities. Jack wasn't the only one that had heard the approach. Jack with liquid movement slid from beneath the cover and slipped on his boots. Jon Macintosh awoke and looked at Jack. They silently communicated with minimal hand signs. Sleeping near to Jon was Lindsey Trenton, and Jon's slight tap on the crown of his head alerted Lindsey. They were all looking in the direction of the pair of orange eyes. Jack, slowly raised a hand that held his pistol, and Jon and Lindsey raised their own weapon. Lindsey held up his primed muzzle loader. Jack motioned to Jon to wait for the animal to step from behind the bush for a clear shot. The surreptitious visitor reversed course and began circling the camp. This presented Jack, Jon, Abe, and Lindsey with a dilemma over whether to wait for a clear shot or to pursue the intruder. Jack indicated his decision to wait. The black hulk approached with very deliberate moves. Jack's acute hearing could barely detect the stealthy creature. The mule began pulling against its tether and rearing, so terrified he broke loose and ran into the forest. The commotion brought Tommy and Walter running back to camp. Now, everyone except the youngest children was wide awake. The men had thrust off their bedcovers and rose in unison clutching their firearms and blades.

The intruder, a large grizzly, let out a paralyzing roar, rearing on its hind legs before attacking. Absent the mule, his prey switched to the humans facing him. The men formed a semi-circle obstructing the demon's path to the women and children. They all opened fire when Jack yelled "shoot!" Bloody wounds appeared over the brute's body, but the animal launched an assault unimpeded. The grizzly hardly flinched and viciously attacked the nearest human facing him. That happened to be Jack. The leviathan reared on hind legs a second time and swatted at Jack with a front paw, knocking him to the ground.

Jack managed to hold on to his pistol as he went down and when the bear took his entire forearm up to the elbow into its mouth, he managed to fire the round directly into the throat of the beast. The animal clamped down on Jack's arm causing terrible pain. Jack waged a counter attack by gouging at the animal's eyes and pounding on its head. The newly arrived Tommy, out of Jack's range of sight jumped astride the bruin and placed his muzzle loader at the base of its skull firing crossways to prevent the ball from exiting and striking Jack.

As soon as Tommy fired the pistol, the bear bucked him off, and he became the focus of the attack. Jack, still attached by his arm, continued battering the bear. As the beast whirled toward Tommy with lightning speed, Jack was suddenly suspended above the ground by centrifugal force, knocking Tommy onto his back as he was attempting to stand. A forceful swipe from a bear paw sent Tommy flying to land in unnatural sprawl a good 10 feet away. After firing his pistol into the hind quarters of the brute, Abe attacked with an axe. After landing a damaging swing of the axe, Abe was sent flying. He crashed pell-mell into the addled Tommy. The two men lay in a heap not fully conscious.

Lyla jumped into the fray by splashing some boiling water between the bear's hind legs. This must have been considered a foul in bear wrestling rules and the seemingly undiminished giant roared while looking directly at Lyla. She started backing away but not fast enough. Jack was carried along as the bore lunged at Lyla. A giant paw knocked her to the ground bleeding and dazed. In the interim Tommy and Abe had righted themselves and rejoined the battle. With the available firearms all discharged, the assault on the bear continued with the weapons at hand. The scene was surreal and frantic with the victor very much in question. Lorna and Lucy had begun re-loading the firearms. Jane kept the children from seeing the spectacle to the best of her ability, but she was unable to shield them from the hideous sounds. Sadly, the older children were experiencing a horrific event that would fuel their nightmares for the rest of their lives.

Walter picked up the axe and landed a blow to a hind leg. Top side Tommy was again stabbing at the threshing head with his ten-inch hunting knife. Then Walter yelled "here Dad" and handed Tommy one of the reloaded blunderbusses. He fired; Bang! The shot blew away a portion of the Goliath's skull, spattering blood and brain tissue over the defenders. The bear froze for a moment and then in slow motion tried to stand. Before reaching his full height, he crumpled to the ground. The powerful mouth fell open, and Jack was able to remove his arm before fainting. Lorna was screaming "Jack, Jack Oh Lord!" Dora was struggling to peak from beneath her mother's clothing to see what was happening and was repeating "Ma-Ma-Ma?" The grizzly lost the battle, but the odds were ten to one. During the heat of battle the men were all wondering if the monster was supernatural and indestructible. The fight with the grizzly felt like a fever induced hallucination. This had been a fight the likes of which they all hoped to never repeat.

Jack lay sprawled on the ice-covered ground, but awake from his stupor. His arm was injured, but his heavy jacket hid the exact nature of the wound. Lyla, covered with her own battle wounds, limped to kneel at Jack's side opposite Tommy. Jack was a bloody mess. He had multiple cuts from the slashing claws but the bites were more serious. Tommy asked, "Can you move your arm? Who am I? Can you see me?" Before Jack had time to respond, Lyla assumed command of the triage. She chose to treat Jack before the others because of his blood loss. "Jack, where do you hurt"? Her deep voice was calm and authoritative as she barked orders like a drill sergeant. "Abe, get something we can put under Jack like a couple of boards and bind them together with a blanket. Hey, I need help over here to turn Jack on his side so we can slide the boards under him. Help me move Jack to the big trunk next to the fire. Lucy, light some extra lanterns. Lorna, Jack is going to be fine; this is no time to panic."

Rolling Jack to his side caused him to gasp for air and moan. Lyla held on to make sure Jack didn't fall from the makeshift stretcher as he was being moved. "Bring blankets and some warmed rocks. Have to keep you warm Jack." Then Lyla used a knife and split the sleeve to expose the wound. Lyla drew a big breath when she saw the gaping laceration. Jack demonstrated normal movement of his arm and hand. When Jack looked at Lorna's horrified expression, he spoke in calm, even tones, "Lorna, I ain't hurt too bad, I'll be fine. Come over and see for yourself." Jack didn't realize how serious the arm wound was. Lyla yelled above the noise, "anybody have a bottle of whiskey? Do we have any laudanum left?"

The injury to Jack's arm was a series of puncture wounds, but after running her fingers over his radius and ulna, she found no obvious fractures. Lyla quickly recognized that Jack had a punctured artery since it gushed with each heartbeat. Because Lyla was a nurse and had worked for a field surgeon in combat zones, Lyla was knowledgeable in the latest life-saving techniques and was convinced, against conventional wisdom, that blood loss kills. Lyla rejected the benefits of bloodletting and leach therapy. She gathered her skirt into a wad and applied pressure to the hemorrhaging wound. Jack's other wounds were slowly seeping blood indicating minor capillary damage. While Lyla held pressure on the deep laceration, Lucy cleaned the other wounds with a whiskey dampened cloth. Jack raised his head and asked for a swig of the bourbon. Lucy poured some in a tin cup for Jack to sip. Instead, Jack took the cup with his left hand and tossed it into his mouth. Lyla said, "Jack, no more, we have better uses for our last bottle. You want a stick to bite down on while I work on you?" Jack repulsed at the idea of having a stick in his mouth let loose with "HELL NO!" Then Jack said, "Sorry ladies that was the whiskey talking." Then Jack in a surprisingly strong voice said, "Kingston, Abe, why don't you boys look that bear over and see if he looks healthy enough to butcher, lotta' meat there. And while I'm thinking about it, somebody reach down in the bear's mouth and get me my pistol."

Bert held a rag torch for Abe and Kingston as they stretched out the legs of the dead bear. First Abe splashed a dipper of water into the bloody mouth and saw the teeth of a very old boar. Several teeth were missing and two, possibly more were broken off. The animal was emaciated, and one paw was missing its toes and claws, likely from a close call with a bear trap. Tommy spoke up and said, "I don't see any sign of disease 'cept some abscessed teeth. He will be tough as leather but we're gonna butcher out the best parts come daylight." The bear was hung from a limb and bled and eviscerated.

It was likely that the bear's limited ability to find food led to the brazen attack. From a bear's perspective mere mules and humans are easier to kill than elk and deer. Because the bear's bite was so defective, Jack's still had his arm attached to his body. And after seeing the misshapen paw Lyla knew that they had been spared more serious injuries. Lyla kept to herself how dangerous a bite wound can be because a bear's mouth is a breeding place for germs. Only a robust immune system would be able to survive such a deep bite. Of course, that was assuming that blood loss didn't kill Jack first. Lyla decided to probe the deep arterial wound with her finger to make sure a broken tooth was not left buried. Checking for a tooth was the right thing to do, there was one about the diameter of her little finger. Lyla slipped it into her pocket. Lyla poured some of the whiskey directly into the wound and then reapplied pressure. Jack was a pitiful sight all pale and trembling. Jack moaned, "Gosh Lyla, that stings."

She asked Tommy to tie a tourniquet a few inches above the wound and told him to tighten it just enough to slow the blood flow but not totally stop all circulation.

Jack's heavy bleeding was slowed by the tourniquet, but it was a short-term tactic. A solemn Lyla told Jack, "Sorry, but I have to cauterize the wound to stop the bleeding. We are getting near. If that doesn't stop the bleeding, there is one even more drastic measure to try." Lyla didn't elaborate on the "drastic" treatment. The last resort Lyla referred to was ghoulish and counter-intuitive. At this point stopping the severe hemorrhaging was the only way to save Jack's life. Lyla called for a powder horn of black powder and placed a second clean hunting knife in the coals to heat. Lyla asked the men to tie Jack's legs and arms to the board. Then she spread the wound and inserted the bright orange blade. There was a sizzling sound when the knife contacted the flesh. Jack let out a deafening scream and fainted. Lyla waited for the hissing sound to stop before withdrawing the knife. She put it back in the fire and peered at close range to see if the bleeding had stopped.

Very quickly she concluded that she had only enlarged the wound when a spray of blood covered her face and chest. Jack gained consciousness expecting to learn that the wound was closed. Lyla was busy and ignored his questioning eyes. Though Lyla had never actually treated a wound with black powder, she had heard a group of army surgeons discussing how effectively it was for searing hemorrhaging blood vessels.

By nature a decisive woman, Lyla lost no time preparing to use the gun powder. Jack's life hung in the balance. "Okay, Jack, I have to do this. Are you sure you don't want something to bite down on?" Jack nodded his head and said please. Lorna placed her twisted scarf in his open mouth. The salt-peter in gunpowder stung, and Jack moaned in pain. When the gun powder was ignited, there was a hissing sound. The explosion sent sparks in all directions. Once the gunpowder was spent, Lyla examined the burned flesh for bleeding, fully prepared to repeat the procedure. She announced, "Peers to have worked, there is no more bleeding; thank you Lord!" Jack had passed out and was for the moment feeling no pain. The smell of burning human flesh caused Lyla to heave with nausea. Lorna had to sit down to keep from fainting, and Jane kept the children distracted by praying for Jack before tucking them back into their beds.

Walter removed the bear's heart and liver and washed them well before dropping them into the soup pot. By this point the battered group's adrenaline was subsiding. Lyla made the rounds, identifying those that needed attention. She spent the next hour cleaning and bandaging the injuries and checking for fractured bones. As a whole, the group had escaped with only minor wounds. Most everyone returned to their bedrolls to rest up and get warm before sun up.

Chapter 11

PASSAGE TO DERBYVILLE

A couple of days before the earthquake, Tommy, Bert, Ian, and Walter had gone foraging for edible plants and herbs. Since that first trip when they encountered the wolverine, the boys were eager to go on these foraging trips. Old Tommy was a human encyclopedia of wilderness survival, and the three boys were already more knowledgeable on the topic of wild herbs than the average adult male. They returned to camp with a mess of newly sprouted dandelion greens, a hatful of water-cress, three bunches of wild onion, and some tuffs of chickweed discovered under an overhang that caught the afternoon sun. The wild greens would add flavor as well as crucial vitamins and minerals to the soup pot. Tommy told the boys that gathering these vegetables would have to be a daily project. His herb foraging had single handedly prevented the danger of disabling scurvy.

Jack's injuries kept him on his pallet with his arm elevated for days. So far there were no visible signs of infection thanks to the germicidal properties of the whiskey. Jack grew weary of being flat on his back but otherwise appeared to be jovial and a capable leader. He was tired of all the fussing over him. "Women can sure carry that sort of thing too far," he remarked to Tommy.

A break in winter weather helped the men improve the campsite. Thawing snow created mud, and that required hauling in gravel and pine needles. The tremendous workload without a hearty diet was turning the robust men into shadows of their former selves. Their clothes hung on them, and their faces were gaunt with sunken eyes. The women and children were faring slightly better.

Hunting the sparse wildlife in the area, the on-going search for wild herbs and greens, and supplying the constant fires with wood kept everyone busy, even the children. The women gathered branches from the surrounding cedar trees to fortify the wind-breaks and add insulation to the sleeping platforms. The suffering campers had a hero in Tommy. His harmonica music, funny stories, and survival knowhow were a game changer. Young Walter's obvious admiration for his father endeared him to the group. Walter unwittingly emulated the undisputed champion of the Long Waggoneers, the man he called Father.

A few days after the battle with the bruin, the Olsen children had carelessly wandered too far from camp. They learned a valuable lesson quickly. The frightened children raced back to camp making incoherent stuttering. The big-eyed Rolf found his voice and exclaimed in a high-pitched voice, "Ve zaw someone, out there, a bigt manz, kind of Indian that, and scary. He vuz just staring zat us." Jack started to get off his pallet, but Tommy pushed him back down and said, "Jack, we can take care of this. You stay here and watch over the women. Me and Abe will go see what the kids found."

Tommy and Abe doubled their fire power by hiding extra pistols on their body and taking an extra knife. Then they struck out to contact the stranger. They walked in the general direction the children had pointed and soon smelled smoke. The smoke trail led them to what appeared to be a deserted camp. As they explored the campsite, a man's voice came from cover, "I'm not here to threaten you, but I am asking you to place your weapons against the tree. Now take a seat on the log. I mean you no harm." Tommy and Abe froze and then complied by standing their blunderbusses against a tree trunk, thankful that their other weapons were out of sight. A stocky, muscular man with black shoulder-length hair approached them cautiously with his long gun pointed at the ground. The stranger took a seat on a boulder on the opposite side of the fire.

The three men were sizing up each other, hoping to judge the intent of the other. Tommy spoke first. "How 'bout you set your gun aside too. T'woud make us feel a might better." The stranger didn't fit any of Tommy's pigeon holes. He didn't appear to be an Indian, but wore buckskins, had shoulder-length black hair, and his pock marked face was clean shaven; for someone in the wilderness, he was uniquely clean about his person. He spoke perfect English without an accent. After an uneasy pause, the young man placed his long gun against a small tree. He returned to the boulder and sat down. The stranger proceeded to introduce himself. "My name is Strider LaBlanc. My mother was a Shawnee and my father a Frenchman. I am on a hunting trip, and your children happened upon my campsite. What brings you to these parts?"

Abe started with, "Zes art wit du wagon traint that gotz stranded by winter weathzer that."

Tommy broke into the conversation saying, "Yep, like Abe is saying we been living in a cave down by the river but had to come out because of the earthquake."

Strider smiled and said "ah, yes the cave, I have camped there many times. So, it collapsed, too bad?"

After some cordial small talk regarding the mild weather and the after-shocks Tommy asked Strider about the nearest town or fort. "We need to trade for a couple of wagons with mules and some staple goods. We got no money to speak of, but we could barter some of our belongin's."

Strider said, "The only place that might be able to help you is on west of here. There is a small trading post with an attachment of army troops about 40 miles west. I can take you there. I'm going that direction."

Tommy replied, "I'll have to talk to our wagon master, and the other men and I will let you know. This winter weather and the earthquake 'bout got the best of us. Sure would like to take our party into town to wait for warmer weather."

After the three men visited around the fire a little longer, Tommy decided it was safe to invite Strider to come along and meet the others back at camp. As it would turn out, Tommy's decision to befriend Strider would have a gigantic impact on the Long Expedition. From all outward appearances Strider was mellow and friendly. The hostility Strider felt toward the invasion of European settlers was well hidden even from someone as intuitive as Old Tommy.

Over a year earlier when Strider had witnessed Tecumseh's speech, he had been so moved by the emotional appeal that he volunteered as a hunter and scout for the confederation of tribes. The day Strider encountered the Long Expedition, he was on a hunting trip for supplying Tecumseh's warriors.

When Strider arrived in the Long camp, he was given a cordial welcome. Lyla took him by the arm and gave him a seat on a wooden trunk and handed him a cup of broth and a piece of jerky. Everyone filed by and introduced themselves. The effects of exposure and malnutrition were glaringly apparent to Strider: something he was well acquainted with. Despite being a total stranger, Strider was treated as a valued guest. Unbeknownst to the travelers they were in a position of terrible jeopardy posed by Tecumseh's war against the white race. The question foremost in Strider's mind was *did these people deserve to die with the rest of the invaders?*

Strider wanted to know more about these people. He would find a way to eavesdrop on their conversation, leave something of value to see if it would be stolen, and observe how they treated each other. Strider wanted to know how they felt toward Indian People. He opened the topic by asking if there had been any Indian attacks on their train.

Jack answered by describing the attack that left Sally Trenton dead and their mules stolen. Once Jack was well into the story, Strider realized that he had heard of the raid from the family members of the village responsible for the raid. He recalled that the white pursuers had killed the warriors but spared the women, elderly, and children. And most remarkable of all, the white men had left behind food for the survivors. Strider stopped Jack and asked, "Are you the fellars that spared the women, elderly, and children, and left food behind?" Jack looked surprised and asked, "You heard about that? Word sure gets around. You hear it from the Indians?" Strider didn't elaborate but with a gesture said yes. After sitting and listening to Tommy play his harmonica, Strider rose from his seat to go for a stroll into the night for some privacy. As soon as he was out of sight, he circled back and hid within earshot. He got an ear full when he became the topic of conversation.

Tommy asked Jack, "What's your take on this Strider fellar?"

Jack rubbed his mustache and after a good long pause said, "Seems kind of secretive and not sure if he trusts us. He doesn't seem dangerous. I'm bettin' he's lonely and would be a good friend to have in a pinch. The Good Lord knows we all need friends. I sure 'preciate how everyone is making him feel welcome. Before he comes back how about we all bow and have a prayer for him. Maybe he will show some interest in the Good Book. It would be a shame for a fine young man like Strider to lose his soul, that's assuming he ain't right with the Lord. Then the entire group bowed their heads and said a silent prayer for Strider. When Ian got up to add wood to the fire, he saw something shiny on the ground. He picked it up and realized it was a ten-dollar gold piece. Ian walked around and showed it to everyone. They all remarked that it must belong to Strider. Ian put the coin in his pocket. Jon said, "I think I sense a deep sadness in Strider, like he's been through some rough times." Everyone nodded in agreement.

Lorna was contending with a teething Dora. The baby was tired of being so confined inside Lorna's clothing and felt warm to the touch. Jack took over with her, but she wasn't any happier with him. Jane volunteered to hold Dora. Jane commenced singing a beautiful Irish lullaby and rocked from side to side. Dora stopped fussing and with big eyes watched Jane's mouth. Within a few minutes Dora was sound asleep. Strider returned to his seat by the fire in time to listen to Jane's lovely song.

When the song ended Strider whispered, "Jane, you have a beautiful voice." He was thinking how everyone seemed willing to help with the baby. So far Strider had not heard a cross word or even a dirty look since he arrived. As he analyzed the Long party, he felt someone peck him on the shoulder. It was Ian, the teenager.

The boy said, "Mr. Strider, did you lose a coin. I found it by where you had been sitting.

Strider made a show of checking his pocket and said, yes, the one I had is not there. "Thanks for finding it for me. Hey, Ian, ya wanna arm wrestle?"

Ian gave Strider a strange look and said I don't think I know how." Tommy interrupted Ian and said, I'll show you how it's done." Tommy rubbed his hands together and plopped down in front of Strider. Tommy held his own for a minute before the more powerful Strider laid him low. Abe decided to pit Ian against Bert, and they went for several rounds with each winning in turn. The boys enjoyed the challenge and had found something new to pass the quiet times.

Strider had the answer to all four of the situations. The Long Wagon Train folks were kind to each other, they were honest, they spoke well of him when his back was turned, and they had voluntarily shown brotherly concern for the surviving Indians that attacked them. Strider was certain that these were the finest people he had ever encountered, white or Indian. Strider was feeling a sense of panic. He wasn't sure his friends would survive the night or the following day. Death was eminent.

The impending slaughter that awaited his new friends was torturing him. He imagined the scalps of the children hanging from the belt of warriors and the women being raped and mutilated in front of their husbands. Strider felt compelled to intervene on behalf of these good people. But was it too late to save them from certain death? Over the next day Strider devised a plan to take their case before Tecumseh himself. He had reason to believe that the great leader recognized that there were good people among the whites. Strider's tug of war between ethnic loyalties was unsettling. Since Tecumseh was known to have White friends and was rumored to be romantically linked to an English woman, Strider was comfortable asking for a favor.

Not a day passed that Strider didn't flash back to his suffering as a child at the hands of the Shawnee. After his mother's death he was sent out to fend for himself. Had it not been for some kindly white people he might have perished. Strider used the time to engage the travelers in conversation, watching for any indication of dishonesty, cruelty, and avarice. He found none and concluded that the members of the Long Expedition were genuine.

After engaging in leisurely conversation for a couple of hours, Strider retrieved the saddle bag that held his food supply and dumped the contents on a table and said, "Hey Lyla, take this food bag and use it for the evening meal." The women and children gathered around the items spread on the trunk, transfixed with amazement. Was that salt, real salt and a bag of coffee, and oh my, a tin of raw sugar? Next, they realized there was a bag of flour and corn meal too. On the very bottom was a slab of cured bacon. Strider smiled when he saw their reaction. He handed the freshly killed turkey to Tommy and said "Its fresh, only killed a couple of hours ago."

Jack rose from his bed and walked to shake Strider's hand. Something about the unwavering eye contact and friendliness on Jack's face made Strider think of Patrick. Ever since he and Patrick had parted ways Strider had been adjusting to the emptiness. Like Patrick, these folks seemed to be honest and caring people, the kind that made pleasant companions. Strider, true to his suspicious nature, was close to accepting these people at face value.

Strider relaxed by the fire and was enjoying the conversation. He caught Dora looking at him, stretching her neck to see above Lorna's coat collar. He said, "Mamm, you sure have a beautiful baby, is it a girl?"

Lorna said, "You guessed right, she is a girl. We call her Dora."

"Would you mind if I hold Dora?"

"You can hold her if she will go to you willingly. Here, try to keep her wrapped in this blanket." Lorna removed Dora from her warm cocoon, and Strider stepped forward and took the wiggling child into his arms in a rather awkward manner. There was no sign of fright, and the baby looked into Strider's eyes with a beaming toothless smile and giggled as she reached out to touch his pock marked face. Strider was instantly smitten with Dora and hugged her to his breast. He recalled playing with infants when he was a boy. He even watched over them at times. As an adult he was passionately protective about their welfare. Strider had suffered needlessly and he was determined to prevent other children including those from his Shawnee Clan from such a fate. When he looked at Lorna, she had a surprised expression. "Strider, Dora doesn't normally go to strangers. She likes you."

Strider felt a rush of emotion and said, "And I like her. She is so sweet!" He realized that his self-imposed solitary lifestyle was losing its appeal. Closeness to such an angelic baby was dredging long buried feelings.

The women began preparing a special meal made possible by Strider's staples. The soup pot now had some salt and a slice of bacon. Little dumplings were spooned into the soup, enough for everyone to have one, and steaming cups of coffee were slowly sipped and left to sit on the tongue. Thin strips of turkey meat were lightly breaded in flour and cornmeal and fried in bacon fat to a crispy brown.

Jack blessed the meal and asked for God's blessings to fall upon Strider. Once everyone had finished eating, Jack stood to say, "Listen up everyone, companions whom I now consider family, this bounty we have just shared was much more than a blessed feast, it is a celebration to honor our new friend Strider. He has chosen to befriend us at a time when we are suffering mightily. This young man has agreed to help us move on to better accommodations. He has blessed us more than he will ever know. I feel that it is only fitting that we end this meal with another prayer. Please bow with me,

Dear Almighty God, we of this traveling family want to ask your protection and continued blessings upon this young man named Strider. May the brotherly kindness he has shown us be to his credit when he stands before your throne on judgment day. In Christ's Name, amen."

The Long Expedition had an occasion to celebrate. Tommy began playing a lively tune, and that called for hand clapping and dancing. The numb extremities and fatigue due to poor nutrition was ignored for a few minutes. Strider was coaxed to join in and for the first time since his parents had perished, he felt a family connection, an emotion he had dismissed as weakness. The cold temperature drove them all back to the relative comfort of their beds, no longer reserved for only nighttime sleeping.

Strider was invited to sleep inside the large sleeping lean-to but declined and chose to erect his one-man buffalo hide tepee. After bedding down sleep evaded Strider. The coming appointment with fate was growing nearer by the hour. Once the attack began it would be too late for Strider to negotiate safe passage. The war parties were only miles away, and Strider was considering several scenarios for saving his new friends. Lying in his bedroll, Strider realized that his core identity had changed. He was a white man, the split ethnicity discarded. He reasoned that the waves of white settlers from Europe were so over-whelming that Tecumseh's mission was decades too late and doomed to fail. Strider was certain that the assembled force of thousands would still be inadequate to change the ultimate outcome for North American. Strider would not allow the slaughter of the Long party. Tecumseh's Great War was doomed to fail.

The following day Tommy and Jon left with Strider headed westward for the fort. Tommy and Jon rode double upon the mule, an experience only slightly better than walking the distance. The padding barely helped soften the sharpness of the mule's backbone. After what they had been through, a few more days of personal discomfort was trivial. They carried along trade goods and coins for purchasing the needed items. Tommy noticed that Strider was being overly vigilant almost to the point of causing suspicion.

While Tommy and Jon were gone, winter weather returned to the region. The only positive aspect to the heavy, wet snowfall was that it insulated the makeshift shelter from the bitter cold. The children were kept tucked into their sleeping blankets most of the time. Maintaining the woodpile became a supreme challenge. The men had to travel ever farther into the surrounding forest to find firewood.

Lyla was suffering with frostbite to her two little toes; she knew that amputation was a possibility but kept it to herself for the short term. Lorna noticed that Dora was still hungry after nursing and increased her solid food. Two tiny teeth appeared on Dora's bottom gum line, and she felt the need to try them out. This prompted Tommy to introduce Bert and Ian to the art of wood whittling. The first of the toys were lacking artisanship, but Dora was pleased. The two boys derived considerable satisfaction from seeing Dora play with her teething ring and a piece of wood that resembled a horse.

After a two-week absence Tommy and Jon were spotted returning. Everyone was eager to welcome them home and watched as they approached. But there was only one wagon drawn by mules and one saddle horse. Tommy announced, "Rumors are flying about Indians being on the warpath. This is it, all we could get them to sell us. The fort is preparing for an attack and keepin' its hoard of supplies. We was lucky we got what we did."

Jack was surprised that Strider had returned with Tommy and Jon and was offering to help. What Jack and the others did not know was that Strider was afraid to leave them to travel alone. Strider was secretly terrified of the thousands of warriors waiting for Tecumseh to sound the "charge." The main group of Indians was camped about thirty miles to the north-east of the Young party. The confederacy of Indians was holding nightly pow-wows and growing in number daily. The speeches and dances had the warriors so stimulated with blood lust a commander like Tecumseh was hard pressed to control them. They were ready to apply their warpaint.

While Tommy and Jon conducted business at the fort, Strider secretly rode out to parlay with Tecumseh on behalf of his friends. The compassionate side of the great leader prevailed, and his respect for his brother Path Strider culminated with a conditional promise of safe passage. Strider returned just in time to join Tommy and Jon on the return to Clinch River. Tommy asked Strider the reason for the red and black stripes painted on his horse, but Strider gave a vague answer that made no sense to Tommy. Strider had tucked away in his saddle bag a piece of bark inscribed with symbols that would grant safe passage to the Long group. Tecumseh promised to send word to the war parties to grant safe passage to those traveling with Strider. The red and black stripes on his horse would signal the stand-down.

Within two days the Long group was loaded up and ready to strike out for the new destination a Calvary Fort. The sub-freezing temperature made traveling easier by hardening what would have been deep mud. All the women and children were crowded into the bed of the canvas-covered wagon. The mule was harnessed to a travois for hauling the overflow of necessary gear. Jack managed to find room for his saddle. The men took turns riding and walking. Jack wanted to make the trip with as few stops as possible. A moon made night travel possible.

On the second day, a war party appeared atop a ridge. Strider yelled, "HALT" Jack reigned in the mules. Strider spurred his horse to where Jack sat on the wagon seat and said, "Jack, signal everyone to stay calm and peaceful. It is extremely important to keep weapons out of sight. I will go to parlay with the war party." Jack and Tommy glanced at each other with obvious alarm but decided to trust Strider to deal with the Indians. Strider jerked his horse around and raced toward the ridge where the war party was lined up shoulder to shoulder seemingly ready to launch an attack. The warriors were decked out in full battle regalia, waiting for a command. The distance was about a half mile, and Jack strained to see what Strider withdrew from his saddle bag before dismounting to speak with the war chief who also dismounted. Tommy pulled a field glass from his gear and handed it to Jack. Jack watched as the two men sat down cross legged on a blanket facing each other and waited for a warrior to bring a lighted peace pipe. The two men passed the pipe back and forth without speaking for a suitable time before engaging in conversation. Jack couldn't make out the object that was handed to the chief. There was a tense period of conversation between the two seated men, and the object was handed back to Strider. After more conversation and much waving of hands, the meeting ended, and Strider returned to the wagon train.

The war party disappeared behind the ridge. Strider gave a brief explanation, "Jack, the war party is from my mother's village. I have a message board granting you safe passage through this territory. The paint on my horse is a signal from Tecumseh. You need to ask your God to help the couriers get the message out to all of the war parties that would otherwise attack us. We are not out of danger, so stay alert. I will do what I can to protect you." An incredulous Jack shook his head to clear his mind and thanked Strider with words that for the moment seemed inadequate. Jack flipped the reigns to re start the team moving.

When the Long expedition approached the small fort, it appeared to be abandoned. Then upon closer inspection it was discovered that the fort had been attacked and was partly burned. There were a number of dead, both soldiers and Indians strewn about the grounds. It was so strange that the bodies had not been collected. What kind of urgency justified leaving the fallen sprawled upon the ground to become carrion? It made no sense.

Only two of the buildings were left undamaged. The larger of the two had a functioning fireplace, so Jack motioned for the group to inspect the interior before unloading their belongings. They removed the bodies of three dead soldiers and placed them in a shed that Jack designated as the morgue.

The log structure was divided into four main rooms and had thick wooden shutters covering the windows. The great room had a large capacity dining table with benches, food preparation counters with storage underneath, and a massive rock fireplace with grates and hooks for cooking. The three smaller rooms had built-in barrack style sleeping bunks, three deep.

Jack called a meeting and asked if there was any problem with moving into the building. No one objected so Jack said, "For now we will make use of this fine building and move on when the weather permits." The log structure was luxurious in comparison to what they had been using as living quarters. Within a day and a half, they were situated in the new building. Strider and Tommy organized foraging and hunting parties to bring back food. Jack supervised taking the wagon into a stand of trees to gather firewood. A small stream flowed parallel to the outer perimeter of the fort ran with clear, unspoiled water. As soon as food, water and firewood were adequately collected Jack ordered that the corpses be given a respectful burial behind the compound. Jack and Tommy watched as Strider painstakingly painted the outer walls of the log structure with the same red and black striped design that marked Strider's horse. Strider had brought along two large bags of the powdered pigment for the job. Since there were no attacks on the decommissioned fort during their stay Strider assumed that the messengers had all gotten through. The abundance of food on the grasslands surrounding the fort helped Jack's group to recover from malnutrition and exposure. Life was mostly uneventful as the days became weeks. Then a most curious event happened. Tecumseh and an entourage of sub-chiefs paid a surprise visit. Several of the party saw them coming and reported to Jack. Jack hurried to where Strider was sawing up firewood. Strider immediately recognized Tecumseh and told everyone to be friendly and rode out to greet the great leader.

Jack felt panic set in as he searched for the correct response to a visit from a man that held the power of life or death over all of them. Jack formulated a strategy on the run. First, express appreciation to Tecumseh, then entertain him, and find something to give him as a gift. Responding in a manner acceptable to the Indian was a tricky proposition. Jack appointed men to carry the benches out to surround the fire pit in the center of the yard and built up the fire. He set a large pot of chicory on to brew and asked the women to bring out cups for serving the brew.

Jack rummaged through his trunk for a suitable gift for Tecumseh. He decided to part with his father's gold watch that John Silas had pilfered. Jack placed the keepsake in a black suede bag secured with a drawstring. Jack took one last look at the inscription on the back of the gold pocket watch.

> By order of the Royal Ulster Constabulary
> Loyal Subject Corporal Llewellyn Breton Long
> Is presented with this time piece
> In recognition of Gallantry and Exemplary acts of bravery
> In the service of King George III of Great Britain
> On this day 21 August, 1762

Bert and Walter collected the Indian ponies and restrained them in plain sight. Helga and Rolf took turns taking the visitors by the arm and escorting them to a seat on the benches. Ian carried a tray and served each guest a cup of hot chicory sweetened with honey. Jack sat upon a bench and had a cup of the brew as well. After a pause Jack stood and escorted Tecumseh and his entourage to the graves of the dead warriors that had been left behind. Jack was so glad they had gone to the effort to place a stone on each grave. Set apart by a few feet were the graves of the United States Calvary officers marked with similar head stones. The Calvary troops had names inscribed on their stones, the only difference. Tecumseh asked Jack's indulgence while he sang a mournful and sonorous chant while making hand motions over all of the graves.

Tecumseh's demeanor was a surprise. His broken English was well understood and polite. He was pleasant and grand-fatherly and carried himself with great personal dignity but without a hint of arrogance. He made a point of making eye contact while shaking hands with the men and bowed to the ladies. He made on over Dora and had her smiling at him. When Helga took Tecumseh's arm to seat him, he playfully accepted and thanked her for her kindness. He commented on her lovely dress and hair bow. He made a point of patting each child on the head. Each Indian, seven in number counting Tecumseh, sat very patiently waiting for Jack to speak.

Jack spoke in a loud clear voice, "Great Leader of the Shawnee, Tecumseh, Puma Across the Sky, revered leader of the Indian Peoples of North America, we are indebted to you for saving our lives. Our mutual friend, Strider tells us of your ability to see the future and to communicate with your gods and spirits. He has told of your brilliant mind. He insists you are a fair man that desires to live in peace with all men of good will. We are honored to have you visit with us and hope you will return. Now, great leader, we have a gift of entertainment for you. Relax and listen to our Jane Macintosh sing a lovely old ballad called 'Barbary Allen.'" Jack nodded to Jane, and she stood to perform the centuries old song with a sad haunting melody. Jane stood in the center by the fire. She began her song very softly but increased the volume as the song progressed. Jane's vibrato did not disappoint in spite of her stage fright.

T'was in the merry month of May
When green buds all were swellin'
Sweet William on his death bed lay
For the love of Barbary Allen.

Jane curtseyed and returned to her seat. Jack rose and thanked Jane for the musical number and then he invited Tecumseh to speak. Tecumseh rose and walked to the designated area. First, he addressed Jane and said, "My ears liked song, thank you. I come to thank you all for good will; you give food for the women, old people, and small children. Sorry warriors attack your wagons. They angry, white people hurt them, so they hurt back. Thank you for bury our dead. Strider say you all good people, Tecumseh stop war on you." He abruptly stopped speaking and returned to his bench. Jack rose and walked to where Tecumseh was sitting. Jack asked the great leader to stand. "Tecumseh, I want to present this gift to you. It once belonged to a great brave man, my father, Llewellyn Breton Long. Since he has passed from this life, I want another great man to have it. Please accept this watch as a token of our appreciation." Jack removed the watch from the bag so Tecumseh could see it. The old man smiled and shook his head in appreciation and thrust out his chest indicating he wanted Jack to pin it on his tunic. Jack held up his hands and said, "First I show you how to set the time. Wait until sun casts no shadow and set both hands to this number at the top of the dial." Then he explained the winding mechanism. Jack pinned the watch to Tecumseh's tunic. Lucy sent Helga to fetch a hand mirror and held it for Tecumseh that he might admire the gold watch. Tecumseh took the mirror and thanked Helga, assuming it to be another gift. Tecumseh removed from his neck a necklace of elk teeth interspersed with turquoise beads and handed it to Helga. Helga turned to look at her parents, and they told her to try out the beautiful necklace. It was indeed a beautiful piece of jewelry and quite valuable. Helga raised the necklace and encircled her neck. She curtseyed and said thank you.

Tecumseh was wise enough to grasp the significance of Jack's gift. For this White Man to part with a treasured family heirloom made a profound statement that was not lost on the wise Chieftain. Tecumseh was obviously thrilled to have a time keeper, but the tribute of respect meant even more. Tecumseh felt the desire to give to Jack an equally precious gift. The one great item in Tecumseh's possession was his mount. The stallion was white with black and brown spots over the rump. The appaloosa's tail and mane were snow white and full. Tecumseh called for the horse to be brought to him, and he paid a very emotional tribute to the magnificent steed by encircling his neck with both arms and rubbing the velvet between his great flared nostrils.

Tecumseh allowed a small breech of his stoicism as he handed the reins to Jack. While Jack held the reins, Tecumseh removed his personal belongings and handed them to the warrior standing next to him. Jack was stunned by the generosity of the gift. Tecumseh looked at Jack and said, "This Nimphkie Messewa, the Lightening Horse; Yours now." Silence reigned interrupted only by the sound of shuffling hooves and some low neighing sounds originating from deep in Nimphkie's chest.

Without further discussion the great Tecumseh smiled, meekly climbed on behind one of the sub-chiefs and waved goodbye as the band of Shawnee quickly disappeared over a hill to the northeast.

Jack was speechless. The nature of the entire encounter with Tecumseh was mind-boggling. Jack was amazed at the intellect and kindly character of a man that many white people would describe as sub-human, uncivilized, and of low intelligence. Jack reckoned that small minded people believe what they want to believe without regard for the evidence.

Jack had never seen such a beautiful appaloosa. He spoke to the horse and allowed him time to get his scent before he mounted to ride bareback. Jack reassured the slightly skittish animal and was able to guide the horse around the camp with the slightest pressure from his knees. The steed's regal size at seventeen hands was awe-inspiring. Nimphkie had stout bone structure and heavy muscling with pronounced tendons that indicated speed and endurance. The dappling and lavish snowy white mane and tail exceeded Jack's vocabulary of superlatives. Nimpky was a horse that he would treasure. Jack was glad he had kept Bones' saddle; it would work with adjustments just fine on Nimpky's larger frame. Lorna couldn't help but notice the 'boy in the candy store' smile on Jack's face.

Once the weather grew warm the Long Expedition disbanded. The parting was painful and drawn out. With tear-stained faces Lorna and Jack turned their handmade cart and travois toward Kentucky, with plans to purchase a Conestoga wagon at the first opportunity. Strider was invited to come along, and he gladly accepted.

Kentucky turned out to be a big state, and the Long family spent months searching for just the right place to put down roots. Jack's right hand regained normal function, and he was eager to man a plow. The little Long family fell in love with Kentucky. After a few weeks of bouncing around on the dirt roads in their well-used wagon, they came upon the perfect little farm. By this time Strider was Uncle

Strider to Dora. Jack suggested that Strider look for property nearby and settle down. Since Strider was unencumbered, he agreed to at least consider Jack's suggestion.

The farm Jack purchased was near a tiny little community called Derbyville, Kentucky. The people of Derbyville welcomed the new comers and offered a helping hand. The farm's log house was ancient and dilapidated. Lorna and Jack camped on the property while they remodeled the house. The weather was warm, and the campsite was shaded by oak trees. The property was well watered by a spring that fed into a creek. Jack was excited about the farming potential of the property. The soil near the creek appeared to be exceptionally fertile due to seasonal flooding.

Only a half mile from the farm's border was a one room school house that doubled as a meeting house for a group of "Christians." A stone's throw away was a small general store and feed mill. It was run by a man named James Stoneker. Brother Stoneker was one of three elders serving the little church and was well respected in Derbyville. From the first Sunday Lorna and Jack attended services at the country church and quickly determined that it was a good fit for their religious sensibilities.

The little community church set out to convert Strider to Christianity but soon concluded according to pastor Stoneker, "He ain't ready to hear the Gospel and needs more time for religion to take holt on him." The good people of Derbyville figured it was only a matter of time till he came around to find The Faith, and in the meantime, Strider would be shown love and included in the social functions of the church. The congregation spent their spare time, what there was of it, in one of three ways: playing a new game they called baseball that closely resembled the British game of cricket; cross country horse racing; and square dancing to Kentucky's version of blue grass fiddle music. Strider could be counted on when there was a get-together. In Strider's mind he had joined "The Church of Chicken Leg and Apple Pie Fellowship."

Lorna bore a son in 1814. Then only a year later she gave birth to twin girls. The Long family loved their new community. Strider, loyal friend that he was had helped Jack remodel his old cabin into a comfortable home. Strider decided to open a livery stable and blacksmithing shop in Derbyville and hired a retired blacksmith to teach him the trade. The community had a barn raising for Strider, and he was in business and making a living none too soon.

Strider was instantly popular with the young single women of the valley. He was much too attractive to remain a bachelor. Among the eligible women vying for Strider's attention was a 19-year-old blue-eyed blond named Bella Townsend. The commitment-shy Strider La Blanc had always enjoyed the company of women but balked at the prospect of matrimony. Bella crashed through that barrier and had Strider moon-eyed and figuratively panting. Jack immediately recognized the state of bliss poor Strider had waded into, having recently walked in those moccasins.

Strider's overly analytical internal voice acted out of an abundance of caution. Strider postulated, debated, staged dry runs and played devil's advocate all with himself. The winning argument's scenario went like this, "If my marriage to Bella is half as good as Jack and Lorna's union, it will sure keep me happy."

It seemed Bella and Strider had a wedding ceremony priority list and going-slow or re-examining was nowhere to be seen. The only constraints were how long it would take to make some minor alterations to the wedding dress handed down from Bella's mother and the time needed to bake a big wedding cake. The picnic would be "pot-luck" where everyone brought enough food for their own family with a little extra. Saturday at 10:00 AM the ceremony was held in Lorna and Jack's front yard under a huge shade tree. With Jack and Lorna's help, Bella and Strider staged an intimate romantic ceremony followed by the biggest, rowdiest wedding reception ever held in that neck of the woods.

Jack's new hobby of horse racing was a way to relax and enjoy the culture of local equine enthusiasts. He had inadvertently chosen the epicenter of horse racing for his new home. After racing Nimpkie four times, he had won no less than a span each time. Derbyville folks were already refusing to bet against him. The local derbies, steeplechases, and single elimination down and dirty horse races infected Jack with the fever.

Jack put it like this, "Horse racing is an itch that I can't scratch enough. Nimpkie is competitive due to Tecumseh's training. The spirited stallion has been praised and rewarded for maintaining the lead when running with other horses and that shaped him into a winner."

Chapter 12

DOUBLE DATING & THE PICNIC

Cheatie mused, "Glenda, hon, measured in years it was a long time ago, but to me it don't seem that long ago. Roy was my first love, my only love. From the day we met something clicked, I always thought we were meant to be together.

I said, "Oh, Mother, I am so looking forward to this section of the book. Please be detailed and go into your emotional responses to Daddy."

"I'll try, but this story is very personal, it is something I was taught to keep private. There was something about the way he looked at me, know what I mean? He wasn't one to hide his maleness. And oh honey, he had hungry eyes, no doubt about it. He considered his masculinity a birthright, part of who he was. Glenda, I don't mind telling you there was no lack of romance between us."

I started laughing and said, "Whoa, remember to keep it clean."

"Let me start with our first date. Oh, my, I loved him so!"

Cheatie walked into the bedroom she shared with Stella Ruth and said, "Why are you all dressed up? Where did you get that dress?"

"Promise not to tell?"

"Cross my heart." Cheatie drew an imaginary x across her chest.

"Okay, well you remember me talking about a fellow I been dating named Grady. He bought it for me from a local seamstress. She had a booth set up at the Throckmorten Bazaar. He insisted that the dress was made just for me." Stella changed the subject and asked, "What time is it? Grady is sposed to be here by six. We're goin' to a picture show named "*Gone with the Wind*" over in Sherman.

Cheatie checked the clock in the living room and reported that it was, "Quarter till."

Stella Ruth was blessed with beautiful fine features; we all considered her to be the "pretty one" ever since she was a baby. Ethel was pretty enough, she always had suitors, and that got her into some trouble but enough about that. As for me I was the 'plain jane' of the family except when I dressed up in my Cheatiebo outfit. Thankfully I outgrew that stage and pretty much grew up blending into the background. That was fine with me.

Beauty plus being the baby of the family should have created a spoiled, self-centered brat, but that was not Stella Ruth. She was kind, loved the Lord, and was always ready to do her share of the chores. But she sure loved getting all dolled up. I'm talkin' eye lash curler, bright red lipstick, and jewelry. Getting ready to go on a date was a lengthy process that could take hours.

The new dress was a soft pastel pink. It had a fitted bodice and scoop neckline. The skirt was hemmed above-the-knee and revealed beautifully shaped legs. The delicious color of the dress complemented Stella's brunette hair. As she stood looking into the dresser mirror, she began humming the song "Charleston." Just thinking about the tune got her feet moving. Stella smiled at Cheatie and began her high stepping version of the Charleston, a dance that had been popular during the roaring 20s. Cheatie joined in the hummed song and did her own version of the Charleston. Cheatie remarked, "Hun, you look just beautiful! Grady's right, that dress is perfect for you."

Stella did her version of the Hollywood Starlet walk and flashed a "sultry" look beneath fluttering eyelashes. Cheatie laughed and said, "Better not let Daddy see that or your chances of going to the movie will be *gone with the wind.*

Stella Ruth decided on her stiletto black patent pumps because she fancied that they flattered her legs. She held her mass of wavy brown hair away from her neck while Cheatie fastened a gold locket.

Cheatie recalled seeing the movie "A Star Is Born." The resemblance between the Hollywood star, Janet Gaynor and Stella Ruth was uncanny. Cheatie remarked that Grady was about to fall in love if he wasn't already. The moment was interrupted by a loud knocking at the front door. Cheatie said "I will let Grady in."

Cheatie looked out and saw two young men standing on the porch dressed like cattlemen. They both wore dark western suits, wrangler's boots, bolo ties and Stetsons. "You must be Grady. Come on in."

The caller nodded and said, "Yes Mamm" as he removed the hat. Cheatie escorted them into the living room. Without the hats Cheatie could see a family resemblance. That Stella knew how to attract the handsome ones for sure. Grady had a confident manner and spoke with the polish of a business man. "I'm Grady and this is my brother Roy. You must be Cheatie. I've been looking forward to making your acquaintance, heard nothing but nice things about you. At the last minute I talked Roy into coming along, thinking we might be able to convince you to make it a foursome. *Gone with the Wind* is being advertised as the best movie of the year. We can wait if you need a few minutes to finish up a chore or something."

Cheatie blushed and thought to herself, *Stella has fixed me up with a blind date again.*

Roy cleared his throat and stepped from behind Grady. "Call me Roy and what should I call you?"

"Just Cheatie will do, it is short for Cheatiebo, a nickname my Poppa gave me when I was a kid, and it stuck."

Roy said, "I am delighted to meet you. Sorry about the short notice, but I really hope you can come along. Otherwise, I will feel like I am crashing Grady and Stella Ruth's party. It's up to you." Roy held out his arms and slowly rotated his body a full 360 degrees. Cheatie blushed a little after looking him up and down. Next, he said, "Never been in jail?" Cheatie was at a loss for words, so Roy continued, using an exaggerated hillbilly accent, "I learnt ta read, rite, and take regular-baths, them's the three 'Rs.' I done some boxin', rastlin, and played football in high school." Roy set the dishes to rattling in the cupboard when he put his dukes up and did some lively shadow boxing. Grady faded into the background, thoroughly amused at Roy's creativeness for getting a date and made some mental notes for future reference.

Grady had always considered Roy to be the imaginative one of his siblings.

Cheatie was intrigued by Roy's sense of humor. The mock "try-out" piqued her interest. She wanted to know more about him. She pretended to be unimpressed, turned her head to the side, and said, "Interesting, but I need more?" Momentarily stumped, Roy paused and then grabbed the first thing that came to mind. He assumed a hunched-over stance and began slapping his chest and thighs in a lively "hambone" performance. This bit of originality cracked Cheatie's stoic expression, and she started laughing. Roy smiled, stood at attention, and said, "You have high standards my dear." He reached inside his collar and withdrew the golden football he wore on a chain and exclaimed "VARSITY"; after a pause he added, "Graduated 6th in my class and—won—."

Cheatie interrupted, "Enough Roy, you handle torture well. I am actually excited to go along. I have been hearing about the movie."

Roy feigned a great sigh and said, "After I rest up and regain my dignity, I will be honored to escort you to the movie!"

Cheatie smiled and said, "Give me time to change, and I will hurry Stella Ruth along. It takes her forever to get ready."

As Cheatie climbed the stairs she paused and looked back to say, "While I'm changing have a seat and no more shadow boxing in this old house, it might fall down."

She confronted Stella Ruth with her hands on her hips. "So here you go fixin' me up again, well this time I happen to like him so there."

Clean and neat was Cheatie's style. Fashion trends felt fake and gave the appearance of being intellectually shallow. Cheatie didn't stress over what to wear and went with an earth-toned geometric print broom handle skirt and a scoop necked black sweater. She whispered, "Stella Ruth, I am impressed, Grady and Roy are handsome for hometown boys."

For a wrap Cheatie chose her hand made rabbit-fur vest and matching high-top moccasins. She brushed her hair and gathered it into a pony tail at the nape of her neck. Lastly, she brushed her teeth and said, "Come on Stella Ruth, we don't want to be late for the movie."

Once on the road to Sherman, Stella Ruth and Grady were in their own world in the front seat of Grady's souped-up jalopy, no doubt the ugliest car ever allowed on the road. Cheatie asked, "Hey Grady, what kind of car is this? What color is it supposed to be?" The car was currently painted in flat gray primer with lighter gray spots.

Grady answered, "Wait until she is painted and restored. Gonna be a beauty. She is a '37 Packard V12 Boat Tail. As soon as I have enough money put aside, I plan to have the car professionally painted 'candy apple red.'" At first Grady and Stella didn't notice that Cheatie and Roy were quite absorbed in conversation. Stella did look back once and thought, so far so good, Roy doesn't seem to be intimidated like the others.

Cheatie kept catching Roy staring at her, and it was a little unnerving. Roy got the conversation going by asking, "What do you do with your leisure time?"

Cheatie replied, "Oh, I don't allow myself much leisure time. I have my own business. I have a few animal traps along elm creek that I check at least every other day. I skin and tan the hides I trap and make them into all kinds of garments. I tried trapping on the Red River, but I mostly trap on the small creeks around the county. Sometimes I drive the family Model-A, but most of the time I ride Girty, our 19-year-old Morgan mare. I sell the garments I create at fairs and carnivals. She held out the lapel of her vest and said, "I made this rabbit fur vest and these moccasins."

Roy was surprised and said, "Beautiful job, can I touch the fur, so soft. What a novel business idea! How is business?"

Cheatie smiled and said, "Good, so far I have a waiting list. I can't keep up with the demand. And I have a home-based bakery. I supply Cherokee bean bread for local pow wows. There is a small Cherokee community out west of town, and I furnish bread for tribal ceremonies several times a year. And then I have some regular customers. Sure keeps me busy. Do you like bean bread?"

Roy asked, "What is bean bread?"

"The next time I bake I'll make an extra box for you."

Roy interrupted and said, "What does it taste like? Made from beans?"

Cheatie answered, "Yes, mostly beans and cornmeal, like hush puppies but with a different taste. The balls of dough are boiled in oil or sometimes water. The ancient peoples also wrapped them in green leaves and cooked them in the coals of a dying fire. Like I said, leisure time is rare for me, but it all sure beats plucking chickens or waiting tables. Like I said, I stay busy but not so busy as to pass up a chance to go to the movie. Thanks for inviting me." Cheatie patted Roy on the shoulder, paused and then said, "Oh my, I must be boring you. I want to hear about you, Roy?"

Roy smiled and said, "Anything I have to say will be boring so how about we change the subject." Cheatie abruptly disagreed and insisted that she really was interested.

Roy shrugged his shoulders and began with, "I've been taking some electrical engineering classes at North Texas State. I've always been interested in technology. There are some mind-blowing advances being made right now, for instance in the area of space travel. Did you hear that they are working on sending a man into orbit and eventually an expedition to the moon?"

Cheatie said, "No, this is all news to me. Do you mean a man could go flying in space?"

"Mark my words, we may see someone go to the moon and walk around within our lifetime. Of course, I don't think we should hold our breath, seems a little farfetched. Another of my interests is genetics, selective breeding and animal husbandry. I have a few pure-bred polled Herefords pastured out on my parent's ranch. I am adding to the herd as my budget allows. Having my own herd has been a dream of mine since I was a boy. I tried my skill at amateur prize fighting but decided it wasn't for me. My two older brothers Sam and Bill have been on the fight circuit for a couple of years and are making enough prize money to pay expenses and then some. Unlike me they are natural-born brutes. After getting the snot beat out of me a few times, I decided to follow a different career path. I do enjoy working out with them. We run laps and lift weights, stuff like that. One of my favorite past times is reading."

Cheatie considered his self-review and exclaimed, "What makes you so studious?"

Roy shrugged and said, "I was sickly as a small child, had asthma and my mother gave me books to read to keep me from boredom, Mom is a reader too. Reading books became addictive."

"Are you still bothered with asthma?"

"No, not at all. By the time I got to high school, the symptoms just up and disappeared."

Cheatie said, "I dropped out of high school, and reading books is not on my list of fun things to do."

The small talk was flowing naturally, and Roy noted that Cheatie was a good listener. Roy spoke up, "Would you like to go on a picnic tomorrow? I will drop by the hamburger joint for sandwiches and soda-pop. You want to sit by a bonfire?" What would you enjoy doing?"

"A fire sounds good."

From a block away the movie house's huge flashing billboard caught their attention. Seeing the sign "GONE WITH THE WIND" was exciting. Roy opened the rear door for Cheatie, and she looked out and saw that the moon had just peaked above the roof tops. "Look, the moon will be full in a night or two."

Roy replied, "The perfect companion for a picnic, a full moon." Roy took Cheatie by the hand and helped her from the back seat. Once the movie started Cheatie leaned over to Stella Ruth and whispered, "That Clark Gable is a handsome fellar!"

Stella replied, "Isn't her dress beautiful, sometimes I wish we still dressed like that." The couple sitting directly in front of them turned their heads and gave them a dirty look. During a sad part of the movie, Roy and Grady started sniffling and rubbing their eyes on their sleeves and whispered, "Oh no." And the four of them had a good giggle. The same cantankerous people looked over their shoulders and shushed them. The ultimate transgression happened when Stella Ruth spilled her bag of popcorn, and it went flying in every direction. Some went down the front of her dress, so she sprang from her seat and brushed the greasy kernels from her dress and did a little shimmy to get the ones in her bosom to fall out the bottom of the dress. A couple of teenage boys wolf whistled and applauded causing laughter among the movie goers. The continuity of the movie was broken, and that brought some boos from the audience. The ones hit with the flying popcorn stood to brush it away, concerned that the butter would soil their clothing.

That was the last straw, and the angry man sitting one row to the front stood and glared at the rude, uncivilized foursome sitting behind and marched to the back to summon the person in charge. The man in the projection room stopped the reel and switched on the overhead lights. The angry customer insisted that the manager expel the unruly people sitting behind him. So the manager followed the man back to where Roy and Grady were sitting. The manager saw the incident as an opportunity prove his managerial skill. He appeared to be about 15 years old and was small for his age. He wasn't prepared for what followed. The slightly built assistant to the assistant was a suspender wearing high pockets with black rimmed glasses and huge ears. The air of authority he displayed marching down the aisle quickly dissipated when he arrived at the trouble spot. His high-pitched voice cracked when he spoke to Roy and Grady. He cleared his throat and addressed Roy and Grady, "Will you please come with me?" Roy and Grady pointed to themselves and gestured "me?" Genuinely embarrassed, they stood intending to publicly apologize. Their sheer bulk and athletic builds so intimidated the former usher that he literally shrank in stature an inch or two as he stood with his head cocked back, looking up at Roy and Grady. Roy reached into his pocket and retrieved a five-dollar bill and handed it over to the flustered boy. Then Roy in his most sincere voice said, "Sir, we are so sorry for the commotion. Please use this toward the purchase of advance tickets for the kind people seated here in front. As for the other folks seated in the two rows around us, I want to treat them to a round of popcorn. Sorry about the interruption to the movie just when it was getting interesting. As a gesture of good will, it is popcorn on me. Start up the popper." Roy looked around and noticed that the entire audience was spreading the word and rushing to line up at the concessions counter.

Roy graciously placed his hand on the young manager's shoulder and accompanied him to the back of the auditorium. Roy said, "I'm Roy, what's your name and how long have you been the manager?"

The boy was obviously flattered and said, "Actually, I'm only the assistant to the assistant manager. My name is Eugene McQueen, and I been in this job since last June."

"Well, it appears you are doing a fine job."

Most everyone lined up for the free popcorn. Roy, good-naturedly spent all of his cash and asked, "Eugene, I'm out of cash, can I pay the rest tomorrow?"

Eugene puffed out his chest and said, "No need Roy, the rest will be written off per me."

Roy stood in the lobby and thanked the people standing in line for being understanding about the delay. Roy was a natural at making 'good ole boy' small talk. Before returning to his seat, he bought a new bag of popcorn for Stella Ruth. Cheatie was relieved to see that the grumblers had taken the free tickets and left the movie house. The movie was restarted as soon as everyone was seated. Cheatie enjoyed the movie but found it a little too melodramatic for her taste but for a blind, first date, she gave it high marks.

The evening was memorable for other than the merits of the cinematography. The occasion of Roy and Cheatie's first date was one of the stories told and re-told at McCawl family gatherings. As far as Roy was concerned, the extra money spent on popcorn wasn't enough to fret over. He would have been surprised if Grady had offered to help pay for the popcorn. Grady was notorious for his avaricious attachment to his money and deserved the reputation as a dyed in the wool penny pincher.

As the crowd of movie goers filed out of the theater, several people waited for an opportunity to introduce themselves to Roy. When a white headed, friendly cuss recognized the name McCawl he asked Roy if he was any relation to Asa McCawl, and of course Roy admitted to being his son. The well-dressed gentleman had an earnest expression when he said, "We need to talk."

The old gent had an air of urgency in his manner, so Roy asked Cheatie to give him a minute and pulled him aside. The man introduced himself as Ken Coats and added that he was classmates of Asa's kid sisters Velma and Callie. If you can spare me a couple of minutes, I want to tell you about a kindness your poppa did on my behalf. Well, to git to the point, he flat out changed my life, saved me he did. I been grateful ever since.

He had Roy's attention, "Wait, ah Mr. Coats, can you start over, I'm having trouble hearing you over the noise."

"Sure, it is noisy, I'll speak up. I have a story about your dad. When I was in high school, I was going to run away from home to avoid the trouble I was in over failing my math class. The math grade was going to prevent me from graduating with my class. As a result, my parents would be publicly embarrassed, and I didn't feel like I could stand seeing the pain my failure would bring them. Since the path of least resistance led out of town, I had my bag packed. Before I left, I tried to go out with your Aunt Callie, I was madly in love with her, you ever see any pictures of her when she was young: beautiful woman, perfection, you might say I was smitten." Roy inclined his head indicating his interest in hearing more. Ken continued. "Well, Callie paid me no nevermind and shared my poem with everyone at the dinner table that night. Asa stuffed my poem in his wallet and reminded Callie that she should let me know that she wasn't allowed to date. Over the next few days, Asa was hot on my trail but not for the reason one would expect, no sir he was trying to prevent me from a terrible mistake. When he finally caught up to me and set me down, he put an arm on my shoulder and spoke in a most kindly tone.

He said, 'Kenny, I'm glad I found you before you left for the circus or wherever it is you was planning to go. I want to share some of my background with you and hope you will reconsider before abandoning your family for an ungodly, dishonest, dog eat dog world where people would as soon shoot you as look at you. Since being orphaned and forced to make it on my own, I figure you need sound counseling. I've seen the ugly side of society, and there are people that prey on young fellars like you. I know because I experienced them first hand. I didn't leave my parents, but they left me with four younger siblings to care for. Died, just up and died fairly close together. Town's folk started to looking for homes for us and when I realized they wuz going to split us up I had a rebelled. Seems the community folks couldn't afford 5 more mouths to feed, so I got my way by raising a big ruckus. They gave up and decided to see if I could handle the responsibility. I was about ready to turn 19 years old. But it wasn't smooth sailing by any means. The only reason we made it good as we did is because our parents had taught us to behave, and we wus ust to workin'. There weren't an hour that went by that I didn't miss them. I wuz determined that nobody would see me cry, but I sure did plenty of it in private. All five of us were scared little urchins, and not sure where our next meal was coming from. Neighbors helped when they could afford to, but times wuz spare, and most folks were struggling to take care of their own. Ken, getting back to your situation, are your parents abusive, do they give you enough food and a warm place to sleep?'

I answered, 'Well sure, they always took care of me. Gave me gifts at Christmas and birthdays. Mom was a great cook and kept a tidy house. They just thought I was smarter than I am. That was the problem in a nut shell.'

Then your father said, 'I can't even imagine abandoning a good family like yours. Please, try to make amends before it's too late or something bad happens. Take my advice and work things out with your father. If it will help, I am willing to talk to him. I'm so glad you took the time to speak with me. Is it okay if I tell Dad about our conversation?'

Ken smiled and said he hoped to be seeing Roy around town and repeated himself. "Asa McCawl saved me, and I will always be grateful."

Roy finally had to excuse himself from the well-meaning people that wanted to extend the visiting and inquire about his illustrious father's health. "It was nice meeting yawl, I will pass along your well wishes to Dad. I have to go, but thanks for being so kind."

Cheatie spoke up, "Wow, those people were so nice to ask about your father. Back to the picnic, forget the burgers, I will fry us a chicken and make potato salad, and maybe some of my bean bread."

Roy said, "That sounds great!"

Cheatie slapped her knee and said, "I love picnics! Oh, would you mind if we check my traps first thing? It is a scheduled day for checking the traps. It won't take long; I only have six traps. They are live traps, and I always make sure that I can use the pelt or I turn the critter loose, I don't want any trapped animals to suffer needlessly."

Nothing about Cheatie was frivolous, or egocentric. She preferred to blend in and give the limelight to others. Growing up on a run-down share-crop farm with a carousing alcoholic father might have given Cheatie an inferiority complex but for Granny Delia. The family matriarch had purposefully instilled the four Wainwright girls with a sense of self worthiness. She reinforced Mattie's parenting by instilling values like charity and honesty and the golden rule. The years of powerful life lessons would always be there in their subconscious minds. Lessons like having a sense of ancestral pride in their Cherokee heritage and living a godly life.

Cheatie was fairly confident that the right man would come into her life when the time was right. Until then she would choose to spend her time with genuine and thoughtful people. Someone that looked beyond physical beauty, stylishness, and trying to imitate the rich and famous. Early indications were that Roy just might fit that bill nicely. Cheatie really, really liked Roy, and he had already asked her on a second date. She felt a little giddy.

The truth of the matter, Cheatie had her own earthy kind of beauty. She was petite and physically fit. Her face was a fresh young version of the legendary Cherokee woman. Her facial bone structure had Cherokee written all over it. Roy preferred Cheatie's natural look. Cheatie had always suspected that love and romance was often nothing more than being in love with the idea of being in love. Like so many of Cheatie's deeper thoughts, she kept her musings on romance to herself.

After that first date with Roy, some of her notions about romance came into question.

Cheatie had every reason to expect the picnic to be a lot of fun, and for the most part it was. Roy wore his individuality like a badge of honor, and his sense of humor was pleasant without silliness. There was just a hint of machismo about him.

Punctuality was important to Roy, and he arrived on the Wainwright porch at the arranged time. He drove an old white pickup truck that had traveled too many rough dirt roads. With the radio playing songs by the likes of Hank Williams and Earnest Tubb, they drove to Elm Creek and parked the truck in the shade of a tree. Five of Cheatie's live traps were empty, and the sixth had trapped a very angry snapping turtle. Roy, mustering his manliness, stepped forward to release the turtle from the trap. He quickly learned to respect the reptile's personal space. At first the turtle opened his mouth as a warning and then with lightning speed struck out with a suddenly elongated neck narrowly missing Roy's hand. His second try to release the trapped critter frightened him even more. On the third attempt he picked up the cage and turned it with the opening down and tried to shake the turtle from the trap. By this point the animal was so agitated it struck at Roy's hand as it fell from the open end of the trap. Out of pure orneriness Roy faked being bitten.

When Cheatie realized that Roy was kidding, she joined him in a good laugh. "Roy, you are a funny man!" Cheatie loved Roy's personality. As it would turn out dating Roy would never be boring.

Soon after freeing the turtle, Roy was clowning as he walked along the trail and slipped down in a mud hole. His entire backside was coated with a disgusting layer of slimy mud that had a few cow patties mixed in. With a swarm of iridescent green flies following him down the trail, Roy performed a Charlie Chaplin heel click. The circumstances suggested that Roy should take a dip in elm creek, clothes and all. Yelling at the top of his lungs, he did a cannonball from the bank. As fate would have it, he had picked a shallow place, and when he stood up in the three-foot-deep water, he was even muddier that before and was bleeding from his mouth. A quick examination by Cheatie determined that he had bitten his tongue when he hit the shallow bottom. Cheatie kidded him about needing to bandage his tongue. In Roy's mind he was now reduced to a caricature of a pitiful drowned rat. Cheatie noticed that he was shuddering from the effects of evaporation.

The Cheatiebo took control of the situation. She asked if he had a blanket or some extra clothing. Roy said no clothes but there is a blanket behind the seat. Cheatie got the blanket and passed it to Roy. She then pointed toward the river and said, "Go into the brush and remove your clothes, take a dip to wash off and then tie this blanket around your body toga style, okay?" I will be here getting a fire started. While you are in the water, wash the mud out of your clothes best you can. We will hang them by the fire to dry.

Roy feeling striped of his dignity followed orders. To resist would just make him look even more inept. He thought, darn, I was really starting to like Cheatie. Now I've blown it with her big time.

Roy stayed gone for the longest time, waiting for darkness. He felt foolish in the toga get up and was trying to get enough courage to come out of hiding when Cheatie came looking for him.

Cheatie yelled from between cupped hands, "I coming to look for you, hope the snapping turtle didn't get you." She walked to the river and yelled, "Roy, you okay? Did that turtle get ya? What is taking so long? I have a big fire going and we still have our picnic dinner to eat."

Roy stepped from behind a bush with a self-conscious look on his face. He held out his palm and said, "If you laugh at me, I might just gag you and throw you in the back of the truck hog tied."

Cheatie took one look and knew that Roy had been humbled. She walked over to him and asked, "How does your tongue feel?" She reached up and ran her fingers through his wet hair rearranging it to point in the same direction. "There, now let me see. This toga you are wearing is not covering you so well, take this scarf and my concha belt and make yourself a loin cloth." Once Roy had the loin cloth in place Cheatie rotated him and looked at his backside. He was exposing a little too much of his cheeks, so she adjusted the scarf to cover a wider area. Then she turned him around and stepped back for a panoramic view. Suddenly her heart was doing a jig inside her chest. "Roy, put the blanket back on; your muscles are making me feel weak keened." Cheatie, caught up in the moment ran her hand over his upper chest. Roy was caught off guard by her frank admiration. Maybe he hadn't ruined his chances with Cheatie after-all. Cheatie took Roy by the hand and led him to the fireside, and they sat upon a log. He was suddenly putty in her hands.

Cheatie asked, "Where are your clothes?"

Roy replied, "Oh, I forgot and left them hanging on a bush by the river. Cheatie said, "Stay put, and I will get them." She jogged to the creek bank and soon found the dripping shirt and trousers and skivvies. Cheatie draped the clothing over a substantial limb and twisted to wring out the excess water. Darkness slowed her return to the fire. Roy was standing without the blanket with his backside to the crackling fire. Her approach distracted him, and he got the tail end of her scarf too close to the flames.

Cheatie yelled, "Roy, you're on fire!" She rushed to his side and used his wet clothing to extinguish the burning scarf just in time. "Roy, are you burned?"

Roy grinned sheepishly and asked, "If I say yes, will it get me a hug?" Cheatie answered, "Maybe, but after another dip in Elm Creek." Cheatie spread the wet clothes on the rigged drying rack. "We'll have to watch that we do not catch your clothes on fire, or you might have to go native all the way home." Roy still looked chilled, so Cheatie stood on tippy toes to drape the blanket over his shoulders. That is when she realized just how broad and muscled his shoulders were.

Cheatie asked, "Are you as hungry as I am? I hope I brought enough for you too. Want to bring the basket over here by the fire?" Roy placed the wicker basket on a flat stone near their log and set the ice filled bucket with the soda pop next to it. Cheatie pulled out two plates, two checkered napkins, and two forks. Roy used a church key and opened two bottles of "Grapette" pop.

"Do you prefer white or dark meat?" Cheatie asked.

Roy exclaimed, "You kiddin', I just like to eat chicken, or chickens. I am so hungry now that I smell the food, I could eat that snapping turtle." Cheatie started placing food on the plates. "Here, I'll start you off with a drum stick and a half breast." Then she spooned a large helping of potato salad on each plate. "And this is a bean bread cake. They look like hush puppies but have a different flavor. Keep in mind that bean bread is better when eaten warm, just out of the cooking pot."

Roy grimaced when he took his first bite of potato salad. Cheatie said, "Roy is it that bad?"

Roy, still chewing was shaking his head and pointing at his mouth. Finally, he was able to explain, "It's my tongue, hurts to eat."

Cheatie looked into Roy's mouth and saw that the cut in his tongue had opened up and was bleeding again. Cheatie got a piece of ice from the bucket and told Roy to hold it on his tongue for a minute. Cheatie spoke up and said, "The potato salad has green onion and pickles with extra juice. Maybe you better skip the potato salad. Your part won't go to waste, you can bet on that." Next Cheatie took some chicken off the bone and shredded it into tiny bites. "See if you can chew on the side away from the cut. Maybe you can swallow without much chewing. Roy let Cheatie put some of the chicken into his mouth, and he managed to swallow.

There he sat, shivering from the evening chill, with Cheatie patting him on the back. Roy suddenly got a vision of himself the way Cheatie must be seeing him. He berated himself, *"Roy, old boy, do you know just how foolish, how pitiful, how buffoonish you must appear to Cheatie? Now that your dignity and credibility are gone, she will always think of you as a joke. You blew it big time. What real man would be sitting on a log dressed in a woman's scarf for a loin cloth that he caught on fire, whining about his tongue that he bit himself? What real man would let an attractive young woman take pity on him? Me, Roy, yep that is me, how dumb!*

Roy removed the blanket from his shoulders and walked to a pile of cut limbs and brush and pulled a load to the fires' edge. He added some very heavy limbs to the fire, and Cheatie noticed the ease with which he handled the heavy firewood. *Cheatie was affected by the sight of his testosterone drenched, well-toned torso and upper arms. Cheatie was thinking, what a beautiful man.* "Roy, you are sure strong, must be the weight lifting." Roy did not answer, and Cheatie decided to concentrate on her plate of food. The awkward moment passed, and Cheatie ate in silence.

Roy, between small bites said, "Cheatie this food is wonderful. So, you made it yourself? Wow, you use just the right amount of seasoning." Then Roy realized that while he was engrossed in his own introspection, he had ignored Cheatie. She just kept eating without looking up. He suspected she had hurt feelings. He cleared his throat and said, "Cheatie, I didn't mean to ignore you. I was suddenly feeling foolish dressed like this. When you were feeding me, I thought, I do not need mothering. I already have a mother, a very loving and devoted mother. I am looking for an intelligent and interesting individual in a girlfriend. My preliminary assessment is that you would more than fill that bill, if I were to be so lucky." Cheatie stopped eating and swallowed the food in her mouth. She scooted on the log until she was touching Roy's shoulder and said, "Roy, I am delighted that we met and should you decide I am not too bossy I would love to be your, ah girlfriend." With appetites satisfied Cheatie and Roy sat quietly absorbing the warmth of the campfire.

Time passed, and Roy broke the silence to check on his drying clothes. "Almost dry, think I will build up the fire one more time." Roy moved aside the drying rack. Then he lifted a huge dead limb from the debris pile and carefully placed it on the fire. Cheatie guessed the limb must have weighed at least 200 pounds yet Roy showed no strain. Roy knew that the wood was old and dry and would easily be consumed before time to head for home. Cheatie's subconscious mind, true to her inherent programing, was scoring Roy as a suitable mate.

Very little escaped Roy, and he felt a tingle travel the length of his backbone when he caught Cheatie in an unguarded moment once again admiring his body, and that caused them both to blush. Roy was thinking how expressive and vivacious Cheatie's expressions are.

Cheatie began humming a sweet melody barely audible. Roy asked her to sing louder. Cheatie began singing the Cherokee Morning Song. She started over and sang the words with a delicate vibrato. Being awash in certain hormones Roy was captivated and even mired in the sweetest sickness known to mankind. Cheatie was afflicted with her own chemically induced personality anomalies. Moon eyed Roy was thinking how her voice was easy on the ears. Cheatie's Granny had taught her the Cherokee words when she was a child. Singing the song brought back memories of the beloved old woman.

> *We n' de ya ho*
> *We n' de ya ho*
> *We n' de, We n'de*
> *Ho Ho Ho Ho*
> *We'n We'n We'n Ya Ho*
> *Ho ho ho ho*

Roy said, "Beautiful! The melody is so different from any music I've ever heard, such an unusual tune, I need to hear it again." Cheatie started over, and Roy listened intently. Everything about Cheatie was dramatically unique: the epitome of a free spirit. Roy had known Cheatie for such a short time, yet he felt the essence of her core being. Would she give him a chance to develop a deeper relationship?

Roy wanted to ask about Cheatie's Cherokee ancestry but thought it might be a sensitive subject. It was as though Cheatie read his mind and began a narrative of her ancestral heritage, a subject near to her heart.

She started by introducing Wathena and Patrick Larson who lived the early 1800s; described the 1811-1812 the New Madrid Earthquakes; lamented the forced relocation of the Cherokee People; described how a remnant of Cherokee avoided the soldiers and fled to the remotest mountains of the Appalachian chain. Cheatie described the treachery of Andrew Jackson that went beyond selling land to pay national debts to protect credit worthiness: Jackson's penchant for violence and cruelty when it served his purpose. Finally, Cheatie was candid about her own impoverished childhood and her father's alcoholism; the hardships of living on a "share-crop farm." Roy was fascinated by her story and encouraged her to continue. He concluded that Cheatie had actually grown into her unique personality partly because of her struggle with adversity.

During the evening Roy thought of many questions, and he was pleased by Cheatie's openness. She concluded her reminiscence with, "Each successive grandmother became the family historian and preserved the memories by way of a tradition of storytelling. Now, in modern times I have access to the written family history preserved in diaries and old Bibles." Neither Roy nor Cheatie wanted to call it a night, but discipline prevailed.

It was 1:30 AM when Cheatie bid Roy good-night on her porch steps. Roy asked, "Can I see you tomorrow?" Cheatie opened her mouth to answer, but the question was answered by her Daddy, Willie Joe instead, who was sitting on the porch swing, hidden by darkness.

"Young man, whoever you might be, I think my daughter has seen enough of you for a while. If you want to court Cheatie, I will have to get to know more about you. I'll be lookin' for you at say 6:30 PM at the Main Street Café Monday evening. Don't be late."

Roy, in a respectful tone said "Yes sir, my name is Roy, and I'll be there Lord willin': Monday, 6:30 at the Main Street Café. Good night Cheatie, I enjoyed the evening. Good evening, Sir."

Cheatie ran up the porch steps and bent to kiss Willie Joe's cheek and then sat down beside him. "Daddy, Roy is a real nice; he is the brother of Grady, Grady McCawl." He reeked of liquor and Cheatie knew not to upset him.

Willie Joe's demeanor changed, "Are they Asa McCawl's boys, Deputy McCawl?"

Cheatie said, "Yes, I found that out tonight while we were at the movie." She would have elaborated on the popcorn incident but sensed that it was not a good time for light hearted conversation. "That's Roy's father okay, The Asa McCawl that competes in the cutting horse competitions and spins cowboy tales. I reckon he's sorta famous in these parts. Do you know him, Daddy?"

Willie Joe knew him, a little too well, and the relationship was not what one would call cordial. Willie Joe quickly cut off the conversation and said he was going to bed. The reason for Willie Joe's abrupt change of mood raised questions that Cheatie let drop. She wasn't in the mood.

When Cheatie learned of the history between the two men, she was embarrassed and was certain that Roy would lose interest in dating her. Cheatie was wrong about Roy; he couldn't care less about her father's past. Roy turned out to be just as individualistic as Cheatie. Were they too much alike to make a match, or would it turn out that they were destined for each other? Only time would tell.

Chapter 13

A NEW BEGINNING

Sunday morning was a time to sleep in for Cheatie. Mattie and Annie Mae usually attended a small community church only a few blocks from their home, within walking distance. Cheatie lost interest in attending after a few sermons. Money in the collection basket was a recurring theme, accompanied with some brazen arm twisting. The collection basket would be passed several times in the same service. Cheatie had read what the Bible said about giving: to purpose and give with a cheerful heart. She decided to wait for a church that didn't try to strong arm people. Cheatie chose to see God in nature and felt close to the Creator when running her traps or sitting on the river bank fishing. Cheatie did believe in the God of the Bible and prayed to him often to help her to find truth and salvation.

Roy knew nothing of Willie Joe's history of public drunkenness and his extensive arrest record. Willie Joe's rap sheet included assault and domestic violence. The life style Willie Joe had lived had taken a toll on his health, and Asa had gone easy on him of late, afraid he might just up and die on him. Many a time Asa had dropped Willie Joe off at his house rather than booking him into jail. "Strong armed" law enforcement was never Asa's style. Underneath Asa's hard shell "don't mess with me" public demeanor was a kindly soul that was willing to temper his response to the citizenry's minor breaches of ethics or lack of impulse control. But when it came to serious crime, Asa was definitely "on the job."

Cheatie was almost 21 and as an adult was determined to guide her own destiny: *if the Good Lord was willing*. The decision on whether or not she would date Roy or any other young man would strictly belong to Cheatie not her parents. She loved her father, but he had destroyed his right to preach morality.

The following day Roy came to the Wainwright front door with a big bouquet of flowers and a gutted river otter. When Cheatie came to the door, she was wearing her robe and slippers and had not brushed her hair. Cheatie not one for vanity, opened the screen door and said come on in.

Roy remarked, "You look rested, I already checked your traps, and this was in one of 'em. I hope I cleaned it okay. I can't stay, I'm gonna get my mom and go to worship service at 10:00 AM. I was thinking our picnic got interrupted, and so I thought we could give it another go this afternoon? I have something to show you. Cheatie hesitated, considering the demands of her business commitments.

Roy coaxed, "Come on, say yes."

Cheatie smiled and said, "YES, I would love to".

Roy said, "I will furnish the food this time. I'll be by about 2: PM. Your father isn't going to shoot me or anything is he?" Cheatie smiled and replied, "Daddy's bark is worse than his bite." As Cheatie watched Roy jog away, she exhaled a big sigh. Being so smitten with a young man was a new experience for little Cheatiebo. *Maybe I am capable of "silly" puppy love after all.*

Right on time Roy picked up Cheatie in the beat-up old white pickup truck. When Roy knocked on the screen door, Cheatie yelled from upstairs, "Come on in Roy, I'll be right down." Cheatie descended the stairs dressed in dark blue dungarees, a white cotton shirt that buttoned in the front, the rabbit fur vest, and matching high top moccasins. Her hair was in a single braid coiled into a knot at the nape of her neck. Her only adornment was a necklace of animal teeth strung on a leather cord. Cheatie's complexion was flawless, and her natural lashes and brows needed no enhancement. She was a natural beauty. Roy thought to himself, "Now here is a real person with depth."

Roy excited to see Cheatie, rushed up and spun her around. "Hello beautiful, you ready to see my business, or ah my means of livelihood?"

Cheatie put her head back and laughed and said, "Business, oh lardy I can't wait."

Then Roy said, "You might need a warm coat, 'cause we will be out until after dark. If you are okay with that, and ah, your father." Eerily on que, the family model A with Mattie and Willie Joe drove into the driveway. Roy walked through the screen door and waited on the porch. He was unsure what to expect. Roy nodded and offered his hand to Willie Joe and said, "Nice to see you again sir." Willie Joe shook Roy's hand but without any warmth. Then Roy extended his hand to Mattie and said, "Mrs. Wainwright, I am so glad to meet you. I have invited Cheatie to go on an outing with me. We will have dinner out, so please do not wait supper on her. I plan to have her home by 10 o'clock tonight. I will take good care of her." Cheatie spoke up and said, "Roy, I'll get my jacket, and we can go." Roy turned and made eye contact with Cheatie's parents and said, "Mr. and Mrs. Wainwright, I appreciate the fact that you are concerned with Cheatie's welfare. She is a very special young lady and a tribute to both of you. Please let me assure you that my intentions are entirely honorable." Mattie and Willie Joe were left speechless with the formality of Roy's statement, and they both nodded, and after an uncomfortable silence Mattie said, "Roy, I am glad for Cheatie to have a nice friend like you." Willie Joe abruptly excused himself with another nod of his head and headed to the backyard. Roy relieved that the encounter had gone so well, waited on the porch for Cheatie. Roy noticed that Mattie was still standing just inside the screen door watching him. Roy addressed Mattie and said, "So Cheatie made her fur vest and moccasins herself? Golly, that took a lot of skill!"

Mattie with a hint of pride answered, "She made them without help from anybody. She even kilt the animals, and tanned the hides. She is right good at that kind of thing ever since she was a child; she learnt it all from my mother."

Roy replied, "Wish I was that handy, but I do like to hunt and fish." Cheatie appeared and kissed Mattie on the cheek and said, "See you this evening. Love you, Momma."

Roy headed the truck in a south easterly direction. Soon they ran out of pavement and bounced around on the wash-board surface for at least 10 miles. Finally, Roy pulled up to a hand-made barbed wire gate and opened it. After securing the gate they drove down a lane with grass growing in the middle. On a slight incline Roy parked the pickup next to some gigantic oak trees. Underneath one of the trees was a rock well-housing equipped with a pulley rack and rope. Cheatie jumped out of the pickup cab and headed for the well. She removed the wood covering and yelled "hello." Just as she expected she heard an echo. "Roy, is the water good, can I take a drink?"

Roy nodded and said, "Go ahead, I been drinking this water all my life, and it never hurt me." Cheatie started pulling on the rope and was surprised at how shallow the water table was. "Roy, this is a shallow well, that must be the reason for all of the heavy woods and undergrowth around here." Roy answered, "Yep, good farmland. Daddy mostly used the cleared fields for growing peanuts, it is perfect soil for peanuts, and we always had a good garden when we lived out here. We spent most of the depression years living out here. We suffered hard times like everbody, but we got along better than most." Cheatie was taking in the surroundings and noticed the corner stones to a demolished structure. "Was this your house? What happened?" Roy stated that it had caught fire, and they decided against rebuilding.

"Someday I just might build a weekend cabin in the same spot. I love spending time down here and tending my cattle." Roy raised both hands to his face and hollered, "Sooouuieeeeeee, Soouie," and then he honked the truck horn several times. Within a couple of minutes, a half dozen lumbering Hereford cattle gathered around the truck. Roy took out a salt block and placed it on the ground and scooped up several buckets of pellets and poured them into a 4-foot-long trough. The heifers were very docile but next to appear out of the brush was the bull, "Old George." He was the biggest bull Cheatie had ever seen. He stood back, pawed at the dirt, and sounded off with a series of scary puffing grunts and then made a higher and louder bawl. Roy spoke softly, "George is a prize Bull, with a great blood line. He cost me a pretty penny. He has never liked strangers, but he will get used to you if you hold the bucket of pellets for him." Cheatie said sure and took the bucket and approached George with her side toward the great massive bull. Roy was struck by her knowledge of how to approach the Bull without challenging him.

"The heifers and Old George are all polled, meaning hornless," said Roy. They are the result of careful selective breeding. About that time a heifer with a newly born calf joined the rest of the small herd to feed upon the pellets. Cheatie was immediately taken with the darling calf and tried to pet her. Her impulsive action triggered the mother cow's protectiveness, and the bellowing, thousand-pound bovine charged Cheatie. After two turns around the pickup, Cheatie was getting winded and dove into the bed of the truck. She hid under a big white tarp to wait for Roy to take control of the situation. As soon as the threat was gone, the old heifer went to claim her ration of pellets, and it was as though the incident had never happened. Roy rushed over to the truck and raised a corner of the tarp expecting to find Cheatie cowering from fright.

As soon as Roy looked under the cover, Cheatie jumped to her full height and threw the tarp over Roy, which caused him to yell at the top of his lungs. Well, Old George must have either been afraid of ghosts or maybe he identified the white figure with the KKK and charged at the shrouded figure. When Cheatie saw that the bull was charging straight at Roy, she screamed, "The bull is charging quick Jump—" she grabbed a flailing hand and pulled him into the pickup bed with not a second to spare. The tarp had fallen over the rail of the pickup bed, and George took out some male aggression on the now lifeless tarpoleum. That is how Roy's old white pickup came to have a caved in fender well. Roy, a sentimental sort of chap decided against repairing the damage preferring to keep the evidence as a conversational prompt and reminder of Cheatie. Suddenly the humor of the situation got both Roy and Cheatie laughing. "Cheatie I didn't know you could move that fast. That was quite the chase. That flying leap into the bed of the truck was awesome. You launched your body off the rail of the bed and made a complete flip before landing on your feet in a squatting position, very impressive!"

Cheatie said, "And George doesn't seem to like things that look like ghosts or KKK goons. Roy, I AM REALLY sorry about the close call, you could've been hurt real bad. I need to think through my practical jokes ahead of time. And that cow, I think she was about scarier than the bull. She really put the fear in me." Roy was still laughing as he helped Cheatie out of the truck bed.

As soon as the feed was consumed, the cattle wondered away into the undergrowth. Roy spread the tarp from the bed of the pickup on the ground and topped it with a blanket. Then he started a fire in the existing pit. He erected an iron tripod, started the coffee pot to boil. Next, he took two cane fishing poles from the pickup. They were ready to bait. Roy took out a bowl of flour with the baking powder and salt added in, a cup of lard, and some buttermilk, and quickly mixed up a recipe of cowboy biscuits. Then he dropped the dough by the spoon full into a greased pre-heated Dutch oven and hung it over the fire. "Now we have to catch our main course, come this way. Cheatie, if you see a grasshopper, grab it and I will dig a few worms. The slough is down there where all of the weeds are so tall. We have perch and catfish waiting to be our supper. Watch out for the bull nettles. We have a bumper crop this year. As they approached the slough, Cheatie heard some very deep croaking and felt the urge to add a couple of the frogs to the pot. Cheatie said, "I hear bullfrogs." When they got closer to the water, they could hear the splashing when the frogs jumped into the water. "You want me to kill a few with the 22 hanging in your truck?" Roy asked, "Sure, but how are you going to get them after you shoot them?"

"Just watch me, a real frogger." Cheatie walked over to a small grove of willow trees and cut a long straight limb with her hunting knife. She split one end with her knife and then drove a short stick into the split separating the two halves. She sharpened the tips to make a two-pronged spear. The last touch was to make barbs on the tips to prevent loss of prey. Cheatie told Roy that she needed to go back to the fire and harden the pole's tips in the hot coals. Roy noticed that Cheatie was comfortable doing things that most girls expect guys to handle.

He yelled out to Cheatie, "Check on the biscuits while you're up there." Cheatie came back munching on a biscuit, with the 22-rifle slung over one shoulder and the smoking stick pointed skyward. Cheatie checked the two fishing poles, first the one with a cork, and the bait was gone, so she reached into the grass at her feet and grabbed a grasshopper for bait. The other fishing line was laying on the bottom, and the bait was still on the hook.

Cheatie reported, "Coffee was boiling, so I took it off the heat. The biscuits are done, and I decided to try one, it's very good." The line with cork moved sideways and then disappeared.

Roy yelled, "got one" and proceeded to pull in a hand-sized blue gill perch. Cheatie walked around to the other side of the pool and after a few minutes spotted a frog. She decided to sneak up on him and gig him with her willow spear. She stabbed at the frog but missed.

Soon she spotted another and was able to impale it. Cheatie handed Roy the struggling frog and looked at the second fishing pole in time to see it bending from pressure.

"Roy, you got something on the line. Here, let me git it. Wow, nice size, blue cat, some good eating." Roy asked how hungry Cheatie was, and she said, "With biscuits, this should be plenty."

Roy spoke up and said, "We have a can of pork and beans to open and some honey for the biscuits.

Cheatie unsheathed her knife when Roy spoke up and said, "Here, I'll clean the fish and the frog while you get the cornmeal batter ready. The iron skillet is in the bottom of the box. Some shortening is in a jar. I'm ready for a cup of coffee, how about you?" Cheatie said, "Sounds good."

The Sunday evening cook-out set the stage for an unforgettable evening, one that would mark the beginning of a magical romance. From this evening forward, Cheatie and Roy were overwhelmed with a magnetic attraction for each other that developed into euphoria.

As soon as they finished eating, Roy built up the fire but decided they needed more light and turned on the truck's head lights. Roy brought two books from the truck.

Cheatie asked, "Which two books did you bring?" In addition to the Bible, Roy unveiled a worn copy of "Tarzan of the Apes." Cheatie confessed that she didn't recognize the title.

Roy rubbed his hands together and said, "Ah, there is a treat in store for you." His eyes sparkled as he read the last chapter of the book of Luke and the first two chapters of Acts.

Cheatie said, "The story seems to jump off the page and come to life when you read it. I've read that part, but it is confusing. I wish you would explain what is really going on."

Roy had used his best public voice and read as though the author Luke was speaking to them. Cheatie, "It's gonna get late on us, and you have to be home by ten o'clock, so we will have to do the Bible study when we have more time. Bow with me while we close our Bible study with a prayer. Roy stood from the blanket and pulled Cheatie up and held her hands,

"Father, thank you for preserving your holy Word. Thank you for sending your son in the form of a man, so that mankind can comprehend your awesomeness. You sent Him as the Messiah, the fulfillment of the promise to Abraham, Isaac, and Jacob. We see your plan, your scheme of redemption unfolding on the pages as we read. We recognize your authority and majesty. If it your will, protect us from harm. Lord help us to be ever mindful of your suffering on the cross. When, in a moment of weakness, we transgress your law, thank you for the promise of forgiveness when we ask. In Christ's name, Amen."

Cheatie, "While you help our plates, I will introduce you to 'Tarzan.'" Cheatie was big eyed and hung on to every word. Roy's vocal inflection and timing made the summary come alive. Cheatie was immediately immersed in the story. After a half hour of "Tarzan" Roy put the books away and said "Stay tuned."

Cheatie said, "The story of Tarzan is so entertaining! Please, I can't wait to experience this great adventure." Roy replied, "Stay tuned." Roy put the books away and turned off the headlights. After that Cheatie and Roy sat upon the blanket and enjoyed the fire. Then Roy looked at his watch and quickly started loading the truck. Roy said as he worked, "Oh my gosh, we are cutting it close on having you home by ten. When they pulled up to Cheatie's house, Roy pulled Cheatie closer and gave her a goodnight kiss.

Then he asked, "Can I come by after I meet up with your dad tomorrow night? I really want to see you." Cheatie just moved her head up and down and said, "Thanks for a lovely evening."

The meeting with Mr. Wainwright was a little strained. Cheatie's daddy looked haggard, definitely prematurely aged. He avoided eye contact and was severely subdued. His first comment was about Asa McCawl.

Willie Joe began with, "I reckon it's okay if I call you Roy, and I want you to call me Willie. I heard tell that deputy McCawl is your poppa. The other night I had no idea of who your family was. I think you can understand how late it was and that we was a might worried. First off, your pappy and I have a history that you are likely aware of. Let's just say the long arm of the law got stretched too far for my likin'. I don't hold anything against you because of him. You seem like a right nice young man, and you need to know that I expect you to behave like a gentleman. I'd appreciate having Cheatie home by 10 at night.

Roy cleared his throat and responded with, "Mr. Wainwright, I didn't know you even know my father. Though I suppose most folks have seen him around. His reputation, what with so many irons in the fire, has got him purty well known in these parts. I will try my best to have Cheatie home by ten at night unless I clear it with you in advance. Mr. Wain- ah, Willie, I want to tell you what a fine young woman Cheatie is: never met anyone like her, not even close." Roy started to comment on her talents when Willie Joe rose from his seat and walked away and out the front door without finishing his coffee. Roy was left alone, mid- sentence and shaking his head at the strangeness of the meeting.

By the second picnic Cheatie and Roy were so drawn to each other it was unthinkable to let a day pass without spending some time together. It was as though the two young people were foreordained to find each other. On Cheatie's porch swing Roy said something that stopped Cheatie's heart for a few beats. "Roy said, "Cheatie I don't mind saying that my vision of the perfect woman for me pretty much looks like you." Then they kissed, it was a prolonged, passionate, and oh so intimate sharing. Afterwards they both had to sit down to recover from a spell of dizziness.

Mattie told Roy, "Anytime you are over this way, feel welcome to come in and visit. I'll treat you like family, so don't be surprised if I give you chores to do."

"Yes Mamm! I would like that."

As the months passed Roy became a fixture in Cheatie's living room. Many a night Mattie would ask Roy to read the scripture and lead them in prayer. Mattie claimed to have an open mind, but when Roy took issue with Calvinistic church doctrine being taught in the Protestant Denominations, she suddenly had pressing tasks that drew her away. Roy was still asked to say grace before meals and to read the scripture, but Mattie let Roy know her philosophy of "to each his own" and finally spelled it out in plain language, "Roy hun, I'm sorry but in my heart, I know God is love and will not condemn me to hell for not interpreting every single scripture just right." Roy changed the topic of conversation.

Roy had come to have real affection for Cheatie's family and vowed to never alienate them by being too forceful with his viewpoints. He liked to quote the old adage, "You can lead a horse to water." Trying to force-feed the Gospel wasn't his style. He prayed for the wisdom to balance that with the scripture that urged Timothy to, "— be urgent in season and out of season—." And there was the verse in Jude that read, "—contend earnestly for the Faith (Gospel) that was once for all (times) delivered unto the saints (obedient worshipers)."

During the early days of their courtship, Roy was able to establish a high degree of credibility with Cheatie. When a controversial biblical topic would come up, she was willing to listen to the point-counterpoint with an open mind. Roy was encouraged by the way Cheatie listened to his Bible teaching. He was especially gratified that her questions were appropriate and relevant. Within a few weeks Cheatie was sitting between Ollie and Roy most every Sunday morning for worship service.

Reading aloud from books like Tarzan was for entertainment and a good way to spend time with Cheatie. Roy was invited to sit on the big plush sofa in Cheatie's living room and read from one of his favorite adventures. Willie Joe had taken a night watchmen's job and was rarely home in the evenings. Cheatie was addicted to Roy's reading. Those were the days before television. With family members around or not, Roy and Cheatie found reading a great way to pass the time together. Roy was persuaded to start "Tarzan" from the beginning by Stella Ruth. When Roy finished the first Tarzan book, he went on to the second volume. It seemed that some of Asa's vocal articulation, inflection and cadence had rubbed off on his middle son.

On a regular basis Roy invited Cheatie to eat with his large and boisterous family. One of the most memorable occasions happened on a Sunday afternoon on a mild fall day. Cheatie was invited for Sunday dinner. She was about to experience one of Ollie's famous Sunday luncheons. Cheatie caught a glimpse of the legendary dishpan of banana pudding being fanned by a grandchild, and she was reminded by the growl of her stomach she had hardly eaten breakfast. The McCawl family home had an interesting story behind it. While Asa and Ollie were getting serious about each other, Sam McClarren was worried that his special Ollie would never have a fine home if she married a poor cowboy like Asa. Sam had been thinking about his savings and what should be done with it. He and Elizabeth decided to build an addition on to the church building, order new song books for the church, donate to the local hospital, and build both daughters a home. The homes were not two room shacks but rather beautiful two-story homes. That is how Grandmother Ollie lived in such a grand home. It had lots of hiding places and was perfect for imagining ghosts in the stair well.

The card tables were set up on the front porch. The food was served buffet style in the kitchen and carried to the card tables on the porch. Once everyone had finished eating it was time for the "42" game to begin. Winners progressed throughout the afternoon tournament style. For hours "the addictive blood sport" would rage on, but when the sun cast long shadows, there would be an armistice. Unabashed bragging, and haranguing, and rehashing of war room strategy was allowed. That was the signal for the ice cream freezers to come out. There could be as many as four or five freezers going. The most popular flavor was banana, with strawberry and chocolate in second and third place. The freezers were still of the hand crank design, and there was no shortage of crankers. The kids were enlisted to weigh down the freezer by sitting on some kind of padding placed over the top of the wooden tub. Once we had completed our freezer sitting tour of duty, we could resume the quest for "lite'n bugs" commonly called fire flies in other parts of the world.

That particular afternoon was one of those unforgettable times that Cheatie loved to talk about in her old age. She remembered the details in vivid technicolor. Shortly after she and Roy arrived at the old two-story home place, Brother Bill drove up in front causing quite a stir. He and the most recent beauty, newly married wife stepped out of a brand-new Studebaker and walked into the home accompanied by a half-grown mountain lion cub on a leash. Cheatie caught her breath because the cub was the spitting image of Klandagi.

Everyone gathered around for introductions followed with hearty greetings and hugs all around. Cheatie had heard all about Billy's celebrity. He had recently been awarded a championship belt and was known to associate with the likes of Hollywood actors and was a business partner of a famous wrestler with long blond hair. Bill and Betty were both fashionably attired in leather overcoats with big fox collars. Betty had the allure and carriage of a movie star. Folks around Gainesville liked to say, "That Billy McCawl is living high on the hog." The professional wrestling circuit had been Bill's ticket out of small-town USA to bright lights and big cities.

Cheatie was eager to get closer to the lion cub and inched her way in that direction. The puma cub gave her goose bumps and brought to memory the words of Granny's Lion Cave Story. There in Ollie's living room, Cheatie revealed that she too had kept a mountain lion cub as a pet for the first year of its life and that she had sold it to a boxer for a mascot. Cheatie was imagining her long departed Granny's reaction to the strange turn of events had she been alive and present; Cheatie didn't rule out the possibility that Granny was present in some form. When Cheatie approached the cub, the rambunctious ball of fur calmed down and focused on her, as though it sensed something different about this human. Cheatie seated herself on the floor beside the cub and offered the back of her hand to be sniffed and licked. Then Cheatie pulled the cub closer and began stroking its fur as she voiced a series of chirps and whistles. The animal moved closer to Cheatie and then climbed upon her lap and lay down. Cheatie spoke in soft calm tones and addressed the beautiful creature as Klandagi.

Roy had his attention directed to Cheatie and the cub by Billy. The brothers were transfixed with the spectacle. A tear ran down Cheatie's cheek, and she hid her face in the coat of the little puma. Roy's curiosity got the better of him, and he approached her a little too abruptly for the cub's liking and Roy was forced to step back.

Roy asked, "Cheatie, what is going on with you and this lion?"

She met Roy's gaze directly and said, "It is ATAVISM."

Roy said, "what on earth is that?"

Cheatie spoke with a monotone and appeared to be detached. "Atavism explains why I am so different. My Granny Delia was convinced that I am a throwback to my ancient Indian great, great, great grandmother Wathena, the Puma-Woman."

Suddenly Roy and Cheatie were unaware of the others in the room. He took a seat on the floor beside Cheatie and the lion cub and asked, "So I'm all ears, please explain the condition or ailment or whatever atavism happens to be."

Cheatie replied, "This is what the medical books say, 'Atavism is a term used to account for the reappearance of an individual trait or traits after generations of absence. Such an individual is sometimes called a throwback. It explains the unexpected emergence of primitive traits."

Roy said, "Wow, you just said a mouth full. I need to digest that bit of information for a while. Oh well, for now Momma says it is time to eat." Roy took the initiative to lead the gathering in a prayer.

When Cheatie stood the cub stayed by her feet and then followed her to the front porch where the card tables were set. Roy seated Cheatie and left to bring her a plate of food and a glass of iced tea. While he was gone Cheatie lifted Klandagi to her lap and the cub closed its eyes and settled down for a nap. Cheatie felt a peck on her shoulder, and it was Billy. He was looking at the cub and said, "Oh there she is. They told me that you had her. You must like animals like me."

Roy showed up with a plate of food for Cheatie, so Billy said, "Here, let me take "Terminator" with me so you can enjoy your meal. I'll touch base with you later. Cheatie reluctantly handed over the "Terminator." Ollie was watching and handed Cheatie a soapy cloth for her hands. Ollie patted Cheatie on the back and said, "Cheatie my dear, I'm so glad you can be with us today. Please enjoy your meal." Roy had noticed to his great relief that the two of them seemed to like each other.

Once everyone had finished eating Cheatie asked Billy for permission to take Klandagi for a walk while most everyone would be absorbed in playing '42.' Roy was on board with skipping out on the crowd, and they had a delightful time playing with the little mountain lion.

Cheatie told Roy, "Her blue eyes will be changing to an amber brown, and her spots will disappear in the next few months. Roy, before long she is going to be too dangerous to keep as a pet. Mountain lions do not make good pets; I found that out the hard way. If he keeps her, he will need to have her declawed and muzzled."

Roy said, "Hey, that's Bill's business, but you can clue him in if you want. I think he was thinking he could domesticate her." That evening it didn't take much for Cheatie to convince Billy that keeping the mountain lion was a very bad idea. The liability issue was a major factor and caring for the animal was admittedly consuming too much of his time. Cheatie offered to take over the care of Terminator until Bill found a permanent solution. She and Roy had some rough and tumble episodes while caring for the saucy pet. After some official complaints, Asa was forced to insist that Roy and Cheatie move the lion to a more secure setting. The Fort Worth Zoo agreed to accept the puma when their female squeezed under a fence into the hyena enclosure and was killed. Cheatie was feeling bad for the cub but rationalized that she had never known life in the wild and would habituate to the zoo. For the first few weeks, she and Roy made a point of visiting the zoo on a weekly basis. Klandagi alias Terminator always recognized them and would rub against the wire enclosure and beg for them to pet her. Roy was ingenious at picking fun and interesting places for dates. Cheatie never knew what to expect next. They were regulars at Bill and Sam's boxing and wrestling matches. They often attended local varsity sports held at the local high school.

Cheatie learned that Roy's status as a former Gainesville Varsity football star never expired. Roy even had his number painted on a pair of bleacher seats. Another favorite place to visit was a park in the Arbuckle Mountains of Oklahoma called Turner Falls. The social group called the Taylor Street Gang made regular trips to the only mountains most of them had ever seen. Cheatie was a game participant in the more rugged outings. Unlike the other females, she never fretted over her hair being mussed or being spattered with mud.

The meeting with Willie Joe at the restaurant had been awkward but civil. Roy let Willie Joe set the tone of the relationship that started with mutual civility and curtness. Roy was much too clever to be rebuffed by poor Willie Joe. On the other hand, he felt compassion for the sad person that Willie presented. As time passed the two men became friendlier, and Willie Joe invited Roy to a backyard cook-out and a jam session of fiddle and guitar music. Willie played and sang sitting upon a chair. Dancing about while playing was now too strenuous for Willie Joe but with a little encouragement from Roy he relived his glory days. Willie Joe perked up and was his old flamboyant and animated self. He enjoyed being the center of attention as much as ever.

Not long afterward Willie Joe's health declined to the point that he retired his fiddle. He just couldn't "play to beat the band" anymore.

Roy's competitive side wanted to learn how to tan hides and to hunt and fish Cherokee style. He jumped in to help Cheatie bake bean bread and even cooked some for his mother Ollie. The exotic bread cakes were actually very tasty, and Roy never missed an opportunity to find new bean bread clients for Cheatie.

The Bible study sessions were going so well that Roy was confident that Cheatie would respond with "what must I do" soon. He shared the exciting prospect with his mother Ollie. During the year of courtship with Roy, Cheatie was surprised when Stella Ruth and Grady called it quits. Stella had found someone even more handsome and romantic. His name was Hugh Ben Harris. H.B. had grown up with the McCawls. Stella Ruth and H. B. were inducted into the Taylor Street circle of friends as charter members. Grady, being handsome and gentlemanly, soon had lovely new lass upon his arm. Her given name was Della, but she preferred to be called by her nick name, Pat.

The year Cheatie and Roy fell in love was 1940. This was a time of world turbulence. Fascism was sweeping Europe and had gained a popular following within the body politic of the United States. Many of America's rich industrialists had been business associates of the top German business moguls. The German regime was now led by the popular Adolph Hitler. By the time the free world awoke to the threat Hitler posed to Western civilization, the Nazi war machine had devoured much of Europe. The German Air Force was bombing the cities of Britain nightly. German submarines had suspended much of Atlantic shipping. The many deadly attacks on American ships were increasing and that fact alone made it inevitable that the United States would be drawn into the near global conflict.

Ever since the founding of the United States, the majority of Americans opposed involvement in foreign wars and wanted to "avoid entangling alliances" a lasting legacy of the iconic and prescient founder George Washington. But the powerful industrialists saw war as the means to greater wealth and power and used their influence behind the scenes with President Theodore Roosevelt and then President Woodrow Wilson to assure involvement in the war.

Cheatie and Roy's wedding took place a few days after Cheatie responded to the Lord's invitation. Cheatie was baptized for the remission of her sins in the small church in Gainesville where Ollie was a long-term member. The informal wedding ceremony and reception was held at the groom's family home, the very home that Ollie's father, Sam had given her as a wedding gift.

In advance of the wedding, Roy and Cheatie's siblings and close friends had concocted an elaborate shivaree. The plan was to kidnap the newlyweds and pitch them into elm creek and then hold them prisoner until daylight. Roy, armed with an intuitive nature intercepted some looks and whispering not intended for his ears and quickly decided that he must figure a way to give the gang the slip and do it with fanfare and aplomb. After all, Roy would have Cheatie riding "shot gun" on the get-away. Roy and Cheatie hatched a counter-plan that would hopefully get them the last laugh.

Following the cake cutting and congratulations, Roy excused himself to visit the bathroom and was mysteriously gone for more than half an hour. Cheatie feigned concern and convinced the guests that Roy must be having a bad case of nerves that gave him reason to sit out much of the reception in an upstairs restroom. Cheatie referred to Roy's retreat from the celebration as "riding the white buffalo."

While Roy was incommunicado, he put the finishing touches on his escape plan. He had managed to visit the bait shop earlier in the day and bought a sealed carton of catfish bait. The bait was not kept inside the bait shop but in a shed out back on the off chance of a leak or spill. Roy looked around and determined that he was alone before raising the hood on Grady's sparkling candy apple red souped-up jalopy. Roy donned a leather apron and some elbow high gloves and used a stick to paint a very small amount of the bait onto the engine block all the while gagging at the foul odor. H.B. had a glitzy yellow roadster that could really eat up the pavement, so Roy inoculated his engine as well, using only a small quantity that could easily be removed with a strong detergent in hot water. Then Roy used a pre-positioned car jack and raised the rear axles of Grady and H. B.'s cars enough to put cement blocks in place, leaving the rear tires just slightly off the ground. Roy imagined the look on Grady's face when he gunned the engine and nothing happened. Off course the hot engine would suck one of the most disgusting odors known to mankind into the passenger compartment.

Roy hurried back to the reception, and when several folks asked about riding the white buffalo, he was wondering what they were referring to; why would I be riding a white buffalo? The reception was winding down, folks were leaving for home, and Roy signaled Cheatie to meet him at the back door of the house. Roy had the white pickup backed up and was ready to speed away. The old truck was so ugly it was endowed with character: caved in wheel well and scratched up paint, vintage deluxe.

The gang had the usual tin cans tied to the bumper and had written all over the windows. Roy pulled their two suit cases from a hidden cubby hole and placed them into the pickup's bed. Roy burned rubber getting out of the driveway. When Grady and H. B. heard the sound, they paused mid-sentence and summoned the gang. Grady yelled, "They are getting away, hurry everyone!" The conspirators all charged pell-mell to the lot where the cars were parked. The helter-skelter manner they piled into the pursuit vehicles resembled the old clown and Volkswagen circus trick with bodies three deep. They started their engines, and smoke poured from the tailpipe, but they remained stationery.

Someone shouted, "Check the emergency brake."

Grady waited for someone to get out and check the tires. By this time both engines were hot and sending out nauseous fumes so foul the air took on a greenish tint. H. B. shouted, "My gosh, what is that smell?" Emmy Lee, near the bottom of Grady's back seat, started gagging and placed her hands over her mouth as she waited for her first opportunity to spring from the back seat. Suddenly the circus act changed to a Chinese fire-drill. The car doors were damaged from being opened so violently they would require the services of a machinist. The escapees were crawling upon the ground searching for a spot where no puke had yet landed. Pink, wedding cake pink was the color of the vicious and chunky vomit that covered the ground.

Roy, spur of the moment circled back by the scene of upheaval before heading out of town. He sounded his horn, and he and Cheatie drove past the scene. The pitiful scene brought a glimmer of pained sympathy that quickly passed as the newlyweds calmly drove the speed limit on the way out of town. Roy blew his horn when they drove past the farmer's place signaling time to drop the suspended banner.

In the end the dirty trick squad was out maneuvered, and the bride and groom escaped to their secret destination un-shivareed. Roy and Cheatie's final segment of the prank came in the form of an unfurled banner that spanned the main road south of town. A gratuity having crossed the palm of the farmer assured the unfurling of the banner. The evening before Roy and Cheatie had been laughing so hard they both had sore ribs and jaw bones. The bed sheet banner contained the following message.

Nice try! Forget chasing us and go fishing.
Use the catfish bait before it goes bad.
Love you all, Cheatie and Roy

The newlyweds honeymooned in Dallas totally unprepared for the course their married life would take. Troublesome times were brewing. Within three months the Japanese attacked Pearl Harbor. The nation's response was one of collective indignation, unified by a spirit of unprecedented patriotic fervor. Roy's response was no different. He hurried to volunteer for the draft but was rejected for health reasons. It was a high school football injury that led to his 4F classification. Thoroughly deflated, he redirected his patriotism by training as a tool-and-die machinist and applied for employment with a defense contractor.

Following his training he was transferred to St. Louis, Missouri where he continued working as a machinist. That's where their first daughter was born. It was a happy occasion but for one detail. Glenda Ruth would always feel cheated out of her Texas birthright. Pat, the second daughter had better timing and two years later was born in the great State of Texas.

Cheatie and Roy compressed what should have been a lifetime together into hardly more than eighteen years. They were devoted to God and His church. They believed in romance, adventure, and close family ties. Parenting their daughters was one of life's great adventures. They thought everyday life should be fun, and it was, for them and more than a few friends and relatives that held the same notion.

On September 24. 1959 it all ended. Roy had been having chest pain for a few days and spent the last week of his life hospitalized. The morning after he was discharged, he experienced a massive heart attack and passed away shortly after arriving at the local emergency room.

www.ingramcontent.com/pod-product-compliance
Lightning Source LLC
Chambersburg PA
CBHW051830020726
47502CB00005B/1712